A TAIL FOR TROUBLE

※❧※

RIMMY LONDON

Rimmy London Cozy Mysteries

Snuggle up... if you dare!

For my sweetest English bulldog,
Gus.
We love you forever and miss you everyday.

Foreword

Rimmy here,

Thanks for your amazing support! I can't wait for you to get started with *A Tail for Trouble*. I hope you love it as much as I do.

I'd love to keep in touch through my newsletter! Sign up at www.rimmylondon.com to get all the Rimmy London sales and news. See you soon!

Cheers,

Rim

Follow on Bookbub

Chapter One

✦

Megan set her hand atop a round, mossy boulder. It was their turnaround point, but she wasn't ready to head back just yet. Fred sniffed at the ground where she'd dropped a handful of trail mix for some squirrels the last time they'd hiked. His big tail whipped side to side, and his legs still had plenty of spring. Clearly, he wasn't tired out yet. He might enjoy his frequent afternoon naps by the fireplace, but he could cover plenty of ground on their hikes too.

"Hey boy," she said, sitting on a rock. He trotted up to her, and she rubbed under his ears where he loved it best. "Wanna go a bit farther today?" Her ginger hair was tucked behind her ears. It had grown longer in the past few months and hung forward, nearly reaching her waist.

Fred let his big, pink tongue loll out as he panted, which was definitely a yes.

"Okay, let's go," she said. Fred sprang into action and loped on down the trail, taking advantage of his long Great Dane legs. "Stay close," she called, having wrapped his leash around a strap of her backpack. The summer tourism season was behind them, meaning the trails were mostly empty. Any hikers she might run into usually knew her and Fred, so she didn't worry about the leash. However, the trails had never looked worse. A windstorm had knocked a few trees down at the end of summer and littered the pathways with branches and debris. Megan assumed it would've been cleaned up in a few weeks. As it was, they were well into fall and the unkept trails remained.

But the trees made up for it with their flashy colors. This was Megan's first time experiencing fall in the coastal Washington state town, and she was in awe. In nearly every direction, there was a patchwork of orange, red, and yellow leaves fluttering in the breeze. The next hour passed quickly as she scanned the surrounding wilderness and basked in its beauty while Fred zigzagged across the trail in front of her.

The incline increased until their trail suddenly skirted across the steep mountainside. The ground was rocky and littered with broken granite like shale; one stacked atop another until it was a slippery mess.

Megan sighed, ready to turn back. The rocky trail was more than she wanted to conquer that day. Plus, she didn't want to return home too late. There was still dinner to make and cleaning to finish before the weekend was through. But when she glanced around, she suddenly realized Fred wasn't anywhere in sight. She called for him, but only silence followed.

Finally, she heard a low whine. Turning around, she looked back across the steep portion of the trail she'd been hesitant to cross and saw him standing on the other side. He'd gone right across the rocky portion.

She called him, patting her leg. He took one step forward

gingerly. But several rocks slipped out from under his foot, almost bringing him to the ground. He slipped and fumbled. Finally, he backed up until he was on solid ground, and then he whined a second time.

A bit of nerves worked their way into her chest. As much as she tried not to look down the mountainside, she couldn't help noticing how far it was to the bottom. Just steep, rocky terrain the whole way down. She looked back at Fred to see him attempt a few shaky steps forward. Then he froze, looking back at her with worry in his big, blue eyes. His thin tail tucked between his legs, and she could see him shaking as he took another step.

The rocks slipped from under his feet, and he scrambled to stay on the trail. His back legs slid off, and he dug with his front feet, finally making it back up.

"Stay, Fred," Megan urged, holding her hands out as she made her way onto the trail. "Stay, I'm coming to you."

She placed her hiking boots cautiously, one after the other. Each step had her fighting to keep her balance. The rocks were dominoes piled into layers of instability. But very slowly, she made her way across, talking to Fred while keeping her eyes on her feet. She crouched low and held her hands down by her knees, ready to catch herself at any moment should she fall.

When she was nearly halfway, a rock slipped out from under her foot. Her knee hit the ground hard. She braced herself quickly before she could slide down. But when she looked up, it was to see Fred coming toward her again. "No, Fred. Stay," she said, but he kept walking. She could see him coming to a difficult spot layered in the thinnest rocks, and she hurried to get back on her feet. "Fred, stay!"

Easing forward again, she watched as the rocks began to

tumble away from where Fred walked. He was hurrying, but a small landslide of rocks was suddenly rushing under his feet. The chaos carried him right off the trail. Down the mountain he went, and she ran for it. With giant, leaping steps, she closed the distance between them as the rocks took her painfully down the mountain. But at least it was toward Fred.

Suddenly, she lost her balance and landed on her backside. But she managed to slide on her heels and rear. Trying to move toward the frightened canine, she spotted blood on his feet as he struggled and dug at the rocks. Nothing mattered more than reaching him before he really began to tumble. If he somersaulted down the mountain, it could be the end.

Finally, she was close enough. She grabbed his collar and hugged him to her chest. Digging her heels in hard, her boots found dirt. It brought them to a stop while rocks still tumbled around them. Shaking and gasping, she held Fred firmly. "I got you," she said. Her voice was raspy, and her breath rushed through her lungs as she tried to calm down. Leaning back, she looked up the mountainside to the trail above them. Climbing up seemed impossible, but she wasn't prepared to slide down the rest of the way either. They'd barely gone a quarter of the distance to the bottom, and both had enough cuts and scrapes as it was. Up was their best choice.

Careful to keep herself firmly planted, she untangled the leash from her backpack and clipped it onto Fred, tying it onto the belt loop of her shorts. It was an unusually warm day for fall, and she chose to wear her shorts just once more before winter set in. Looking down at the cuts along her knees and shins, she wished she would have stuck with pants.

But there was no changing that now. She rubbed Fred's back and took a deep breath, pivoting so her toes faced the mountain. She lifted one foot and dug her hiking boot through the rock to wedge it down deep. With her weight on that foot, she lifted the other and did the same, anchoring it into the dirt. Each step took far too long. The sun began to hang low in the afternoon sky, but at least they were moving in the right direction. If it took the rest of the day, she didn't care.

She held Fred's collar as they went, thankfully able to keep him from sliding back down. His steps were scrambled, and his feet left marks of blood on the rocks. Her heart ached at the sight. It left a gruesome trail behind them, but she made a point of not looking back. They were almost halfway up when she felt a spark of encouragement that they would make it safely.

Suddenly, both feet slid out from under her. She landed flat on her stomach and began to slide. The rocks scraped her legs and arms, but she managed to dig her hands in, and remarkably, Fred stayed where he was. The leash was taut between them, and his head was turned to her. If she slid another inch, she would take him down the mountain. She pressed her hands in as hard as she could and tried to get her feet under her again. The rocks seemed piled beneath her, and she couldn't find the bottom. She continued working, digging in with her knees and her feet, trying everything she could think of. Her grip was already failing, and she needed to climb up soon or she'd fall.

"Megan!"

She heard her name but didn't dare move.

"Hold on, I'm coming."

This time, she recognized her friend Santiago's voice and relief washed over her. As a forest guide and rescue volunteer, she knew Santiago would have supplies and equipment. The sounds above her were encouraging. She could make out the whiz of rope as it rubbed together and the clinking sound of what she imagined were carabiners. Still, she didn't risk moving and only hoped desperately that he would reach her at any second.

She managed to wedge one boot into the dirt and hung there from her hands, her weight mostly on one toe.

"Look out!" Santiago shouted. Rocks began to tumble around her, and Megan tucked her head just as a few whizzed past. She glanced up to see Santiago had anchored a rope to a tree and had a harness around his waist. He began to repel down toward them. In only a matter of minutes, he was there.

"I've got you," he said, just as his hands came around her waist. He lifted her up and held one arm around her as he wrapped the rope around her waist and tied them together. "Hold on to me," he said, grabbing Fred's collar. Megan wrapped both arms around his middle, and they made their way up together. He fed the rope through his harness and continued up without a single slip. Such a difference from the struggle it had been on her own. With just a simple piece of equipment, the mountain became perfectly safe instead of the treacherous beast it had been before.

When they were back on the trail, they stayed tied together until they made it to the safety of the trees and a nice flat trail. Santiago loosened the rope around her and went back to retrieve his anchor from the pine tree.

Megan's legs were shaking, and she was completely

drained. She sank to her knees. Fred lay down beside her, licking his feet. "Oh, Fred," she ran one hand down his silky coat. "I'm so sorry." The pads of his feet were cut, but they didn't look as bad as she'd feared. Only the deepest one was still bleeding. She held his paw in her hand, considering if he might need stitches.

Santiago returned, and the moment he reached them, he tossed his rope and harness on the ground with his backpack. Thank goodness he worked with the forest service, or she might've been leaving the mountain in a life-flight helicopter instead.

Suddenly, he lowered down and wrapped his arms around her. "I can't believe you came out here alone," he said, resting his hand tenderly at the back of her head. "I'm so glad you're okay." He was breathing hard, as if the moment had shaken him just as much as it had her.

Megan was overwhelmed by the emotion in his voice. She never would have believed how incredible it felt to be in his arms. As much as she'd always thought of him as a college kid, he was every bit the man just now. His long, sandy brown hair was held back in a ponytail that somehow smelled incredible, even after running around in the woods. With a smile, she thought it was quite possible he took better care of his hair than she did. It made her want to laugh, but she was too tired.

After a few silent minutes, Santiago sat back on his heels. His arms slid away, but his hands found her wrists. He turned them over, surveying the cuts along both. They weren't severe, and Megan wasn't especially excited for him to see the damage to her legs. She was sure something was still bleeding.

His eyes lifted from her hands to peer into hers. Brilliant

turquoise blue, like the sea on a sunny day. He could win contests with those eyes. He shook his head and creases formed between his dark, sleek, Spanish brows, a nod to his ancestry. "Why would you take these northern trails?" he asked. "They're not safe, especially this year. Usually, we've gotten equipment back here and had them groomed and maintained, but..." He just shook his head, clearly awaiting an answer.

Megan sighed, and a few strands of ginger hair whisked away from her face. Her hands lifted to her head, feeling the scraggly mess of disheveled hair. Threading her fingers through it, she shifted so she was sitting down with her legs out in front of her. "I'm sorry," she said simply. "I live here so I can be in the forest a lot." She shrugged. There was really no more explanation to offer. "Why has it been so hard to get them cleaned up?" she asked.

This was the first time going so far down this particular trail, and the results were a little discouraging. But hearing Santiago speak, it sounded like there was more reason than just clumsiness or poor navigation. She peered back at him, awaiting his answer. His honey-and-almond skin was enviable, especially when compared to her own pale, natural-ginger variety. So smooth and gorgeously pleasant. A real keeper, this one. He'd make some younger woman very happy one day.

But at the moment, he wasn't answering her question. His gaze was downturned, and he stared intently at her legs. Megan glanced down to see the blood and cuts had become caked with dirt. Pine needles were stuck throughout the mess, and she wished she'd thought to brush them off at least a little. She reached down, but he held a hand out, stopping her. "No, don't touch it. Let me get some antiseptic." He stood and returned to his backpack, unzipping a side pouch. "Looks like Fred will need some too," he said, glancing at the poor dog still licking the pads of his feet.

"It's not nearly as bad as it could've been," Megan said, giving a gentle smile. "Thank you so much," Her throat suddenly tightened. "I don't think we could've made it up on our own."

Santiago returned without answering, and his expression was a bit firm as he used a water bottle to wash the dirt from her legs. She studied him, trying to guess what might've set him off. He washed her legs clean and pulled a cloth from his backpack, patting her skin dry.

She reached up and touched his arm. "Santi."

Finally, his eyes lifted. She could see the color in his cheeks, attesting to an inner anger she didn't understand. "Are you really that upset about me taking a trail on my own? Or... what's bothering you?" she said. "If this is about Kenneth, just say it." She knew he had a small crush on her and that he resented her billionaire boyfriend, but she'd said nothing about him. It was just the only thing she could think of that might've put the foul look on his face.

Santiago set the cloth down on top of his backpack and opened the bottle of ointment. "No, it's not about him." He gave Megan a brief smile. "I'm mad at myself. These trails should be closed. The Rangers tell me they've never had trails in such disrepair before, but now it's obvious they need to be closed. I just wish I would have done it sooner." He glanced up, settling deeply into her gaze. "Before you got hurt... and Fred too."

He began to dab ointment on her cuts, and she tried her hardest not to flinch. "But why are they so bad?"

He touched a particularly deep cut, and she caught her breath, flinching away.

His face was apologetic as he looked back at her with the tube of ointment in his hand. "They say all the funding for maintenance and infestations just vanished this year." He shrugged and turned back to her legs, dabbing the ointment more gently this time. "I keep waiting for them to say it came in late. We were waiting all summer." He turned to his backpack and dug out some bandages. "But it never came." Pressing the bandages onto her legs, he covered the deepest cuts in silence. Megan mulled over his revelation. It was disheartening to hear the funding was cut, and it sounded like it rarely happened. But at least tourism season was over, and hikers would be few over the winter. As long as they closed the most dangerous trails, maybe they could gather some additional volunteers to help with the others.

"Can you help me with Fred?" Santiago asked. Megan glanced over to see him kneel next to Fred while the big dog licked his feet.

"Absolutely," she said, pushing off the ground. She sat next to Fred's big head and pulled him away from his feet gently, smoothing her hand down his long, floppy ears. He whined and pulled from time to time, but he trusted her. She knew it. The way he looked up at her when Santiago bandaged his deepest cut had her heart melting.

"It's okay, Fred," she said, bending down to kiss his nose. "Good boy."

Santiago zipped his supplies up and handed her a water bottle. She opened the top and tilted it for Fred, creating a stream that he lapped at, although he didn't seem to like the water getting on his face. He sneezed and turned away, having only gotten a few good licks. Megan smiled, rubbing his head. "Do you think he's okay to walk?" she asked, even as Fred hopped to his feet. He sniffed around, lifting his bandaged feet up unusually high. But other than that, he acted just fine.

"Yeah, he's good." Santiago glanced down at Megan's legs. "How about you?"

She accepted his hand and rose to her feet, feeling little pain. With a smile, she nodded at Santiago, and they started back at a slow pace. Even as they hobbled home, Megan's thoughts mulled over the state of the trails. For a small tourist town, it seemed like grooming the trails would be essential. No doubt some bossy politician with deep pockets was making all the decisions. Still, she vowed to get to the bottom of their little problem. How hard could it be, anyway? It was simple. They needed safe trails, and that was all there was to it.

Santiago's hand brushed against her as they walked, and then his fingers softly threaded through hers. His grip was supremely comforting. Megan knew she needed to let go before he assumed too much. But she didn't. In the back of her mind, she felt a small epiphany. It seemed sometimes... simple things could get complicated rather fast.

Chapter Two

Toasted sourdough. Roast beef with melted pepper jack cheese, green leaf lettuce, and garden-fresh tomato. Megan wrapped the hot sandwich in red checked paper and placed it in a small plastic basket, adding a sliced deli pickle and a bag of local kettle chips on top. Her Salty Subs sandwich shop was becoming quite successful. The customer was an older gentleman with graying hair, and his eyes widened as he accepted his sandwich. "Wow, looks wonderful!" Glancing back as he went to his table, he smiled. "Thank you."

"You're welcome," Megan said cheerfully, turning to the next customer. They ordered grilled cheese with a cup of tomato soup, and she got to work. It seemed she finally had a service that people were in need of. Sandwiches.

She'd been able to bring in a good income for the past month but finally decided to close each day at 4 p.m. The café at the end of the boardwalk had live bands and patio lighting. It was just too exciting for people to turn down. She rarely got customers in for dinner, so it just made sense to close early. Plus, this way, she had more time to spend with Fred. She glanced behind her to where he slept on his overstuffed doggy pillow. His paws were crossed over his face, and he looked sound asleep.

Only a few more customers stopped in before closing time. The shop was empty at 4 p.m., leaving her free to turn the little sign in the window and lock the door. Fred danced around beside her, having woken from his nap with boundless energy... as always. Megan, however, was exhausted. Her hiking adventure the day before had left her overly tired, and the cuts on her legs made it difficult to sleep. She yawned and reached for the leash on the wall. Instead of exploring today, she just wanted to take the back trail through the woods and head home.

But Fred wasn't having it. The second she attached the leash, he bolted for the front door. "Whoa!" Megan stumbled forward until Fred jumped up to balance his front paws on the door. She looked longingly at her bike along the back wall. But an energetic dog would never let her veg out on the couch, so she admitted defeat and unlocked the door.

On the boardwalk, the sun had just begun to set. It reflected off the storefronts and glittered on the watery horizon. The ocean was unusually calm, leaving a beautiful display of light and color. The sunset would be glorious, she was sure. But, before they set out to the beach, she wanted to check in with her favorite neighbors. First stop was Crystal, who owned a beautiful handmade jewelry store. Her best friend, who'd perfected a look she liked to call casual glamor.

When Megan and Fred walked into the shop, there was a group of young teen girls giggling around a necklace display. They each held a necklace and chatted about which one was best. Megan directed Fred to the back of the shop, where there was a workbench with tools and lights. Fred quickly plopped down on a small rug by the wall, where Crystal left a handful of chew toys for him. He picked out his favorite squeaky bone and began making music.

Crystal was hunched over a delicate string of emerald stones and without looking up, she laughed. "Looks like Fred knows his place around here," she said. Tying a knot in the plastic strings, she set her project down and turned to Megan.

Her glasses magnified her beautiful, dark blue eyes, and Megan couldn't help but laugh. "The bug look is pretty on you," she said.

Crystal laughed with her before removing them and walking around the bench to give her a quick hug. "Thanks," she said. "I can always count on your honesty." She gave Megan a nudge of her elbow. Then her eyebrows rose. "By the way, I have a proposal."

Fred lifted his head at the change in her tone, as if he suspected an adventure. Megan glanced back at him and then turned to her friend. "What is it?"

"Well," Crystal linked her arm with Megan's and began to walk about the store, moving up and down the aisles and straightening items as they went. "I wanted to go visit my father in Seattle this weekend, and I'd love to have some company." She eyed Megan through a brief pause. "I know your parents are in Seattle," she continued, "so maybe we could make it a double visit. Haven't you said they wanted to see you? What do you think?" Crystal shrugged with the question, as was customary for her. It was a personality trait that Megan secretly adored. Especially when paired with Crystal's delicate frame and slender shoulders.

But now, Megan paused as she considered leaving for the

weekend. She'd hoped to get a little furniture shopping done for her home and maybe some remodeling. She'd chosen a paint color for the interior walls and was anxious to get started. But traveling to Seattle with a friend would be much safer and more fun than going on her own. And she was really missing her parents.

She stopped near a small display of charms and looked back at Crystal. "I think that's a great idea," she said, glancing at the big, solemn Great Dane eyes watching from the corner of the room. "Can Fred come along?"

"It wouldn't be a trip without him." Crystal stepped in front of Megan and pulled a small charm from the display, lifting it in the palm of her hand. It was a tiny sandwich, detailed with layers of sliced turkey, pickles, tomatoes, and even hoagie buns with little sesame seeds on top. "I ordered these in honor of your shop." She held it out to Megan. "This one is for you to add to your charm bracelet."

"Aww." Megan took the little sandwich, laughing. "It's perfectly adorable. Thank you." She pulled the cuff of her sweatshirt back, revealing a beautiful silver bracelet with a tiny blue scooter as its only charm. It was dedicated to her first attempt at a shop, renting scooters.

"Here, let me." Crystal took the sandwich charm and added it to the bracelet. "Hopefully these are the only two, right?"

"Right," Megan laughed. "No need to start up a dozen businesses." A sense of dread pricked at the back of her mind, and she pushed it away. She was just going to have to make sandwiches work because changing the shop a third time was out of the question. If money was going to be tight, so be it.

Her phone rang, and she pulled it from her pocket to

find Kenneth Bradburn's name on the screen. Crystal's expression quickly became heavy with teasing. But she only finished attaching the charm and headed back to her work-table. Megan answered with her insides feeling fluttery. "Hello, Kenneth,"

"Megan!" His voice blasted in her ear, and she moved the phone away a bit. Wind was blowing in the background as if he were driving a convertible with the top down. "How are things going in Seacrest?"

"It's going great," Megan said, glancing at the front door as it swung open with a jingle. Santiago walked in, glancing over at her. His face melted into a warm smile. Megan returned his smile and then swallowed, remembering her hand in his. "Uh," she turned, focusing on the phone call again. "It's a little difficult to hear you. Are you driving?"

"Oh." Kenneth paused for a moment, and Megan waited. The guy was a billionaire, which meant he was always busy. He called her between appointments, meetings, and even parties. She adored hearing from him and enjoyed imagining his thick, full hair and pleasant, deep brown eyes. Even his Magnum PI mustache was adorable. She waited anxiously to hear if he would be able to come out to Seacrest anytime soon.

"Is that better?" His voice was lowered, smooth and buttery, just the way she liked it. The sound of wind in the background had silenced too.

"Yes," Megan said, feeling Santiago's eyes on her. Had she been smiling? She wasn't sure. Still, it was no secret she was in a relationship with Kenneth. She had nothing to hide. Regardless, she couldn't stop the heat from entering her cheeks as she thought about Santiago watching her. She looked back, but he'd joined Crystal at the workbench. With a sigh of relief, she concentrated on the phone again. It was utterly silent.

"Sorry," Megan said, "I'm at Crystal's place."

"I see," Kenneth said, his voice retaining its deep, rich tones. "No problem at all. I'm driving back home right now and wishing you were with me. Highway 101 is beautiful." A gust of air blew into the phone as if he'd sighed. "Thought I would give you a call. I miss you."

Megan glanced behind her, turning to the front window as she answered. "I miss you too," she said, her heart aching with the words as she thought of his arms around her and his kiss on her lips. "When can you come out again?"

"Well, about that," Kenneth said.

Crystal appeared, leaning into her view with a shrug. "My dad isn't answering," she whispered, glancing at Megan's phone. "But we should just run out there and say hello. What do you think? I haven't seen him in a long time, and this weekend the weather is supposed to be nice."

Megan nodded. "Sure," she whispered back.

"I'm leaving for the UK and Germany in a few days," Kenneth said.

"What?" Megan was shocked. "For how long?"

"Just for the weekend," Crystal whispered.

"No," Megan shook her head with a grin, patting Crystal's shoulder. She turned around, addressing Kenneth again. "How long will you be away?"

"I'm hoping only a month," he said, although his voice was reserved, as if he knew it was a long shot. Megan's heart plummeted, sinking heavy in her chest. She swallowed, trying to revive her spirits enough to answer. "Would you..." Kenneth cleared his throat. "Would you want to come with me?"

"Oh," Megan said, so shocked, she didn't know how to answer. But she knew she couldn't possibly leave. Her shop was just taking off. Plus, her relationship with Kenneth had only just begun. Going on a month-long vacation with him wasn't something she was ready for.

All this scrolled through her mind as she hurried to respond. But Kenneth beat her to it.

"I... I know it seems too soon for something like this," he said, "but the thought of being away for so long is making it nearly impossible to leave. So, I thought I would just bring you with me." He laughed, although his voice was shaky, as if he knew how tense she was. And possibly, he was tense too. "It's probably more of a daydream than actual reality. Don't feel bad if you have to say no. I understand."

"Well, really I wish I could say yes." Megan took a few steps, glancing back to see Crystal had returned to her workbench. Santiago's eyes were trained on her, and she turned around again. "It's just not the right time, uh, with my shop and everything. I've only just gotten started."

"I understand." Kenneth's tone had flattened, and his voice was quiet. She could hear the engine of his car cut off as if he'd just pulled into his garage. It was likely a gorgeous mansion overlooking the same Pacific Ocean that was next to Megan, just beyond the boardwalk. She glanced out the window to see it glistening in the sun.

"I hope you don't mind me calling you all the time then," Kenneth said with a shallow laugh.

"I'd love that," Megan said, biting her lip. She wanted to see him so badly, but she couldn't leave Seacrest. Not right now. "I'll call you too." She wrapped one arm around herself, gazing out the window and wishing he was with her. "I'll miss you," she said quietly, assuring the words wouldn't be overheard.

"Oh—I've got another call," he said, his voice rising. It woke her from the moment, and she straightened. "Can I call you back tonight?"

"Yes, of course." Megan ran a hand through her hair. "I'll talk to you then."

"Goodbye, Megan," he said. Somehow, he always managed to say her name in a way that had her smiling. She closed her eyes, fighting the urge to say yes to his offer. But they were nowhere near ready for something like that.

"Bye," she said quietly. The call ended, and there was only silence. She held the phone to her ear as she gazed out at the boardwalk and the ocean beyond. The sunset was just beginning. At 5:00 p.m., the colors of the sky were becoming bold and beautiful. If she walked out to the beach, she could watch the display of the sunset compete against the forest's display of fall behind the boardwalk. It was quickly becoming one of her favorite things.

"How's Kenneth doing?"

She turned to see Santiago standing beside her, also gazing out at the sunset. He gave her half a smile. "I hope I didn't make you uncomfortable yesterday. You know, holding your hand and all that." He crossed his arms, glancing down for a moment. "Just making sure you didn't fall." He winked, as if he knew how perfectly transparent his lie was. Then he sobered, looking out the window again. "Seriously though, I understand that you're in a relationship..." He turned to her with his green-blue eyes glowing against the sunset. "And I respect that."

"Thank you, Santiago."

His arm came around her in a side hug, and she returned

it, squeezing him back. "Anytime. Just promise me one thing." His arm dropped, and he faced her, his expression chiding.

"Yes?"

"Promise me you won't ever go hiking alone." Concern pulled at his usually cheerful face, and she knew he was speaking candidly. His concern was heartwarming, but she also wasn't one to make false promises, and this would definitely be one. After all, she lived alone in the woods with miles of trails out her back door. Hiking was going to be part of her life. Still, she didn't want him to worry.

She reached forward and took his hand. "I'm never alone." His gaze warmed, and his hand tightened around hers. "I've got Fred."

He swung around to look back at the Great Dane, who'd fallen asleep on his rug, and Megan glanced over too. Curled up with his big head off one side, his mouth was hanging open, and his tongue trailed to the floor, leaving a puddle of slobber.

"Somehow, that doesn't make me feel any better," Santiago said.

She gave his hand a squeeze and let him go. "Don't worry about me. I definitely know which trail not to take. And after you figure out how to get the funding, they'll be groomed and ready in no time."

"Me?" Santiago eyed her reluctantly.

"You can't fool me anymore." She bumped him with her elbow as she made her way back to Crystal. "I know who you are. Not a simple college kid, but bred from a family that rules over the jewelry and tech world..." She turned around, dipping her chin and raising her eyebrows. "Internationally known business gurus. I'd say you're quite capable of figuring out where a handful of funding went, eh?"

He fought a smile. "I guess the cat's out."

"Oh, it's out," Megan said. "It's out and already knocked the cookie jar off the kitchen counter." She laughed, and Crystal joined in, smiling at Santiago through her bug-eye glasses as they all gathered around the work table. She held a tiny pair of pliers in each hand.

"By the way" Crystal's bug eyes turned to Megan. "Margaret wanted to talk to you." She turned back to her work, clamping a small metal piece at the end of a long row of white beads. "She said it was urgent."

"Oh," Megan glanced back at the sunset. "Maybe I'll head over there now, then it won't be too dark on my way home."

"You riding your bike today?" Santiago asked.

"Yep," Megan smiled. "All by myself."

Santiago rolled his eyes, but a smile played on his mouth.

"C'mon, Fred!" Megan called.

The big dog's head popped up, making his collar jingle. He snatched the squeaky bone and leapt to his feet, scrambling across the smooth floor. Megan attached his leash and waved goodbye to her friends. In the doorway, she paused and looked back. Santiago sat on a stool, looking over the table at the necklace Crystal was constructing. They had become such a wonderful part of her life, and she was so grateful for them. She didn't want to go messing any of that up.

Fred jerked on the leash, and she flew out the doorway and onto the boardwalk, running to keep up. She wrapped the leash around her hand and held it tight. "What's going on, Fred?" She laughed, the words jostling as she ran. But the moment they came to Margaret's shop, Fred screeched to a halt in front of her door. It was wide open, and her bookstore was busy, full of shoppers and kids.

Just inside the door was a beautiful, long-haired calico. The feline was crouched low to the ground, and a warning growl hummed through its body.

Megan could feel the complete power from Fred, everything about to explode. He was standing still and trembling with anticipation. Her grip was firm on the leash, and she said his name carefully, "Fred, "

But it was too late. He dug his claws into the boardwalk and lunged.

Chapter Three

✣✣✣

"**A**argh, Fred!" Megan stumbled, trying to hold the huge dog back. For the most part, it was working, but the cat didn't seem to have an appreciation of its own mortality. Tail lifted high, it pranced on its toes and rubbed against a bookshelf. Then the feline sauntered entirely too close to Fred and arched its back.

Fred went for it.

Megan landed on her knees. Her arms were stretched out in front of her as she gripped the leash with both hands. "No, Fred!" she shouted, catching the sound of a few giggles from the shoppers around her. Thankfully, the cat climbed to a top shelf almost touching the ceiling. Fred yawned impatiently and plopped his rump to the floor.

Margaret appeared with a handful of dog biscuits, as if she'd heard the commotion and knew exactly what had happened. She handed the treats out for Fred, and he gobbled them down. "I'm sorry, Megan," she said. "I should've warned you about my new companion."

"No, it's okay," Megan said, still trying to catch her breath. "It could've been worse, I guess. I'm just glad I was able to hold him back long enough for your kitty to climb up there."

"Well"—Margaret glanced back at the kitty—"just don't walk under her, or she'll pounce on him."

Megan glanced back at the feline licking her front paw ominously while her tail flicked up in regular intervals. "You're serious?"

"Unfortunately, yes," she said. "We've already had three incidents where both customers and their poor pooches ran out of here in fright. Neither one's returned yet, and I'm rather hoping they will. I'd like for my sweet little Snickers to make amends."

"I see," Megan said, keeping a tight hold on the leash. Fred looked much too interested in every flick of movement from the feline. "Well, the reason I came in is that Crystal told me you needed to speak with me?"

"Yes!" Margaret reached forward, grabbing Megan's hand. "I'm asking for your help," she sighed. "Come with me." They walked to the back of the store, where Margaret had a display case of jewelry, although none of it was for sale. They were treasured memories of time spent with her mother back in England and a connection they shared. Behind it was a cozy little room with shelves of books and old newspapers. The furniture, however, was new. Two comfortable chairs and a modest sized couch circled a portable fireplace that was plugged into the wall. It was all very English looking, and Megan imagined it reminded her very much of her life before the boardwalk.

Margaret sank into one of the chairs and gestured to the other. Megan sat quietly, waiting.

"I'm exhausted," Margaret said. "As you know, the food truck festival here has finally come to an end. We retired our truck until next summer and I have to admit, it was a success." Her eyes twinkled back at Megan. "A very big thanks to you. But it also took more out of me than I'd expected. I'm having trouble keeping up with tasks here in my bookstore, and I wondered if you might be able to help."

"Of course," Megan said, sitting up a little. Fred lay down on the rug, but every now and then, he would turn back to the store. She kept a good hold on the leash. "What was it you needed exactly? I do have my own shop up and running now, but I close at 4 p.m. every day."

"Yes, here's the thing," Margaret said. "I host a regular story time on weekdays at one o'clock, and I would really love it if you could take over for me. Temporarily, of course. Maybe for a month?" Her eyes searched Megan's face tentatively. "I could have Desmond watch your place during that time." She leaned forward, whispering, "He's not the greatest at story time. The kids complain that they can't hear him, and he doesn't make good voices."

Megan smiled. She could imagine that. Desmond had come a long way in maturity, but the young teen might not quite be ready for story time. "I'd love to, Margaret," she said, smiling at the woman's obvious relief.

"Oh, thank you," she breathed. "I can't tell you how helpful this will be. Can you start tomorrow?"

"Tomorrow?" For some reason, Megan felt a fluttering of nerves in her stomach. Why were young children so intimidating? Most likely, it was because of their honesty. If they didn't like the way she read the books for story time, they'd be sure to let her know.

"Or I could probably get Santiago to do it." Margaret's

gaze was abnormally sly. "You two are both so personable and full of youth and life. Compassion and soul." She sighed, looking a little starry-eyed. "I can't help but think of my dear husband before he passed. We were a good match too."

Megan was sure her cheeks were crimson. "Oh no, it's not like that between us," she said, fighting the urge to press her hands to her hot face. What was Margaret talking about? Her and Santiago had never even gone on a date before. "We're just friends."

Margaret's smile only widened. "Well then," she said quietly, "very good friends aren't unlike a couple in love. I only meant it's nice to see a relationship like the one you two have." She paused, turning back to Megan and Fred. "That's all."

Megan smiled but couldn't think of anything else to say. She only stood when Margaret did and followed her back through the bookstore. Snickers, luckily, was being adored by two kids, leaving her free to drag Fred out of the shop. But her thoughts remained with the conversation she'd just shared with Margaret. She really did enjoy her friendship with Santiago. He was so different from anyone she'd ever met. She felt a connection and peace when she was with him that she'd never felt before.

Something stirred deep in her heart. But in the next moment, she brushed the feeling away with a deep breath of cool fall air.

"C'mon, Fred." She walked briskly down the wood planks of the boardwalk. "Time to go home."

"Now kids, we've got one last story here. Who thinks they can guess what it is?" Megan held the picture book to her chest, wrapping her arms around it as if she were trying to hide the back cover. She knew full well there were little pieces showing, and she watched the kids' eyes squint and strain to make them out.

One little boy raised his hand, tilting in his crisscross position as if he were going to lift off the ground. "I know!" he said in a high-pitched voice full of excitement.

She pointed at him with a smile. "Yes, Gabriel?" He had quickly become one of her favorites. She guessed he was about nine years old, and his cut-off shorts and T-shirts matched his shaggy overgrown hair and tan skin. It always had her thinking that he was living her dream childhood. Smiles and laughter were frequent with him, and he never missed a chance to offer to help. Now, he grinned back at her with confidence.

"It's about a horse," he said. His little gaze had caught the creature half-hidden behind her hand.

Megan gasped dramatically, leaning to the side to look at the picture. She uncovered it to reveal a unicorn and dragon. "That's very close," she said, smiling back at him. "Should we turn the book around and see what's on the front?"

"Yes!" Shouts rang out from the group of children. Some sat with younger siblings on their laps, and others crawled around behind the group, paying little attention. But when she turned the book around, even the crawlers stopped to investigate.

"The Haunted Castle of Make-Believe," Megan said, accentuating the words and enjoying the way each little pair of eyes widened. "Now this sounds like a book I want to read. Raise your hand if you want to read it too!"

Hands shot into the air along with squeals and giggles. Megan looked across the group to see one younger sibling had fallen asleep on their big brother's lap. A little girl close to the front with her long brown hair in a ponytail was gazing open-mouthed at the book. Megan pointed at her. "Kelsie, would you like to help turn the pages?"

The little girl jumped from the ground. "Yes, yes!" She hopped to Megan and stood directly in front of her, blocking everyone's view. Protests rang out from the group, but Megan held her hand up, stopping them. She winked at the group and guided the young girl to her side.

"Now, just wait for my signal, and then you can open to the title page."

The week had gone so well, Megan was beginning to think she'd like to take over story time indefinitely, even if she had to leave poor Fred at the shop every time. Margaret's feline, Snickers, had taken to sitting on her lap occasionally, and Fred always seemed a little peeved with her when she got back. In truth, it was a big commitment, so she hadn't asked Margaret just yet. She wanted to be sure first. Still, the little faces had grown on her. Especially Gabriel. He had a way of cheering the entire room with each comment and steering the kids in the right direction. Just a simple, *this is fun* or, *thanks for reading to us,* always brightened her mood. Being one of the oldest kids, it was clear the others looked up to him.

"Here you go, Miss Megan." She turned around to see Gabriel with the haunted castle book in his hands. He held it out to her.

"Thank you so much, Gabriel," she said. "Are you coming to story time tomorrow?"

"No." He looked like he was trying to make a sad face,

but the excitement inside was too great and instead, a wide smile pressed at the dimples in his cheeks. "We're going camping!"

"Wow, camping." Megan glanced out the window at the heavy cloud cover. "Isn't it a little chilly for that?"

"It's not." Gabriel shook his head, and his sandy brown hair fell into his dark brown eyes. He brushed it back. "Not when you have a tent and a dog. My dog is a yellow lab. His name is Tank, and he's huge! He sleeps right on top of my sleeping bag, and I'm not cold at all."

Megan smiled, picturing the boy and his dog. She couldn't resist tousling his hair a bit. "Well, I can't wait to hear all about it on Monday. Take lots of pictures so you can share with us, okay?"

His mouth dropped open with this new opportunity, and he nodded as if it were an important assignment. "I will. See you Monday!"

"Bye, Gabriel."

He skipped outside where his mother was waiting. Her hair was darker and smoother than Gabriel's, but there were similarities in their appearance. She held a leash, and at the end of it, sat a very large yellow lab. Megan hurried out the door, waving at the woman. She was young, likely younger than Megan. As the woman held out her hand and smiled with the same dimples as Gabriel, Megan found herself liking her immediately. "Hello," she said, "I just heard all about your camping trip and about Tank—oh!"

The big, yellow dog jumped up, wrapping his front legs around Megan so his head was nearly level with hers. His face was huge, and his big tongue lolled out one side of his mouth like Fred's always did.

Megan laughed, rubbing the big dog's neck with both hands. "Well, hello there."

"Tank!" Gabriel's mom gave the leash a tug, and he released Megan, settling his feet on the ground again.

"It's okay," Megan assured. "I have a Great Dane, so I'm used to big dogs. But before I had him, that would've terrified me."

"I'm sorry, he's just very friendly," she said. She held out her hand again with the same dimpled smile. "I'm Amanda. Nice to meet you, Megan. We live just north of here in the little town of Duthenger."

"Duthenger?" Megan hadn't heard of it before.

Amanda nodded. "It was settled by Irish settlers nearly a hundred years ago. It never really grew the way that Seacrest has." She winked at Megan. "But I'm glad."

"It sounds amazing," Megan said. "I'll have to drive out one of these days."

"Yes, you should," she nodded, then glanced up above the roofline of the shops to the trees beyond. "It's funny how small a circle we live in. Everyone gets used to their daily routines. I've never actually camped out here in Seacrest even though it's so close. But we're going tomorrow for the first time."

"I heard." Megan smiled at Gabriel, and he beamed back at her. "I hope you have a great time. It was very nice to meet you." She leaned down, giving Tank a pat. "And you too, of course." His tail wagged the way Fred's always did, thwapping Amanda's legs as it went. Megan laughed. "You're a good boy."

"Have a great day, Megan." Amanda gave her a wave, and she and Gabriel started down the boardwalk at what Megan liked to call a Seacrest pace. Peaceful and revived, it just seemed to happen naturally here.

Megan thought back to her days working in an ER as a young twenty-something nurse. She was grateful for the experience and the opportunities of helping others, but it had taken so much from her. It kept her so busy saving lives that she'd never actually had time for living. But here in Seacrest, she was providing a different kind of service. One that saved them in a different way. She crossed her arms and leaned against the front of Margaret's bookstore, considering if this was where she was meant to be. She'd promised her friend Allie, nearly two years earlier, that she would chase her dreams, but was this opportunity really the best path for her life? She gazed out at the ocean, wondering.

"Just heading back?" Megan turned around at Margaret's question. The older woman held a bundle of books in her hands. "I know Desmond enjoys being his own boss at your shop every afternoon during story time." She smiled and nodded her head as if agreeing with herself.

Megan smiled. "I appreciate his help. I suppose I need to head back there now. Just got distracted for a moment. It's a beautiful day today. I've never been here over the winter, but so far, it seems very mild."

Margaret's eyebrows rose, and her glasses slid down the bridge of her nose a quarter inch. "Well, don't let it fool you," she said. "This coastline is notorious for high winds and low temperatures for at least a couple of months of the winter season." She winked. "It'll come. Just be glad it hasn't yet."

"Do people come out to the boardwalk in the winter?" Megan glanced back at the shops.

"No, it's pretty slim with shoppers when the weather is

bad for a long stretch of time." Margaret adjusted the books in her hands. "Some shops close completely through December and January. Although, I like the look of string lights and wreaths in December, so I stay open."

Megan smiled. "That sounds cheerful."

"Yes," Margaret agreed. "Speaking of which, it sounded very cheerful in your story time today. Are you going to be able to continue with it? I don't want it to be a burden with your shop."

"Oh no, it's no bother." Megan looked back at Margaret, hesitating only a moment before she knew for sure. "In fact... I'd like to take it on indefinitely if you're okay with that. I mean, I suppose the winter won't have many kids coming out, but I sure have enjoyed it."

Margaret released a big breath. "Oh, thank goodness." She laughed briefly. "I've been hoping you'd be able to. Taking an hour or two in the afternoon to rest has been the only thing keeping me going. I really appreciate your help."

Megan crossed her arms. "Are you sure there isn't anything else going on, Margaret?" she asked. "I know the food truck festival was busy, but have you been in to see the doctor lately?"

Margaret patted her arm, smiling sweetly. "You're a dear," she said. "I know it's in your blood to ask, but I'll be just fine. These old bones take longer to recover when they're tired. A bit of reality is all I'm experiencing. But I appreciate your concern, thank you."

Margaret made her way back into the little bookstore. "I'll see you tomorrow," she said. By now, Fred was probably starting a bit of trouble. He always seemed to know when she'd been away too long. The past week, she'd returned to find him chewing everything from the chair legs to the back door. He even stole a menu and shredded it to bits one day. But she couldn't blame him. It was probably frightfully boring to be sitting in a sandwich shop watching food go back and forth all day.

When she came in the front door, the tables were full of customers enjoying their orders. She spotted Desmond at the cash register. He handed a woman and her daughter their sandwiches and then a receipt, thanking them. Megan went to the back to check on Fred since he wasn't lying on his pillow. When she opened the door, she found her office empty. The storage room across the hall was empty too, although his leash was still hanging in its place on a little hook by the back door.

"Desmond?" she asked, feeling nervous about the idea of Fred racing back to Margaret's place and tearing it apart. She bit her lip, hearing Desmond respond with a *yeah*. "Where's Fred?"

"Oh, he had to go out." Desmond leaned into the hall-way, giving her a wave. "It's only been ten minutes or so. I'm sure he's fine."

"I told you not to let him out," Megan said, trying not to sound irritated, although she couldn't stop it from building in her chest.

"I'm sorry, but he had to go," Desmond shrugged. "I didn't want a small pond here on the floor, so I let him out. It's fine, go check for yourself." He nodded his Salty Subs hat at the back door.

"Okay, thanks." Megan decided to drop it, telling herself that Fred was fine. Sure, he liked to get into more trouble than a sea lion in a sardine shop, but that didn't mean he couldn't control himself. He was usually very well behaved. Regardless, she couldn't help but hold her breath as she opened the back door. Before she could take a single step, Fred raced across her view, panting hard. A yowl came from somewhere ahead of him, followed by the sound of claws scratching against the wood planks of the boardwalk.

Fred was most definitely *not* fine.

Chapter Four

By the time she caught up with her canine and dragged him back to the shop, Megan was exhausted. Plus, she had the strange feeling that he was laughing at her from time to time. His big blue eyes would shift in her direction while his nose wrinkled on one side, lifting his cheek to expose a few teeth. It was a grin most cunning, so she couldn't help but laugh.

"Fred, you're going to have to be friends with Snickers eventually." She closed the door to her office and sat in her rolling chair. He glanced back at the door as if he were going to sprint off at any moment. She propped her elbows on her knees and took a moment to breathe. "Margaret is my friend, and I'm going to be spending a lot of time at her bookstore." She rubbed under Fred's ear, and he finally sat with a snort. "Besides, the kids at sharing time would love to meet you." She leaned to the side to look into his eyes, but he purposefully averted them. "I can't do that unless you learn how to behave around a cat. You've seen cats before, right? Why is it so hard with Snickers?"

If Megan could hear his thoughts, she would know that Snickers was an obnoxious tease and a know-it-all. Fred felt perfectly justified in chasing the bushy-tailed tyrant away.

With a sigh, Megan stood and stroked his back. "I'll get you a bowl of water, and then you're staying in here until closing time. Settle in and take a nap." She kept a tight hold on the door and squeezed through, closing it behind her.

"Do you think you could take over the shop on Saturday?" Megan asked Desmond. He'd been wiping down the counter, and he paused at her question. A grin brightened his young face, and he stood tall, facing her with a confidence that was very new to him. Megan loved to see it.

"I could, but it would mean closing early at one or two. I made plans to go hiking with some friends, and we wouldn't want to go too late." He ran one hand through his dark, bushy hair and then shrugged. "But if you can't find anyone else, we could go hiking another time I guess—"

"No," Megan said, a little frustrated at herself for not finding a replacement sooner. "Let me see if I can have someone cover the last half of the day. Maybe Santiago could come in at noon? Do you know if he's working Saturday?"

"Santiago?" Desmond shrugged. "Nah, I don't know. I think he pretty much works whenever he wants though, so you could just ask him. He's loaded too, did you hear? His parents are major jewelry tycoons, and he's like the heir of their company or whatnot."

"Yeah," Megan sighed. "I heard something like that." She'd been the one to prove his innocence after his parents thought he was smuggling from the company and had him thrown in jail. But at least he was out, and his parents seemed at least a little humbled by the whole thing.

Desmond shifted his weight, looking uncomfortable with

all the silence between them. "Uh," Megan said as she began stacking empty sandwich baskets and set them on a lower shelf. "I'm sure he can do it. I'll let you or Margaret know. Thank you."

"So, where ya going?" Desmond walked around the counter and took the lid off a garbage can, tying the bag into a knot.

"To visit my parents and Crystal's father too." Megan supposed it didn't sound very fun, especially after Desmond gave her a slight grimace, as if he were trying to smile but couldn't figure why. She laughed. Her response as a teenager would've been similar. "It'll be a nice getaway, especially for Fred. I think he needs some time away from Margaret's new kitty."

"Oh, yeah," Desmond laughed. "They don't like each other much, do they?" He lifted the garbage bag over his shoulder and walked back down the hall to throw it in the dumpster out back. As much as Megan had been a little skeptical of hiring the young teen, he'd shown his worth. In the shop, the tables were empty, and the customers had gone. She grabbed a rag and a bottle of cleaner.

๑๕๕

THE BIKE RIDE HOME WAS UNEVENTFUL, ALTHOUGH SHE'D had to drag Fred the first few feet. Delighted with the prospect of running back to Margaret's, he'd been a little on the wild side. But he got the idea soon enough and was perfectly behaved while she rode on the trail. The number of times he'd sprinted off after a squirrel, or sometimes at absolutely nothing at all, had lessened in recent months. She was happy not to be dumped off her bike into the leaves and pine needles, and he seemed content to run along beside her. The thought struck her that he just might enjoy her company as much as she did his. Being terrified of dogs her entire childhood made this idea rather novel. Her heart warmed as she took the steps to the back porch and leaned her bike against the side of the house. She knelt next to Fred and rubbed his neck. "Good boy, Fred." It was such an amazing thing to have a dog like him in her life. How much had changed since she'd come to Seacrest.

She went inside to call Santiago. He was a good friend but asking a favor at such short notice had her feeling a little guilty. Even so, she wanted to get it over with as soon as possible. His voice was cheerful when he answered, and she cut right to it. "Would you be able to help with my sandwich shop on Saturday? It would only be from noon to four and Desmond would be there for the first hour or so. I'm sorry to ask you so late notice, but I'm heading to Seattle with Crystal this weekend and it was a fairly last-minute plan—"

"Megan," he fell into the laughter that was always so charming coming from him. "Relax, it's fine. I'd love to serve sandwiches on Saturday. It was exactly what I hoped for when you called. I told myself, just maybe Megan will ask me to make sandwiches."

Megan laughed. "You're sure you don't have other plans?"

"Nope," he said. "I'm just walking trails today, but we're going to have to do a major overhaul of the trail you and Fred took. We need machinery out here that can dig out that pathway and wire mesh to stabilize the rock above it. That's our main concern, but we're just waiting for the funding. For now, I just put stakes and caution tape up to close the trail." He sighed. "People rarely pay attention to the signs, but it's all we can do for now. At least it's not peak tourist season."

"Well, when I get back, I'd love to help with the trails or whatever else you guys might need. Consider me a volunteer." Megan had missed spending time with Santiago. He always had her feeling more interesting, funny, and all around amazing when they were together. Plus, he and Fred had a great connection. She looked over to see his big blue eyes were watching her with interest. No doubt he heard one of his favorite voices on the other end of the phone.

She flipped the switch to the fireplace and sank into the couch. "Thank you, Santiago. I really appreciate your help."

"Anytime, Megan." His voice was deep and sincere. "You have a safe trip this weekend."

She thanked him again and hung up the phone, thinking of the first time they'd met. His eyes had been a shock to her, glowing pools of turquoise on a tanned face. The next thing she'd noticed was his hair, long and wavy, threaded with sandy blond as if he spent his summers in the Caribbean. And then there'd been the flash flood that almost carried her house away... she'd noticed that third.

She grinned and pushed off the couch. It wasn't going to be exactly the trip she'd wanted. She'd realized that after calling her parents and finding out they were on vacation in Mexico. It was a little disheartening that she knew nothing about it. But then, she would just have to be a better daughter and call more regularly. At least they were enjoying themselves.

Fred had taken up camp in front of the fireplace, and she went to pack their bags for the next day. A twist of excitement rushed through her at the thought of an actual girl's trip. Sure, it was just going to Seattle to visit former

Governor Chambers, but it was still a trip with a girl. It counted.

The evening passed quickly, filled with cleaning and organizing so her return home from Seattle would be met with an orderly house. She slept well and woke early, energized by her excitement. The morning flew by and story time with the kids was fun, although she missed Gabriel. It would be good to hear from him when he returned from his camping trip.

Before she knew it, she was lifting a duffel bag, blanket, and pillow into the trunk of Crystal's car. It was a roomy sedan and looked brand new, but her friend insisted it was fine if Fred sat up on the backseat. Megan gave him as much of a warning look as she could, crossing her fingers that he would be the perfect gentleman on their trip.

"Your dad knows I'm coming, right?" Megan asked, after they'd traveled down the highway for an hour or so, making small talk about the little towns they passed.

Crystal hesitated, glancing at her from behind reflective sunglasses. "Not exactly, but it's fine. I told him I was coming to visit, and he said he's planning on it."

"Should we call him up just in case? I'm sure he has appointments and parties all the time," Megan said. "I'm not totally comfortable just barging in on Governor Chamber's life."

"Megan, he's not the governor anymore." Crystal smiled, keeping her eyes on the road. "He does teach a college class on Saturday, but it's only a couple of hours. It'll be fine. And Cambridge is beautiful. You'll love it."

Still, Megan's apprehension grew the more she imagined simply popping in at the Chamber's mansion.

"Besides, I called him a few times this morning, and he's

not answering." Crystal spoke at a road-trip pace, matching their easy, scenic drive. Soon enough, they'd be engulfed in city traffic. Still, she seemed to be enjoying the getaway as much as Megan.

Or rather, Megan *had* been enjoying it. Now she was just worried that no one knew she was coming. She shifted in her seat, trying to brush off the unease and simply enjoy it. Besides, if he was anything like his daughter, Governor Chambers would be kindness itself. Megan glanced back at Fred to see he was embarking on his favorite activity while driving. Sleeping. He was stretched out across the entire back seat, looking supremely comfortably.

"So Megan." Crystal checked her blind spot and changed lanes. "How are things going with you and Kenneth?"

Megan felt an entirely new wave of emotions, especially when it came to talking to Crystal about her relationship with Kenneth. Seeing as how Crystal and Kenneth had dated years earlier, it just felt a little awkward. Or maybe it was that she wasn't entirely sure herself how things were going. "Well," she studied the cars around them on the highway as she spoke, "he's heading out of the country for at least a month, but he calls pretty regularly. So, that's nice."

"I guess he travels a lot," Crystal said. Her expression had fallen a bit, as if she'd hoped to hear something different.

Megan didn't want to give her the wrong impression. She sat up a little. "I'm okay with it though. I never expected him to move out here and change his life. But honestly, I don't plan to change mine either." She shrugged. "I've loved getting to know him, and I admire him a great deal... but other than that, I don't know what will happen with us. Our lives are so different."

"They are," Crystal said. Her eyes flickered to Megan's

and then returned to the road. "I guess you never know." She seemed agitated, her eyes scanning the road too quickly. Finally, she turned back to Megan. "So, there's nothing between you and Santiago?"

Megan only stared back, unsure of how to answer. Of course there was nothing going on, but... why was she asking? Finally, she shook her head and Crystal sighed, turning her eyes back to the road.

"Would you mind if I asked him out then?" She glanced back at Megan and shrugged. "I've been wanting to but wasn't sure if you... if there was anything going on between you two."

"Oh... well... no, nothing," Megan said. It was true, but somehow she wanted to argue with herself. Santiago was quite a bit younger than her, but it was no secret that he had a crush on her. Still, even though she didn't want to date him... suddenly she realized she didn't want Crystal to either.

The realization hit her like a sneaker wave on the shore. For the next hour, she couldn't get the idea out of her mind that she might possibly be harboring feelings for him. She pictured him in her mind, feeling her heart warm at the thought of his gorgeous smile and incredible eyes. Then she switched to Kenneth, and her heart warmed just the same.

Great.

So, now that she was completely unsure of herself, she was just going to have to sit back and watch Crystal make a move? She looked out the window, biting her lip. It was fine, she didn't want to stop her friend from going out on a simple date with Santiago. After all, she'd had plenty of time to say something and had only told him no. Repeatedly. But suddenly her stomach was churning. She couldn't imagine them kissing or Crystal being in his arms. It practically crushed her to think of... so why hadn't she known it before?

"You're sure it's okay?" Crystal asked.

Megan flinched. She'd been so deep in thought, she forgot to answer. "Yes, I'm sure," she said. But inside, she was still a battlefield of indecision. From day one, she believed Santiago was too young for her. She'd even told him that herself. For goodness' sake, she was thirty-one, and he was only twenty-three! But then... so much had happened between them, and for the first time, she found herself thinking of him as a man instead of a college kid. In her thoughts, she traced the lines of his face, imagining him while her heart burned with a sense of loss. How could she be so hurt losing someone she'd never even desired?

Her phone rang, and she pulled it from her bag. On the screen was Kenneth's name, and she swallowed hard before answering. Kenneth was an incredible man, and she considered herself lucky to be with him. There were plenty of reasons why he would be better for her than Santiago.

"Hello, Megan." His voice was the same, melted-chocolate luxurious. But somehow, it didn't affect her like it had before. Something was different, even though he hadn't changed one bit. If that was the case, then Megan had to figure something. Because if Kenneth wasn't the one doing the changing, it only meant one thing. Megan was the problem.

Chapter Five

"I'm sorry Miss Crystal, but he hasn't come in yet."

Megan appraised the secretary. A woman not much older than her, with short brown hair and eyes and a petite build, all wrapped up in a very elegant pantsuit. However, her face was visibly stressed. She couldn't hold still, and her hands fidgeted about even as she waited through the small pause of maybe a minute.

Finally, she abandoned them and turned back to organizing things on her desk, as if she couldn't handle being sedentary a moment longer. Fred walked around her desk and sniffed at the woman, and she jumped. "Oh my," she said, setting one hand on her chest. "He's a big one, isn't he?"

"Fred, c'mon," Megan shortened his leash, bringing him back. "Sorry about that," she said. "He's friendly."

"Yes, how nice." The secretary pulled out a folder and began flipping through the papers inside. "Your father is expected to be back soon, though, if you'd like to wait. He has class in one hour. He should be in by now. Have you spoken to him today?"

Crystal frowned. "No, not for a few days, actually. He said something about a field trip with his students?"

"Yes." The secretary's brow furrowed as she went back to the papers in her hands. "They went to the Natural Resources building this week but got back Friday afternoon." The phone rang, and the secretary dropped the papers to her desk. She sighed, looking exhausted. "Why don't you go ahead and wait in his office," she gestured to the door across the hall. "I'm sure he'll arrive any minute now." She picked up the phone. "Hello, Mr. Chambers's office."

Megan followed Crystal into her father's office. The blinds were drawn, and Crystal switched on the lights. A big walnut desk sat in the middle of the room with two tall bookshelves behind it. Large sitting chairs faced the desk, and Megan sank into one, letting Fred's leash go. "Where do you suppose he is?" she asked, leaning her head back to look at the ceiling. She closed her eyes. They'd gotten a hotel room the night before and finished up their trip that morning, but somehow it was still exhausting.

"I don't know," Crystal's voice was more somber than usual, and Megan glanced over to see she'd opened the blinds and looked out on the city beyond. "To tell you the truth, I'm getting worried."

Megan pushed up from the comfortable chair and got to her feet. She surveyed the room. "Do you think he came in at all this morning?" she asked, running her hand across the smooth desk. There was a paper organizer on one side and a wooden cup of pens in the middle. Besides that, there was only a little ceramic figurine of a caterpillar. It sat in the center of the desk with the price tag still attached.

Megan picked it up and read the label out loud. "Washington's Closet." It appeared to be a simple memento. She looked at Crystal. "Do you know where this came from?"

Crystal turned around, frowning at the ceramic caterpillar. She walked back to Megan and peered at it. Pinching the small tag between her fingers, she shook her head. "No idea... Washington's Closet," she muttered. "What is that, like a gift shop?"

"You got me," Megan shook her head. "I've never heard of it."

"Well." Crystal sighed, handing it back. "I don't know. It's been a long time since I've been back at his office. Maybe it was a gift." She wandered the perimeter of the room, touching a vase and the windowsill. "He's only ever left once." Her voice was quiet. "It was after an election. He and my mom had been arguing constantly. Finally, he stormed out, saying he'd be back in a week. We don't know where he went and couldn't get hold of him. It was really tough on my mom, trying to answer everyone's questions and keep their struggles private at the same time."

She turned to Megan. Her arms were crossed, and she rubbed her hands over them as if she were cold. "They decided to buy two separate homes after that. They haven't officially divorced, but they don't see each other very often now. I'm fairly sure it's coming."

The door swung open. The secretary stood in the doorway, face flushed and eyes wide. "Do you think you could take over for your father?" she said to Crystal. "I had no idea he wouldn't be in, so I have no sub, and his students are already in their seats. His class starts in five minutes."

"I thought you said it wasn't for another hour—" Crystal objected.

"No, no." The secretary's hands waved in front of her. "I

forgot on Saturdays that his class is earlier. You'd just have to go off his lesson plan. It's on his computer under a file folder named lesson plans."

Megan fought back a grin, but when she glanced at Crystal, her friend looked terrified. In the corner of the room, Fred looked up from where he'd lain down. Megan shrugged. "I can help, if you want."

Crystal looked to be struggling with the idea, but eventually, she nodded. "Okay, I suppose we could just read over his lesson plan and cover as much as we can."

"Oh, thank goodness," the secretary breathed a sigh of relief. She stuck her hand out. "I'm Carleen, by the way. Nice to meet you."

Fifteen minutes later, Megan and Crystal were staring into the eyes of more than a dozen curious college students. Megan had agreed to take over the introduction after she noticed sweat gathering on Crystal's forehead, but she made sure to bring Fred with her for backup. It was nice to have all the curious eyes on him instead of her.

She cleared her throat as if attempting to gain the attention of the room. But it was unnecessary. Silence remained, and she fidgeted with her hands. "I'm not Mr. Chambers, obviously." She cleared her throat again. "He's been detained, and from his lesson plans, I see we're supposed to be starting a recap of your visit to the Natural Resources building in Seattle. I'm Megan, by the way, and this is Fred." Fred sat down and scratched at his ear, clearly telling the class he was more interesting than anyone else. Megan let her gaze wander over their faces, giving them a bit of time to digest her words. "Anyone want to start us off?"

There were whispers around the room, especially from a group of three boys near the back. Finally, seeming egged on by the others, the young man with spiky black hair and noticeably blue eyes rose to his feet. He raised his hand in a greeting. "I'm Drake." He gestured to the boys sitting around him. One had curly brown hair, and the other had unnaturally white-blond hair. They both had dark eyes and smiled back at her pleasantly. "This is Vance and Carter. We, uh, were in charge of the video presentation." He pulled a laptop from his backpack. "I guess we could just show it and then talk about our conclusions?" He waited for Megan's response.

"That sounds great," she said, relieved to have someone take the lead. "So, just to catch me up on this project, what was the object of your visit? Was it simply to get to know the purpose of Natural Resources?"

A young woman in the front raised her hand. "I can explain," she offered. She waited until Megan nodded and then straightened in her seat, gesturing energetically with her hands as she spoke. "Okay, for three weeks before our visit, we wrote up budget proposals for the Natural Resources department. The purpose of the trip was to take our knowledge of the federal funding they receive and divvy it up based on what we believed were the most important aspects. Then we were going to compare our notes to their actual budget and see how close we came."

Megan nodded, impressed. "I like that idea," she said, turning to the young man. He was still messing with his computer and a cord he was trying to connect to the projector machine. She turned back to the class. "So, before we see the video and talk about conclusions, what were some of your guesses?" She scanned the room. "Where did you feel the money should go?"

A young man with dark, shoulder-length hair raised his hand. "The study of habitats and habitat preservation."

Megan nodded. "I love that. Anyone else?"

A young woman signaled to Megan with a peace sign. "Prevention of hazardous waste contamination."

"Yes," Megan agreed, "very good thought."

"Upkeep for national parks."

"Invasive species prevention."

"Clean water initiatives."

Megan folded her arms, smiling back at the group. "Very good ideas," she said, encouraged for the future of the state and especially her little town of Seacrest. "I'm curious to see what your visit concluded." She turned around to see Drake standing next to his laptop. A video was already projected onto the screen and paused. "You ready?" she asked.

He smiled. "Yes ma'am." He leaned in, scratched Fred, and then nodded to his friend Vance, who flipped the lights off. The video started, and the boys sat down to watch. Megan pulled her chair back and turned it around so she could see as well. Crystal dragged a chair over and sat beside her, peering up at the screen. She still seemed tense and worried, and Megan hoped the video would help her to relax just a little. It seemed strange that the governor's daughter would be intimidated by a little college class.

"...and here we are!" Carter narrated from the video, turning it to his face briefly as he flashed a huge grin. The class around them giggled. The video showed students unloading from a small travel bus. There was a rather architecturally bland building, although the trees and bushes around it were neatly trimmed and added much needed relief from the tan brick structure.

A paper landed in Megan's lap, and she jumped. "Sorry,"

Carter whispered, crouching down in front of her and Crystal. He handed Crystal a paper too. "I just wanted to give you a breakdown of what we came up with for a budget. This was like our hypothesis, and we're supposed to write up an actual budget this week after comparing what we learned from the senior manager of NR." Fred licked Carter's face suddenly and he laughed, sneaking back to his seat.

"Thanks," Crystal whispered back, turning to smile at him. It was the first interaction she'd had with the class, and Megan glanced back to see Carter looking a little stunned. He smiled back and then turned to the video, as did Megan and Crystal. Fred plopped down on the floor with a loud sigh. It was too dark to read the paper she'd been given, but Megan was glad to have it. In the video, the class was a cheerful bunch and much more outgoing than they seemed that morning. Perhaps the change in their instructor had left them a little standoffish.

"This is the front guard to the building," Carter's voice continued while the video showed an officer in a bullet-proof vest and uniform. He didn't smile at the introduction and only nodded curtly. "We're heading to Mr. Williamson's office now. Let's see if our predictions on budget are anywhere close to actual. Katie, what do you have to say? Think we're close?" The video panned to a girl with golden skin and long blonde hair. She grinned with pursed lips and reached for the camera, pushing it away. "That's a yes, folks. She thinks we're spot on."

The class giggled again.

They came to an office and a man dressed neatly in tan slacks, a blue shirt, and a maroon tie. He looked about fifty. He smiled and waved at the camera. "Hello students. Charlie Williamson, pleased to meet you." He stepped forward, extending his hand. "Hello, former Governor Chambers. It's nice to see you again, old friend."

The camera panned and zoomed out to see Crystal's father. He was just like Megan remembered him from his time as governor except with a bit more silver in his dark hair. His broad smile was a trademark, and he flashed it as he shook Charlie Williamson's hand. "It's a pleasure to see you as well," Mr. Chambers said. "Thank you for agreeing to meet with my class."

"Come in, won't you all?" Mr. Williamson stepped out of view of the camera, and the video continued into a sprawling office with lofty city views. It felt like a high-class high-rise instead of the dull government building it was on the outside. There were *oohs* and *aahs* as the students wandered the space and gazed out the windows.

The recording panned back to Carter again as he'd spun the camera around in his hands. "I've given this copy to Mr. Williamson, and he's reviewing it." His eyes widened with intrigue. "Let's see what we've got." The world whizzed by and stopped to focus on a desk. Mr. Williamson sat down behind it and had a few papers and a laptop spread out in front of him. "Uh-huh," he mumbled. "I appreciate what you've done here..." He scribbled atop their budget numbers, occasionally turning to his computer and back again. "Nope." He drew a line across a portion of the budget and began scribbling again. Finally, he sat back and took a breath. "I think we've got it. You weren't too far off, just a few things here and there. Good work, everyone."

A few quiet cheers were heard in the background, and Mr. Williamson laughed. "Thanks for stopping in." He stood and handed the revised paper to Mr. Chambers. "Don't forget to visit the gift shop downstairs." He chuckled and leaned in close to the camera. "It's really just a mini market that expanded recently to include books, magazines, and trinkets."

Megan turned to Crystal. "A gift shop," she whispered.

Crystal nodded.

"Bye, Mr. Chambers."

Megan turned back to the video to see a young woman with long, black hair holding Crystal's father's hand. It seemed they'd meant to shake hands but ended up simply staring back at each other. Although Mr. Chambers' face was out of the picture, the interest in the woman's eyes was obvious.

"Ooooh!" someone called out at the back of the room, whistling. The class laughed, but Megan could only think of Crystal. She had to be wondering so many things at that point. She'd seemed okay with the idea of her parents splitting up, but was she really?

The video continued, jumping from the office to what Megan assumed was the gift shop. The sign at the front flashed past. *Washington's Closet.* Megan held her breath, watching intently. An employee waved at the camera, welcoming the group. She was young and looked college-age herself. Her hair was the longest Megan had ever seen, reaching well past her hips. It was brown, thin, and very straight. "Hey guys," she said cheerily, "come on in. Grab a snack or feel free to purchase anything from our critter's corner. Every purchase helps support the health and vitality of our national parks and protected species." The camera panned the area, and Megan spotted a display with dozens of different ceramic creatures. She didn't see the caterpillar, but this had to be where it came from. Next, the view switched to the students filing back onto the bus. Conversations were loud and excited before it cut out.

The lights in the classroom flickered on, and Megan blinked away her blinded vision. She meant to address the class again, but Crystal beat her to it, walking to the middle of the class quickly and closing the laptop. For a moment, she was silent, and the tension in her eyes seemed to quiet the whole room. She nodded at Drake. "Thank you for your presentation," she said. Then she turned to the whole group. "Mr. Chambers is my father, and I'm afraid he's missing at the moment."

Conversations started up here and there. Crystal wrung her hands together as she waited for them to quiet. Finally, she lifted one hand, speaking over the noise. "Excuse me," she said politely. Then, with a loud voice she tried again. "Excuse me!"

The room hushed.

"Thank you." She began pacing and stared at the floor as she spoke. "I haven't been able to get hold of him for a couple days now, and he missed this class without telling anyone ahead of time. That's not like him. I'm hoping one of you can tell me something." She faced the class. "Has anyone seen him or heard from him today?"

Megan glanced back at the room, hoping. Silence hung heavy in the air until a girl with pixie-cut brown hair raised her hand. "I think the faculty at NR had some kind of dinner after the field trip. I heard that lady with dark hair tell him about it. Maybe he went to that?"

"Okay, I'll check on it," Crystal said. "Anything else?"

The girl sat down, and it was silent again. Then Drake stood. He shrugged and glanced around the room. "Honestly, I think Drea's right." He gestured to the girl who had spoken first. "He was talking to Mr. Williamson and his secretary like they were all going to go out that night."

"Yeah, but what about the ride home," Crystal said, sounding a little exasperated. "What about when you got back to the school? Did he drive anyone home? Did he mention if he was staying late at the school afterwards?"

"The school?" Drake asked, his eyes narrowed.

"Yes, the school!" Crystal shouted. Her voice was shaking. "Here. Right here!" She pointed at the ground. "When was the very last moment you saw him after the field trip?"

"But, uh, ma'am..." Drake shifted his weight, looking uncomfortable. "He didn't ride home with us on the school bus. He stayed at NR and said he was going to catch a ride back. I, uh, don't think it was what he'd planned. But maybe..." He swallowed. "Maybe there was someone he wanted to spend time with."

"Excuse me?" Crystal's voice was a warning, and Drake's mouth clamped shut. He shrugged and sat down in his seat. Crystal scanned the room as if waiting for more.

It stung at Megan's heart, and she joined her friend at the front. "I'm sorry, everyone." She said, "We're just very worried. We had no idea Mr. Chambers stayed at the building." She scanned the faces, sure someone out there was holding back at least a small piece of information. "Please let us know if you hear from him or know anything at all. And can I just ask..." She hesitated, glancing at Crystal who looked mostly frozen. Megan was sure the same thing was going through both their minds. What if all this worry was caused by a weekend fling? "Are you absolutely positive he didn't come back on the bus?"

Again, it was Drake who answered. His voice was hollow,

as if he were thinking the same thing. "One hundred percent certain, ma'am. I'm sorry."

Megan held his gaze for a moment.

But Crystal only swished one hand through the air. "Class dismissed."

Chapter Six

❦

"Tell me what you're thinking," Megan said, looking back at Crystal and hardly able to wait another second. Her friend only gazed across the classroom. The students were gone, and she hadn't said a word since.

Now, her stormy blue eyes flickered back to Megan. "I have no idea what to think," she said. "There are so many possibilities right now. We just need to find out a little bit more. I wish he would call me." She gazed at Megan with turmoil swirling in her worried expression. "Where could he be?"

"What if we run out to his house and see if he's there," Megan offered, rubbing Fred's back. He was still sleeping at her feet and had begun to snore. Trips really seemed to take it out of him. "That ceramic caterpillar on his desk proves he came back to the school, doesn't it? What if he got sick and just forgot to call in to his secretary? Maybe he's just sleeping off a fever."

Crystal took a breath, nodding. But the lines of her face

didn't ease. "I left him so many messages," she said. "I thought for sure he'd get back to me before we even got here. What could possibly be keeping him?"

Megan's thoughts turned to the woman at the end of the video with long, dark hair. She thought of her as she watched Crystal stand and loop her purse over one shoulder, staring out the window.

"We should stop in at that Natural Resources building too," Megan ventured. "Olympia is on our way home, so it would be easy enough." She waited for Crystal to turn around. Finally, she did. There was more discouragement in her fallen expression than Megan expected. But Crystal only nodded and made for the door.

"Good idea," she said, her voice sounding weak. "Let's go to his house first."

Don't you mean your house? But Megan kept the question inside and jiggled Fred's leash, waking him. He lifted onto his big feet and walked out to the hall with them. It seemed he was utterly bored with college.

They turned down a very sleek stone driveway. Crystal entered a code at the gate, and it slid open. She pulled in slowly and stopped in front of the garage. But when Megan turned around to get Fred, she gasped. The back windows were filthy and covered with smudges and nose marks from Fred. "I'll have to clean your car when we get home," she offered. Crystal didn't own any animals, and her house was always spotless.

But now, when she turned around and saw Fred's nose artwork on the window, she only smiled and shook her head at Megan. "No, it's okay. I don't mind." For a moment, she stared at Megan with a peaceful expression. Then, finally, she broke the silence. "I'm really grateful you both came. Thank you." Her eyes looked misty, and Megan couldn't help giving her a quick hug.

"I'm sure everything is fine," she said, smiling when she stepped back. "Let's go check it out. Okay?"

Crystal took a deep breath and nodded back. "Okay."

Fred dashed from the car the first chance he got, but Megan didn't bother with the leash. There was plenty of yard for him to roam, all surrounded with solid stone walls. She left him to it as they made their way up the front steps. The house was just as grand as she would have imagined a former governor's to be. Inside, it was cloaked in marble and designer furniture. The artwork was beautiful but non-specific, mostly nature, as if aiming to please a wide variety of people.

They walked through the entrance with a gorgeous chandelier that held long strings of glittering crystals hanging in a tapered spiral. Megan gazed up at it. "Wow," she mused. It was like long, diamond fringe. But when she brought her attention back to Crystal, her friend was gone. "Crystal?" Megan turned down the hall instead of continuing into the kitchen and living area. There were multiple rooms, most with the doors wide open. A library filled with books was first and then a small sitting room. Next, were two bedrooms and a final room at the end of the hall with its door closed.

She knocked lightly and twisted the handle. It looked like a master suite, albeit an incredible one. A sitting area greeted her with a large stone fireplace and luxurious white sheepskin rug. It opened into a spacious bedroom with a king-size bed and a wall of windows that looked out on a private cobblestone patio. Potted flowering trees and patterns of moss were placed artistically, and tall willow trees stood at the back of the outdoor space, framing it in. It was beautiful. Just like every other room in the house, it was immaculate. From the looks of the perfectly placed bedding and pillows, she'd wager he hadn't come home the night before. Or perhaps a cleaning service had already been there.

Wandering around to the other side of the bed, she spotted something on the hardwood floor. She bent down and picked up an earring. It was long and silver, shaped like a teardrop with a single emerald dangling off the end, glimmering back at her. She peered under the bed but didn't see another one. In the bathroom, it was more of the same immaculate perfection as the rest of the room, aside from the earring. Megan checked every drawer, finding only neatly folded towels and essential items like toothpaste and floss.

One of the hand towels was crooked and in a house so perfect, she couldn't help readjusting it. She returned to the hall. "Crystal?" she called again, coming through the kitchen and enormous living room. Another fireplace stood tall and grand.

"Up here," Crystal's voice came from the upper level, and Megan climbed the spiral staircase, running her hand along the glossy banister as she went.

"Hello?" She made her way down the hall and past a huge theater room.

"At the end of the hall," Crystal's voice rang out again, and Megan followed it into another master bedroom. This one was high enough to look out on a park and the hills and mountains beyond. Crystal stood holding a paper in her hands. It was creased in two places, as if it had come from an envelope.

"Here." Crystal held it out, and Megan took it cautiously. It was a letter made out to Stephen. She quickly glanced at the bottom to see it was signed, *Love, Alyana*. It very much looked like a love letter, but the wording was so vague that she couldn't be certain. The person spoke about enjoying their time together and appreciating his willingness to help in a tough situation.

Megan looked back at Crystal, whose eyes were trained on her intensely. "Do you know who Alyana is?" she asked.

Crystal's jaw hardened, and she squared her shoulder. "I don't," she answered, but there was suspicion hiding in her words, and Megan could read between the lines easily enough. Suddenly, she didn't want to show the earring she'd found in the bedroom on the ground level. But she had no choice. Crystal's father was clearly not in the house, and they needed to use every bit of evidence they could to figure out where he'd gone.

Slowly, she lifted the earring from her pocket, holding it out until Crystal had taken it. She peered at it as if it were from another planet. Megan took a heavy breath. "I found this on the floor in the bedroom downstairs. The one at the end of the hall."

"The guest bedroom?" Crystal asked.

Megan shrugged. Was that a guest bedroom?

Barking came from outside, loud and agitated. Fred wasn't one to bark needlessly and Megan took a tentative step toward the stairs. "I'm just going to check on him... you okay?" She waited until Crystal pulled her gaze from the earring.

"Ehm... yeah." She stuffed the earring in her pocket and followed. "I'll join you."

When they got to the front door, the barking had stopped. But Megan checked outside anyway. The second the door swung open, she meant to call for Fred, but a squirrel flashed across the ground at her feet. She shrieked and jumped back as it skittered across the wood floor.

"What is it?" Crystal was practically hiding behind the door. But before Megan could answer, Fred leapt up the steps and charged in, barking so loud it hurt Megan's ears.

"It's a squirrel. Wait, Fred!" She shouted as he hurdled completely over the couch and skidded across the stone floor of the kitchen. He dug his claws in and raced around the island, barking.

The critter appeared again. Megan jumped back as it raced out the door and up a tree. Fred was right behind him, hurdling the steps and barking incessantly.

With a sigh, she pushed the door closed. "I'm sorry." She turned back to Crystal. "Did he do any damage?"

"I don't think so," Crystal said, walking into the kitchen. They both inspected the floor and the cabinets and then the couch. But everything appeared to be scratch-free, which seemed like a miracle to Megan. Crystal was less impressed, and she sat down at one of the barstools, lost in the contemplation Megan was beginning to get used to. It seemed most of her friend's communication was done in her head.

Megan sat on the barstool next to her. "What are you thinking?" she asked.

After a few minutes of silence, Crystal's eyes wandered over to her, and she leaned back in her barstool with a squeak. "Well, I know what you're thinking," she said with a brief smile. "And first, let me address that."

She pulled the earring from her pocket and set it on the counter in front of them. "My mother doesn't wear long earrings, but it doesn't mean my father is having an affair." Her eyes returned to Megan's. They weren't defiant or shocked, only still. "It doesn't. I know it looks that way, especially after watching that tape and hearing he didn't return home on the bus. And then, finding this," she tapped the delicate piece of jewelry. "But you have to believe me, my father isn't the cheating type." She turned from the earring to Megan, looking deeply into her eyes. "I can't help thinking there's more going on here. I'm worried about him."

"Has anyone called the police to report him missing?" Megan asked. "If you really feel he's in trouble, we don't want to waste a lot of time."

"You're right, but..." Crystal stared off in the distance again. "Let me call my mother first. Maybe she's heard from him."

She pulled her phone out and began pacing the room and Megan listened intently to one side of the conversation. Crystal was calm and casual and only brought up her father after a few minutes, asking if she'd heard from him in the last day or two. There was a long pause and Megan watched as Crystal fidgeted and returned to the barstool, swiveling back and forth. Her mother's voice chittered in the background, and Megan could tell she was speaking very quickly.

"Yes, I know that," Crystal said. She turned and rolled her eyes at Megan. "Mom, all I'm asking is if you've heard from him. He—" She paused with her mouth open, obviously having been interrupted. "But—" Again, she waited. Her expression was becoming more tense.

Finally, she shot to her feet. "Mother, listen to me! Dad is missing. He's been missing for 24 hours now and didn't show up to teach his class this morning. Have you heard from him?" This time the pause was quieter. Megan couldn't hear if her mother was responding or not. Maybe she'd just hung up the phone. In any case, Crystal continued holding the phone to her ear and appeared to be listening to something.

After a few minutes, Crystal sighed but didn't look relieved. "Okay, then I think I should file a missing person's report. I'm going to give the local police a call." Again, she waited. "I understand that... yes, I realize it could be difficult. But Mom, what if he's really in trouble?" She glanced at Megan and sank into the barstool again. "Okay, I'll let you know. Love you. Bye."

With a groan, Crystal crossed her arms atop the counter, and her forehead landed on top with a thump. "I wasn't expecting her to take the news so personally," she mumbled into her arms. "I got the fifth degree of, why would your father ever talk to me, and you do realize it's been months since I've heard from him. Ugh, Megan. This is not how I expected my visit to go." She rolled her head to one side, looking over at Megan with tears in her eyes. "I don't want to hear that they don't love each other anymore. I just want things to magically get better."

"I know." Megan set her hand on Crystal's back. "I'm sorry. That's rough, but..." she couldn't help feeling the pressure mount with every tick of the round clock in the kitchen. "We have to report him missing. The more time passes, the more dangerous things could get for him if he really is in trouble."

"Okay, okay." Crystal brushed at the wetness under her eyes and typed out an internet search quickly, selecting the local police station. "At least I know someone at the station. Maybe that will help."

But when the call was answered, and she requested an Officer Morel, Megan could hear the woman on the other end of the line say he wasn't available. Crystal continued with her explanation, giving a very convincing case for a missing person. But it was clear the woman wasn't in any hurry to jump in. "And where can we contact you, Miss?"

Crystal gave her phone number, and the officer continued blandly, "Let me first assure you that ninety percent of missing person reports are solved without any police intervention. Especially adults. It could be very likely he will show up in the next day or two. We will do what we can for now, but unless there is evidence of foul play, we won't start an investigation until five days have passed."

"Five days?" Crystal's voice echoed in the big house "But what if something really happened to him? That's too long to wait! He's a former governor, don't forget. That has to account for something."

"Yes, ma'am." Her voice was no less dry. "That's why we bumped it up to five days instead of seven."

Crystal exhaled with a look of disgust. "Can you have Officer Morel call me, please?" The woman agreed to let him know she called and then said goodbye. "I can't believe this," Crystal said, turning to Megan with irritation lining her face. "How can we just sit around for four more days?"

Megan gave Crystal a look that she hoped held the appropriate amount of sympathy, but there were thoughts in her mind that wouldn't be still. Suspicions that had to be ruled out. She'd been considering each one of them during the phone call, and now they had the perfect amount of time to do a little digging of their own.

She turned her barstool to her friend. "What if we go down to the Natural Resources building right now?"

Crystal looked a bit suspicious.

Megan knew she'd already ruled out the idea that anything was going on between her father and the woman in the video, but she had to admit it was suspicious. "I know it's Saturday," Megan continued, "but maybe someone will be there cleaning or getting some extra work done. Who knows? We have time for a day trip. What do you think?"

Crystal straightened, seeming to buoy herself up a little. "Natural Resources is open on Saturdays, actually. Not every office will be open, but we can still look around a little."

Fred's barking suddenly burst to life outside, and they both turned to the window. It sounded different this time. It sounded vicious. But the barking was coming from the back. Megan hurried to the French patio doors, expecting another squirrel was teasing the Great Dane. But when she looked out the windows, she gasped.

A man clung to the top of the perimeter wall, and Fred was stretched up with his front feet on the stone, barking wildly. The man turned, meeting her gaze. He was pale with honey blond hair and wore jeans and a gray T-shirt. Before she could move, he jumped down, disappearing behind the red granite stones.

Chapter Seven

✦❧✦

"Yes, officer, I'm sure," Crystal repeated. She'd explained the situation three times already, and Megan could tell she was losing her patience. "Can you just send someone down here to check it out please? Thank you. And is Officer Morel around? No? Okay, thank you for your help. Goodbye."

Crystal tossed her cell phone on the couch and continued her pacing. She'd completed at least a hundred circles around the living room already, and Megan was getting dizzy. "Are they coming?" Megan asked.

"Maybe," Crystal shook her head. "They probably think I just want attention or something. I'm a little old for that, wouldn't you say?"

"Well, if we don't know whether they're coming, let's just go." Megan abandoned her barstool and glanced at the note Crystal scribbled out in case her father returned. The clock on the wall ticked away, reminding her that it was already past three in the afternoon. She wanted to get going.

They drove with Fred spread out across the back seat,

taking his usual afternoon nap. When they finally arrived and parked in a half-empty lot, he was breathing peacefully, his lip flapping with each breath.

"Let's crack the windows," Megan said. "I'm sure this won't take long." The late afternoon was cool and cloudy as they made their way inside. It seemed a little emptier than Megan would have expected, but Crystal was probably right about not everyone being there on the weekends. They passed an indoor courtyard with skylights and potted ferns. It was a pretty area, although small, and in the middle was a circular cement planter with a bench all the way around. Along the back was a gift shop.

"Washington's Closet," Crystal said, reading the sign above the doors. "Here it is." She had her hands clasped together but looked calm otherwise. With an unsteady glance at Megan, she walked inside.

There were fanny packs, magazines, and a wall of books. One shelf held varying flavors of homemade jams while another had T-shirts and even onesies with different critters and landscapes on the front. Everything showcased the state of Washington and its parks and wildlife. It was a beautiful little shop, and Megan found herself lost in its quirky, whimsical style. She touched a paper butterfly that hung from the ceiling many others.

"Right here," Crystal said.

Megan turned to see Crystal next to a wooden tree display with pegs on every side. Ceramic figurines dangled from the pegs. Megan joined Crystal and searched through the rodents, insects, sea-life, and mountain animals. A few of the spots were empty, but each had a label.

"Search for the caterpillar," Megan said, gazing over a

large beetle and a skink. But aside from the monarch cater-pillar, there were no others.

"I don't see it," Crystal said, having circled the display a few times over. "Maybe they changed the labels."

"Can I help you?"

Megan turned around to see the girl from the video. Her long brown hair was tied into a braid that swung like a rope about her hips.

"I order these from an artist up north," the girl said. "My manager didn't like the idea, but they've been our most popular items." Her slender lips broke into a wide smile. "It's nice to be right."

"We're looking for a caterpillar," Crystal said, from around the other side of the display.

The girl lifted a monarch caterpillar, letting it dangle from her fingers. "Right here," she said.

"No, not that one." Crystal joined the girl next to Megan. "It's one someone bought just the other day. It has very pale coloring, not bright like the monarch."

"Oh." The girl laughed, slapping her thigh. "It must have come from our tansy ragwort display. I had to take it down because my manager was getting complaints about it being too controversial, although I can hardly believe anyone would object to controlling noxious weeds and infestations."

"I'm sorry, what?" Crystal's nose wrinkled with the ques-tion, showing her utmost confusion.

"I have to agree," Megan said with a laugh. "What?"

"Here, follow me," the girl said, glancing about the shop. But they were the only customers, so she led them through the back door into a storage room with shelves and boxes of organized products. "I haven't sorted through it all just yet." She came to a few boxes on the floor behind a row of shelves. Sitting down on the concrete, her braid swung forward across her legs. She snatched it and flung it behind her. "Have a seat," she said, patting the concrete next to her. "I'm sure we can find it in no time."

Megan glanced at Crystal, and they sat down next to the girl.

"I'm Sandy, by the way," she said, reaching a hand forward and shaking their hands in turn. "Nice to meet you. So, why do you want this particular caterpillar?" she asked, as she pulled out bubble wrapped figures. She handed one to each of them and they began unwrapping.

"It was just a, uh, beautiful little figurine," Crystal said, unwrapping a giant hornet. She wrinkled her nose at it and wrapped it back up. Setting it in the box, she lifted out another bundle of bubble wrap. Megan finally uncovered her figurine to find a big black beetle. She sighed and wrapped it again, reaching for another.

"Here it is," Crystal said. She held her palm open, revealing the caterpillar from her father's desk. It was gray with dark red spots trailing its body and long bristles all over.

Sandy stared at the figurine and frowned. "Huh," she said, peering back at Crystal. "I guess I can see how you wanted to find it." She reached for the little figure, lifting it from Crystal's hand. "This is a Gypsy moth caterpillar. They're an invasive species in Washington. All of these are." She set it back into Crystal's hand. "That's how I came up with the name for the display. Tansy ragwort is a noxious weed."

"So, why were people complaining about these?" Crystal asked. "What did they say?"

Sandy handed the caterpillar back to Crystal and closed

the box, sliding it back with the others. "Well." She stood with a sigh, brushing her pants off. "I don't know what they said or who they were, but they had to be fairly important because my boss didn't even question it. He just had me take the display down immediately. It's frustrating because... well, my father supplies farmers all over the state with farm equipment. He's talked to a lot of them about the damage done to crops and natural habitat because of these harmful pests and—"

"Do you think you could ask for a name?" Crystal asked.

Sandy glanced between the two women; her eyes narrowed. "I... well yeah, I guess. What's so important about that caterpillar?"

"Oh, nothing," Crystal said. But she bit her lip as Sandy tilted her hips to one side and rested her fists against them. "Well, okay," Crystal said with an impatient breath, "but promise me you'll keep this between us."

The girl shrugged. "Sure, fine. I don't have a problem keeping secrets."

"Thanks." Crystal hesitated, rubbing her hands along her arms. "My father came here yesterday with a group of students. Mr. Chambers. Do you remember him?"

"Governor Chambers?" Sandy smiled. "Sure, I do. He's got to be one of the nicest guys. So, you're Crystal then?" Her eyes widened with her smile. "That's incredible." She held her hand out again. "It's so nice to meet you."

"Yes, thank you." Crystal shook her hand quickly. "The problem is, my father's missing. He didn't return to the school yesterday and didn't show up to teach class today. I haven't been able to get hold of him." Crystal leaned forward, and her voice hushed to a whisper. "But this was on his desk at the John F. Kennedy School of Government, so we know he returned. We just..." She sighed. "Well, we have no idea what to think. Do you know anything that might help?"

Sandy ran one hand down her braid, glancing at the door. "I'm sorry you guys, but I really don't..." She glanced back at the gift shop. "I need to keep an eye on the shop—"

"Sandy," Crystal grabbed her wrist, but when the girl turned around, she released her. "I'm worried about him. Really worried."

"Okay, but I didn't even hear what they were saying, okay? I just know what I saw and what it looked like..." Sandy chewed on her bottom lip, clearly nervous.

Crystal's eyes narrowed, but she took a slow breath, nodding back at Sandy. "Go ahead," she encouraged. Megan could see she was forcing a calmness on her face that wasn't real. Her tension showed in the creases between her smooth brows.

"Well, when the students were browsing the place, he went into the hall with a woman," Sandy's eyes were on the floor as she spoke, but they flickered up to Crystal's. "Just talking and stuff, but it looked pretty serious. I think the girl was even crying at one point." Sandy shifted her weight from one foot to the other. "He, uh, gave her a hug, and she left while he stayed here with the class. One of the girls noticed and asked who the woman was, and he said they were just old friends." Sandy paused, clearly having more to say as she looked tentatively at Crystal. She took a deep breath. "But when the woman was walking away, I heard him say, 'see you tonight.'"

"The woman works here in the building?" Crystal asked, not missing a beat.

"I think so," Sandy said. There were voices coming from

the shop, and she took a step toward the door. "At least, she probably does because I know I've seen her before." She grabbed the door handle and pulled it open. "I'm sorry I can't be more help."

"No, it's okay," Crystal assured her. "Thank you." But she glanced back at Megan with wide eyes and flushed cheeks. It was obvious she was nearly panicked.

"Let's go see who we can talk to upstairs," Megan said, sure the employees were close to calling it a day. Plus, Fred was bound to be slobbering on her windows again by now. "Maybe we can chat with her and clear this all up."

Crystal sighed. "I sure hope so."

They took the elevator to the top floor where the senior manager worked... along with his secretary.

And there she was.

A circular desk greeted them as they got off the elevator, and the woman from the video was typing away on a computer. Her hair was luxurious and dark. It was by no means as long as Sandy's hair, but it was thick, wavy, and very shiny. She looked up and smiled as they approached, and Megan couldn't help but feel a sense of doom at how beautiful she was. Her eyes were an exotic green and hazel mixture that glowed in contrast with her dark hair. Her skin was fair and smooth, and her full lips and smile were dazzling. Megan kept her gaze away from Crystal for fear of being too transparent with her worries.

"Hello," the woman said, shining her glorious smile in their direction. "How can I help you ladies?"

There was a moment of silence before Crystal managed a reply. "Yes, we'd like to speak to the senior manager, please."

"I'm sorry, but Mr. Williamson is out of town for the

next ten days. Can I leave him a message or possibly answer your questions in his place?"

"Sure," Crystal said. Megan could hear the hint of challenge in her friend's voice, and she held her hand up, claiming their attention.

"Maybe we should, uh..."—she looked intentionally into Crystal's eyes—"talk about it first?"

Crystal shook her head. "No, it's fine. I'm sure she can answer my questions." She turned back to the secretary. Megan wanted to interrupt, but her phone chimed, and she turned away from the desk to search for it in her purse.

Digging it out, she saw Drake had sent her the field trip videos she'd asked him for. "I'll just be just a second," she said. Taking a few steps away, she started the first video. In the background, Crystal asked the woman's name and Megan strained to catch the woman's answer. Alyana Cheshire. So the note they found was from her, and likely the earring too.

She brought her focus back to the videos. They were mostly repetitive of what she'd already seen, and she skipped through them impatiently. It wasn't long until she found just what she'd been hoping for.

A conversation was going on behind the camera while the view was tilted. It caught Crystal's father and Alyana standing down the hall from the gift shop, talking.

"I'm sorry, but you're wrong."

Megan glanced back to see Alyana looking a little red in the face with her voice rising as she spoke to Crystal. "I don't know what you're talking about. I never even spoke to him aside from saying hello when his class was with Mr. Williamson."

Megan turned back to the video, watching the screen as Alyana wiped a tear from her face and stepped into

Governor Chamber's arms. It was definitely more than a mere expression of friendship with the way she sunk into his arms and held him tightly. Her hands roamed his back, and she snuggled against him. A full minute must have passed before she stepped away again. Watching her lips, Megan could make out the thank you she uttered.

The camera angle corrected and panned back to record students leaving the gift shop, and the narrator began summarizing again. Megan paused the video and backed it up until the screen was frozen on an image of Alyana and Mr. Chambers embracing.

She walked back to the desk in the midst of Alyana denying yet again having seen Mr. Chambers. Leaning against the counter, Megan held her phone out. "Oh, I think you did much more than say hello," she said, glaring back at Alyana as she began to squirm. "Unless this is how you greet everyone?"

Crystal leaned in to look at the screen, and her eyes narrowed. She turned back to Ayana. "I'm going to be very forward here, since it's clear you've been lying to me, and I don't appreciate it. You were overheard making plans to see my father last night. I want to know where you went."

Alyana's expression turned into shock, and she covered her parted lips with one hand. "Your father?" she gasped. "So you're... Crystal? I didn't recognize you."

Suddenly, Alyana stood, recovering from her shock. She wore a short pencil skirt and tall black heels, her legs slender and long. Anger swelled in her eyes, and she shook her head. "No, I'm sorry. This is not appropriate. You can't come here and demand to know personal details about my life." She stepped around the counter like she was going to walk away, but Crystal stood in front of her, blocking her way.

"Please," Crystal begged, her voice losing all the roughness from before. Alyana's anger immediately softened. "Please, I need to know what happened and where he might have gone." Crystal's voice broke, but she continued. "He's missing, and you could've been the last person to see him."

Alyana's beautiful green eyes widened, and she looked from Crystal to Megan, who gave a small nod of confirmation. With a sigh, she ran one hand through her dark hair. "So if he's really missing, have you spoken to police?"

"They won't do anything for five days." Crystal took a step back, clearly giving Alyana the option of leaving. "But I worry that will be too late. I'm begging you. Please tell me what you know."

For a moment, it looked like Alyana would simply walk past them, but then she crossed her arms, sinking back on her heels. She glanced behind them and then down the hall. "We weren't together for long last night," she said quietly, staring down at the carpet with her voice low. "We were acquainted through his work as governor, and we became"— her eyes tentatively found Crystal—"close friends during that time."

"How close?" Crystal demanded.

"Frankly, that's none of your business," Alyana said. But even though her response was harsh, her words were soft.

It didn't seem to matter to Crystal. Megan watched as her friend crossed her arms in front of her and stared pointedly into Alyana's eyes. "Did you have an affair with him?"

"No," Alyana responded quickly and closed her eyes, bringing one hand to her face and pressing her temples. After a heavy sigh, she looked back at Crystal. "He did help me through a very difficult time when my husband was unfaithful. We were both struggling and leaned heavily upon each other, but nothing happened between us."

"There's no ring on your finger," Crystal said.

"That's because we divorced a year later. Infidelity is difficult for any relationship to recover from, and regrettably, mine never did." Alayna held her gaze firmly.

"How can I trust your word?" Crystal asked.

Alyana walked past her. "I suppose you have no choice." She pushed the button at the elevator and turned back as she waited. "Please know I respect Stephen very much. I... well, I love him. If I hear anything, I'll let you know."

The elevator opened, and she stepped inside, pausing in the threshold with her hand on the door. "And if you find out his whereabouts, I'd appreciate you doing the same." She selected a button and gazed back at them soberly until the doors slid closed.

Chapter Eight

Megan could make out Fred's irritated expression the second she stepped outside. He sat upright with his big blue eyes trained ahead and refused to look at her as she approached. Crystal was quiet as well. She hadn't said a word since they'd watched Alyana disappear into the elevator. Megan decided to give her time to digest everything they'd learned, but if she didn't start talking soon, she'd run out of patience.

"I'm sorry, Fred." Megan pulled the door open, and he leapt out, shaking his coat. She held his collar and rubbed his back, lowering down in front of him. "It's barely been twenty-five minutes," she said, watching his eyes shift from one spot to the other, avoiding her. "I love you, Mr. Fred Astaire," she said, leaning in close until her nose was practically touching his.

Finally, he sniffed at her face and released a big, slobbery tongue, planting it on her cheek. She laughed, kissing the top of his head. "That's a good boy." She stood and turned back to Crystal who was staring back at the HR building.

"C'mon, let's go for a little walk," she said, linking her arm with her friend's.

Crystal sucked in a sudden breath, blinking as if she'd been temporarily frozen. She allowed Megan to tow her along to a strip of grass and trees that bordered a small decorative pond. Fred perked up and pulled ahead, zigzagging in front of them with his nose to the ground. Three mallard ducks floated together at the far end, but they began to glide closer, likely in hopes of an offering of breadcrumbs.

When they reached the water's edge, Megan dropped the leash and let Fred wander.

"She never answered our questions," Crystal said.

Megan turned back to her. "No, she didn't. But she might not have any information on your father."

"She didn't tell us where they had dinner," Crystal folded her arms, looking out on the pond. "Or if she left first or my father did. Did he take a cab? Did anyone hear where he planned to go after?" She blew out a breath of frustration. "If she really cares about him like she claims, wouldn't she do all she could to help find him? I mean, she just left us there with hardly a discussion. What do we do now?"

Megan reached down and picked up a pebble, tossing it into the water. The ducks scurried closer, leaving v-line trails behind them in the pond. She smiled. "As much as I wish we could hop in the car and just hunt him down ourselves, we can't do that. Let's contact everyone you know who are friends with your father or who work with him. Someone out there might have at least a little information." She shrugged. "And then we head back to Seacrest tomorrow, I guess. We both have shops that need to be run."

"Yes, we do." Crystal sighed and lowered to her heels, pulling a blade of grass. She tossed it in the water, and the closest duck snatched it in his bill, guzzling it down. "Do you think it's safe to go back to the house?"

"Sure." Megan placed two fingers in her mouth and whistled for Fred. "We've got a guard dog, and we can check in with the police on the way. Whoever that man was, he didn't seem keen on running into anyone. As long as we leave some lights on, I'm sure he'll stay away. Plus, if your dad comes back, we'll be the first to know."

"All right." Crystal stood and stretched her back. "Let's go then. If the police aren't at his house when we get there, I'll give them a call."

WHEN THEY ARRIVED AT CRYSTAL'S FATHER'S HOME, Megan was relieved to see a patrol car parked on the street. Two officers were walking back from the house. They paused when they noticed Crystal and Megan driving up, one of them lifted his hand in greeting.

"I'll just pull up right here," Crystal said, parking on the street behind their car. She parked and got out quickly, hardly glancing at Megan. It was clear she was nervous, and Megan rushed to follow her, hoping to be of some help. But by the time she zipped her coat up and joined them, they'd already started up a conversation. The officer was speaking to Crystal with a gentle smile on his face, looking calm and unconcerned. He spoke softly and Megan would bet he thought of Crystal as a sensitive, overly worried person. But that wasn't her friend at all. She was strong and driven, the type of person to start up a business with her own sweat and tears instead of letting her father's career pave her way. She was tough, and Megan admired her immensely.

The officer paused his soothing speech and silence hung in the air. Megan suspected he was waiting to be agreed with, but she also wagered Crystal wasn't about to do any such thing. She joined the group and gave each of the officers a quick smile before turning to Crystal. Her gaze was stony, and she crossed her arms, nodding as if taking it all in.

"It's our understanding that he was invited out with colleagues last night?" one officer asked.

Crystal nodded. "Yes, but I haven't been able to learn if he went or not. I know he didn't go home on the bus with the students."

"Right," the officer nodded. "Well then, we may just need to give him more time. Maybe he just stayed out too late or needs a few days to recover from the festivities of the night."

"I see what you're saying, and in any other circumstances, it would make sense." Crystal was staring at the ground, but when she looked up, the smiles on the officer's faces waned. Her expression was firm. "But my father is in trouble. I can feel it. Nothing about this situation makes sense. He wouldn't leave his job without talking to a single person. He might not have known I was coming to visit, but he would at least contact the secretary at the school. Or even one of the students." She shrugged. "Anything. Something."

"Ma'am." The taller officer placed his hands on his hips and glanced back at their car, as if eager to get going. "I'm sorry, but this isn't the first time he's run off without mentioning it to anyone. And I believe you know that. I don't mean to cause additional pain, but in the past, there have been times when he's acted impulsively without considering the effect to those around him. Especially his family."

"That's enough," Crystal said sharply.

"I simply want to illustrate why we believe we need to give this case a few more days."

His voice was kind, but the words felt harsh to Megan. She couldn't imagine how much worse they must be for Crystal.

"Can you understand that, ma'am?" he asked softly.

Crystal took a heavy breath and nodded. "Yes," she said quietly. "Thank you for stopping by."

The officer nodded, glancing back at the house. "Everything seems to be in order at home. I believe the alarm was left off, which explains why we weren't notified of an intruder if there was one. Be sure to set it again."

"Yes," Crystal repeated, turning to leave. Megan followed beside her. "Thanks again."

The officers responded politely and left, and Megan felt a rush of disappointment. But she also felt curious. It seemed there were enough rumors going on about the governor's life that maybe, possibly, he left without talking to anyone. It wasn't impossible, as the officers pointed out. She wanted to side with her friend, of course. But they had no idea what her father did the night before. Maybe he'd just stayed with a friend or... acquaintance.

She glanced up to see Crystal watching her. "I'll just"— Megan hurried to open the car door for Fred—"get him out of here, and we can go inside."

Crystal didn't answer, but as soon as Fred leapt out the back and Megan closed the door, the locks engaged. Megan hurried to catch up to her as she walked quickly back to the house.

"They said they checked things out, but let's just do a quick sweep to be sure," Crystal said, pausing at the front door. She glanced down at Fred. "He can come inside with us for a while."

The house was just as before except for Fred's loud feet on the hardwood. He wandered down the hall, sniffing around excitedly. "I hope he isn't too wet," Megan said, spotting a trail of water droplets from his wet coat. "Maybe I should have him sit on the rug by the door."

"No, he's fine," Crystal's voice was almost harsh. "It doesn't matter anyway. The cleaning crew will take care of anything before my dad even has a chance to notice—" Her voice caught, and she sank down into the couch.

Megan walked around her into the living area, not sure what to say. Crystal's head was slumped, leaving her pretty blonde hair as a curtain around her grief. Before she could say a word, Crystal took a deep breath and brushed at the tears on her face. She sat up and pulled her hair around one shoulder, running her fingers through it. "I'm sorry, Megan. This hasn't turned out to be the trip I was expecting."

"There's no way you could plan for something like this," Megan said, joining her on the couch. "You really don't need to apologize. Don't feel bad for anything because I'm glad I can be here for you. But Crystal..." She hesitated, but there was an urgency in the air that pushed her on. "It seems entirely possible that your dad might have just hooked up with that secretary woman. She seemed to be pretty shocked to see you. Maybe he regretted it and just skipped town for a few days."

Crystal shook her head. "No, that's not it."

Megan chewed on her lip, wanting to argue. But she also knew it wasn't the right way to go about things. She was there to help Crystal, not just boss her way around the problem. "Okay," she said, taking a different approach. "There's one thing we haven't considered yet."

Crystal turned to her quietly, waiting.

"Does he still work for the government?" Megan stood, pacing in front of the large windows. "Or does he have any political enemies? His job makes him somewhat of a celebrity, and threats to people in his position aren't uncommon, right?"

For the first time, there was a glimmer of energy in Crystal's eyes. She stood and walked up to the window aside Megan. "He always got a lot of threats, some directed at our whole family too. I mean, it's not impossible. It would be the perfect timing for someone to make a move when he's taking the class on a field trip and they're traveling. Lots of commotion and distractions. No one even noticed he was missing until he didn't arrive at class this morning."

"Exactly," Megan agreed. It wasn't her first suspicion, but it was one they could freely discuss. Besides, it was entirely possible her father hadn't even gone out to dinner with that secretary. Maybe she was angry at Governor Chambers for standing her up.

Out the window, the sun had already gone down. The sky remained light, but it was the fleeting tail of daylight that quickly became absorbed in color with each passing second. A final show of brilliance before the night.

Fred's growling came so quietly, Megan hardly recognized it at first. But as it grew, she turned to the hallway. She could hear his feet stepping one at a time on the floor, as if he were approaching someone dangerous. But she couldn't see him yet.

"Fred?" she called with Crystal scooting in closer until she stood right beside her. When Fred came into view, he was walking toward the front door. His hair was bristled in a way that sent chills through her body. His growling grew louder.

A knock tapped on the glass next to the front door, and Crystal jumped, letting out a startled yelp. Megan linked her arm with Crystal's, and they moved to the side, peering out the long windows. It had become very dark in just the last few minutes, and the glass was warped for privacy, leaving only a hazy outline. She couldn't even tell if the person was male or female.

The knock came again.

Crystal squeezed her arm and walked ahead. "Who is it?" she asked, her voice echoing a little in the big house. There was no reply.

"We don't have to open it," Megan whispered. "Who even knows we're here?"

"No one," Crystal whispered back.

"Crystal Chambers?" a woman's voice called from the other side of the door. She knocked a third time. "I need to talk to you."

Megan snuck closer to the door, turning back to Crystal. "It sounds like Alyana."

Crystal nodded and seemed to take a moment to steady herself. Then she walked to the front door and turned the lock, inching it open only a crack. "Yes?" she asked.

"Hello," the woman whispered. Megan leaned to one side to try to glimpse if she'd been right. "May I come in?"

Crystal hesitated and then pulled the door open wide. "Sorry, we've had trouble with security today."

"Fred!" Megan looped one finger around his collar just as he tried rushing forward. He stretched his nose out, sniffing at Alyana. Then he snorted and circled around, finally sitting down. She released her tension with a heavy breath. "Sorry," she said. "He chased someone out of the yard this morning, and I think he was remembering it."

Alyana's sculpted eyebrows rose. "Smart dog."

"Yes." Megan scrutinized the woman quickly, trying to decide if she looked like the type to break up a marriage. It was difficult to say. She definitely kept things perfect. From the smooth wavy hair of her head to her perfectly manicured and pump-wrapped toes, she was done up nicely. Megan glanced at Crystal next, already quite sure this was a difficult moment for her friend, especially with what Megan had accused the woman of only moments earlier.

Alyana removed the purse strap from her shoulder, wrapping it around the purse as she took a few steps forward. She seemed quite comfortable in the house, and Megan was sure Crystal took notice.

"There's something I need to tell you about your father and I," Alyana finally said. She was looking at the dark windows where her reflection shone back at her. Megan glanced at it to see Alyana's face was illuminated by the overhead lighting. It gave her reflection a very ghostly feel. But then, when she turned to face Megan and Crystal, she could see her face really was getting paler by the second. Megan could already guess the reason. She almost wanted to excuse herself to give Crystal a little more privacy.

"Why don't you sit down," Crystal offered. The three women went to the living area, with Crystal and Alyana sitting on either end of the couch and Megan taking the chair across from them. "Do you have any information about my father?" Crystal asked, hope ringing with each word.

"Yes," Alyana set her purse beside her on the couch and faced Crystal. "I'm sorry I couldn't talk earlier. I..." she hesitated, glancing between the two women. "Well, I don't think you quite realize what you're getting into. Or what you may be getting into. Honestly, I'm not sure of it myself. But I can't stop thinking that there's something big going on. And now Stephen goes missing..."

"What do you mean, exactly?" Crystal asked. Megan squinted, trying to guess what the woman would say. It didn't sound like she was about to confess some serious misstep in her life. But what else could it be?

"I've been suspicious of certain things going on at the office for about a month now." Alyana crossed her legs under her pencil skirt, creating flattering lines that showcased her toned thighs. "The reason I invited your father to dinner last night was to talk about it." Her gaze settled on Crystal. "But other people in the office overheard, and before I knew it, we had a half dozen coworkers coming with us, and I never got the chance to talk."

"Hmm," Crystal's response was curt, and her lips pursed as she looked back at Alyana. "And what was it you would've told him if he came to your place?"

Alyana's back straightened, as if she detected the challenge in Crystal's words. A muscle in her jaw twitched, and she glanced at Megan before flicking her hair back with her hand. "I would tell him that someone in the department is stealing. Someone big. Someone powerful. Powerful enough to keep it secret." She let her words sink in, and her expression darkened as she gazed into Crystal's eyes.

"So, why didn't you tell us this before?" Crystal's face had gone pale. Now, she seemed to be challenging the truth of Alyana's words completely.

Alyana sighed, but she didn't appear to notice Crystal's

skepticism. "I know it sounds crazy, but I thought the office might be bugged."

"Bugged?" Crystal scoffed. "You're serious?"

"Yes, I am." Alyana gave her a firm glance. "By the way, what is your problem? I'm trying to help. You said you wanted to find Stephen, so let's see what we can do about this."

"Yes," Crystal's voice was shaky, hovering on the edge of instability, "and his name is Governor Chambers. I want to help him because he's my father, and I love him. But what I don't understand, is your concern in all this. I saw the video of you two hugging. I saw the way you looked at him. You can't tell me there's nothing there." Her eyes clouded, and she swallowed hard, looking away for a silent moment.

"All I want"—Alyana stood, looping her purse over her shoulder again—"is to find out if there's anything illegal going on behind the scenes at my office. This is a professional problem and a professional visit. I didn't come here to be accused."

"You're lying." Crystal stood as well, staring her down.

"Look." Alyana's face flashed with anger, and she took a sudden step closer to Crystal.

"Whoa, hold on here." Megan skipped forward, standing between them.

Alyana held her hands up defensively. "All I want to say is, I do care deeply for your father. There are some things I haven't told you." Her eyes stared cooly back at Crystal. "But it's my business, not yours, and it has nothing to do with him disappearing. I don't owe you an explanation for anything. Let's just... try to be on the same team." She stepped forward, holding her hand out. A business card was pinched between her fingers. "Here's my number."

Crystal's expression hadn't changed. Except for the tint of red in her cheeks, she looked quite calm. She finally tore her eyes from Alyana's and took the card.

"It was nice meeting you both," Alyana said. "Goodbye." She left without looking back, closing the door softly behind her.

Chapter Nine

❦

"Wow," Megan breathed, glancing at the floor when Fred began snoring. He was lying stretched out on the carpet, blissfully asleep.

"I don't believe her," Crystal said, wandering to the kitchen island. She took a seat on a barstool, holding the card with both hands and studying it. "There's a lot she's not telling."

"Well, maybe," Megan agreed. "But why would she come out here if she wasn't really trying to help?"

"I don't know, but I don't like it. I don't like her." Crystal tucked the card in her pocket and sighed. Fred's snoring grew louder, and she glanced down at him as well. Finally, a smile broke across her face. A small one, but it was a relief to see it. She crossed the room, rubbing her face. "Here's the thing," she said, clasping her hands behind her back as she walked. "Alyana suspects something is going on at work, and she claims that's why she needed to speak with my father." She spun around suddenly, facing Megan. "But she doesn't work with my father. He works at the school. She works at the Natural Resources building. So, who's her boss? I know they mentioned his name in my dad's class, right? Do you remember?"

"No, I don't." Megan pulled out her phone. "But I have the videos right here. He's even on one. Let's take a look."

Crystal sighed. "Okay."

They watched the videos from start to finish and then watched them again. They paused them, played them in slow motion, and set the volume to full blast. Megan was looking in the background, in the corners, anywhere that might show some sign as to where Governor Chambers had gone. Was there someone watching him in the background? Following him? Were there any strangers in view at all?

Not from what she could see. The only thing they discovered was the shot of him and Alyana together, but watching it set Crystal off every time. She grumbled about Alyana relentlessly, venting all her frustrations about her parent's relationship and suggesting that if only there weren't women like her getting in the way, her parents would be happy.

Megan set her phone on the coffee table and leaned back on the couch cushions, the late hour pulling at her. "Charlie Williamson," she said, turning to Crystal. She was also slumped onto the couch. It was luxuriously soft and difficult to resist. Her head tilted back toward Megan, and her features twisted in confusion. "Huh?"

"Charlie Williamson is the senior manager at the Natural Resources department. He's the one on the video." Megan ran one hand through her hair, closing her eyes. "I mean, he seemed nice, I guess."

"Maybe he knows something—wait." Crystal sat up suddenly. "Didn't Alyana say he was out of town for a little while?"

Megan yawned. "Yeah, ten days. Why?"

"What if that's the answer?" Her voice grew louder. "It's as simple as that. They were both at the dinner, and then somehow my dad ended up going out of town with this guy. We don't know where he was going. Maybe it was official business, and he needed to bring my father to help with... something. Maybe Dad even tried to leave a message or trusted the wrong person to get the word back to his secretary." She adopted a sour expression with the last word she spoke, but it broke into something close to a smile. "What if it's that simple?"

Megan had to agree that it was at least possible. "Don't you think Alyana would have called this Mr. Williamson by now and asked? And why wouldn't your dad answer his phone?"

Crystal swiped one hand in front of them. "Oh, he does that all the time. Or, at least he used to. When he was on a business trip, he'd turn the ringer all the way down and leave his phone in his bag. He would say he meant to check it in the evenings, but he almost never did. It drove my mom crazy."

She looked down at the card. "I'm going to call Alyana before it's too late, and she's asleep." She pulled her phone out. "If you and Fred want to take the first bedroom on the right." She pointed down the hall. "It's got the best bed."

"Sounds amazing, thanks." Megan walked down the hall, collecting her bag she'd left by the front door. "C'mon, Fred." He'd been watching her and jumped up at the invitation, hurrying to catch up. He began exploring the room while she opened her suitcase, laying her day clothes over the back of the chair to breathe. She took her pajamas with her to the shower. She glanced into the room to see Fred curling up at the big rug by the fireplace, so she tried a few switches on the wall before finding the right one. Flames jumped to life, and she could practically hear Fred sighing with happiness. She smiled. "Be good."

Soaking in the hot water felt amazing. She tipped her head back and let the water stream over her face and hair. What had started out as a nice girl's getaway for the weekend had become rather dizzying. She didn't want to admit it to Crystal, but it was overwhelming. Sure, she wanted to help her friend, but she'd also been looking forward to a getaway. Some down time. The chance to truly relax. This trip had become anything but that.

Her phone rang. She turned the water off and hurried to wrap up in a towel. Snatching up a second towel, she twisted her wet hair up and reached her phone just before the answering message could come on. "Hello?"

"Megan!" his voice boomed in her ear.

She immediately slumped into the nearest chair, wishing she was in his arms. "Oh, Kenneth. It's so good to hear your voice." Above anyone she'd ever met, Kenneth had his life together. Inheriting a huge company had only brought out the professional in him even more. He was up to the task and then some. He had disagreements with his parents every now and then, but who didn't? Besides that, he knew how to make a person feel safe. She could really use that right about now.

She lowered her voice. "You wouldn't believe how this trip has turned out."

"Why?" His tone changed instantly. "Is anything wrong? I can be there by tomorrow afternoon if you need me—"

"No," she laughed, although the gesture was touching. "No, it's fine. I'm okay, it's just... not at all what I expected."

"How's that?"

"Well." She tucked her feet up under her, pulling the towel tighter. "For one thing, Crystal's father has vanished. She came all the way out to visit him, and no one knows where he ran off to. If you ask me, it might be a case of a previously powerful man trying to regain a bit of attention."

"I don't know," Kenneth said. "I've met Governor Chambers before, and he doesn't strike me as someone who would sneak off without telling anyone. Crystal hasn't even heard from him?"

Megan paused for a moment, remembering that Kenneth and Crystal had a history together. They traveled in similar elite circles and dated briefly, back when Kenneth was younger and more carefree. He admitted to playing the field a little carelessly. But the reminder that he'd been so close with Crystal had her feeling slightly off balance, like she was the outcast of the bunch.

"Megan?"

She started, rubbing at the goosebumps on her arms. "One second, sorry. I'm freezing. Let me get dressed." She set the phone down and then paused, thinking it was strange that she'd said it like that.

"I just got out of the shower," she explained as she pulled on her pajama shirt. But it still felt wrong. Why was she telling him she was in the shower? She didn't want him picturing her standing there all naked and cold... "I mean, I'm just getting ready for bed." She swallowed, looking over at the bed. Maybe she was the only one feeling awkward. He hadn't said anything since she told him she was cold and undressed. Maybe he wasn't uncomfortable at all, and she was just making everything worse.

"Hello again," she said, picking up her phone again, crawling onto the bed and crossing her legs under her. "Sorry about that."

There. Sorry about everything. If he was uncomfortable, she'd just blanket-apologized for it all.

"You know, Megan," he said, his voice suddenly so buttery smooth, she couldn't help but close her eyes at the sound of it. "I love how bluntly honest you are." He chuckled, and somehow it made her cheeks turn crimson with embarrassment. She reviewed everything she'd said yet again, feeling ridiculous. No doubt he was used to polished, classy women like Crystal. Not clumsy, casual, wilderness-loving girls like her.

"Sorry, I'm sure you didn't need to know all that." She tried to swallow the embarrassment down, but it remained lodged in her throat.

"You have nothing to apologize for, Megan. I promise." He cleared his throat, a casual Segway. "I need to head to a late meeting," he said, sounding like he was walking. "So, I don't have as much time as I'd like, but let me see if I can get in touch with a few people who might be able to help find Crystal's father. How's she doing? Is she pretty worried about him?"

Megan didn't want to hear Kenneth's concern for Crystal. It was childish of her, but she was instantly jealous. Still, she was glad they were all friends. She just wasn't sure where exactly her and Kenneth stood... that was the real problem. "She's definitely worried. But Kenneth?"

"Hmm?"

"She thinks he might be with a man named Charlie Williamson. He's the senior manager of Natural Resources for the state of Washington."

"Oh," Kenneth sounded surprised. "Thanks, I'll look into it. Just send me a text anytime if you guys hear anything or just... if you want to."

She smiled, noticing the way his voice softened. "I will," she promised. "Goodnight."

"Get some sleep, Megan. I'll call you tomorrow." The softness remained, and she loved it.

"Bye." She took a deep breath, savoring their conversation. It'd been too long since she'd really let herself fall for anyone, and Kenneth was a good man. But there were differences between them that seemed too big of a hurdle. Much too big. How, for example, would she ever leave Seacrest? Kenneth's vacation home was there, but he spent most of his time in Southern California. She already knew she didn't want to leave. Which meant... what? She'd stay at his vacation home alone and await his occasional return? That was a definite no, or they'd turn out just like Crystal's parents, living two separate lives until it became easier to stay apart.

There was a gentle knock at the door.

"Come in." Megan slid to the edge of the bed as Crystal appeared. "What did you find out?" She could see from the look on her friend's face that she'd found out something. Her impatience had her on her feet before Crystal could answer. "Well?"

Crystal smiled. "I was able to talk to Alyana, and she said she'd give Mr. Williamson a call and call me right back. She said she hadn't even thought of the possibility that they were traveling together. Let's hope we're on the right track."

"Let's hope," Megan agreed. She walked to the window.

But instead of staring out at the night, she looked at her own reflection, trying to see past the surface to her future. What should she do? "Also," she said, turning around. "I spoke with Kenneth Bradburn, and he said he was going to make some calls and see what he could find out."

"Kenneth?" Crystal's nose almost wrinkled. "I guess that's fine. I just don't want the whole world knowing what's going on. Not until we figure out where he went."

"He won't say anything," Megan promised, sure of herself. Kenneth must have been very young and immature when they'd dated because now he was a very reliable person. Crystal cast Megan a glance that had her tensing. She knew where the conversation was headed, and she wasn't quite ready for it.

"Are you two getting serious?" Crystal smiled, giving her a teasing glance. "I mean, if you don't mind my asking."

"I don't mind," Megan lied, continuing her vigil at the window. "I'm a little unsure myself. It's hard to know much of anything when he's gone for so long at a time."

"Yes, I remember," Crystal said.

Megan turned to her friend, studying her face a moment. Her features were delicate, but she was strong. A very capable person who knew a lot of the world and how it worked. She shook her head. "He's different, Crystal." Megan felt the words clear to her bones. "I'm sure he would be very sorry to be reminded that he hurt you, and I don't want you to think I'm with the same man you were. People change."

Crystal's jaw hardened. "Do they?" Her tender voice was full of pain. "Do they, really? Like my father, for example, who I thought had changed. Here he goes and leaves me in a wake of uncertainty like he did my mother for so many years." She rolled her eyes, and they shone in the lamplight. "It's no wonder she couldn't put up with it anymore."

"I don't know, Crystal." Megan set her hand on Crystal's back, wishing to be of some comfort. "We just can't say for certain until we find out the truth. Right now, it could be anything that took him away."

Crystal's phone rang, and she pressed the speaker button. "Hello?"

"Crystal, it's Alyana." Her voice came through confident and proper. A very professional tone. "I was able to get hold of Charlie Williamson and you're absolutely right. He said Governor Chambers traveled with him." Her breath blew into the phone in a sigh. It was the only sign of exasperation, as her voice remained totally calm. "He said he'd be sure to have him call you and set things straight with his work as well. I guess it was a bit of an emergency, although he didn't go into detail about that."

"An emergency so big that he couldn't pick up the phone and let anyone know he was leaving?" Crystal's voice had risen, and she walked the perimeter of the room, agitated. "Even if his phone dropped out the window of the airplane, he could use a friend's. What could possibly explain this?"

"He didn't know you were coming to visit, Crystal," Alyana said, with her voice sounding very much like a mother's.

Crystal straightened abruptly, frozen in place. "I see," she said. "Well, thank you for letting me know. I suppose he should call the police station too and straighten things out there. Would you tell him for me? Thanks. Have a wonderful evening."

She hung up without waiting for a reply and threw her phone into the hall. It smacked against the wall and crashed to the floor.

"Crystal," Megan hurried to her side to see tears trailing down her cheeks. "I'm sure he has no idea what today was like for you—"

"No, of course not." She swiped at her cheeks angrily, storming into the hall. "I'm so sorry I ever brought you on this trip, Megan. I'll drive you home in the morning." She swung the bedroom door shut behind her.

Fred jumped up from his cozy spot, staring at the door. He crossed the room and touched his nose to her hand. Megan rubbed his head. "It's okay." She sighed and sat on the edge of the bed. "Just a whole lot of commotion over nothing." The Great Dane's big, boxy head settled on her lap. "I think right now, you're the only thing I'm sure about." She smoothed her hand over his silky fur. "You and me."

He blinked a few times and then closed his eyes.

Having Kenneth call... hearing his voice. Their relationship was something she appreciated so much; how could she say no to having him in her life? But then, she couldn't exactly lead him on either. And if she was being completely honest, that was a narrow line she'd been walking for a while now. Their relationship was one almost solely of goodbye kisses. He was the ideal man... but he was never around. And she wasn't about to beg for someone's attention. Not again, anyway. Her first engagement had been quite enough of that.

But then, it wasn't a fair comparison. Kenneth was a thousand times the man her fiancé had been. Still, she needed to have a talk with him. And she would. As soon as she was back at Seacrest and things were settled, she'd give him a call and let him know she wasn't ready for an exclusive relationship right now. There was no rush, really, with him being out of the country for a few months. But as soon as she could, she'd give him a call.

It was the right thing to do.

Chapter Ten

❦

Monday came just as it did every week. Except this time, it felt different. Megan stretched her neck side to side as she walked. She wasn't coming from a nice stint of weekend rest like she usually did. Days spent doing things she loved and relaxing with Fred. Hiking in the woods and combing the beach. The tension of the past two days lived in her still, making it hard to concentrate on menial tasks and exhausted to think of an entire week ahead.

Crystal brought her home the previous afternoon, just as she'd promised. Although, there'd been very little conversation on the way, and anything they did talk about felt entirely superficial. They were dancing around the real issues or avoiding them completely. Once, Megan mentioned returning to Seattle for another visit, and Crystal nearly drove off the road.

Megan sighed, brushing her hair back and fiddled with the key. The lock at her shop was old, but she considered it charming. Inside the front windows, she could see it was clean and orderly, and she made a note to thank Santiago. A brisk wind whipped past, and she shivered. The temperature had gone through a shift while she'd been away, dropping nearly twenty degrees. It was downright cold. She pulled her coat tighter, sinking into it as best she could. A sudden rush of sadness came over her her as she remembered Crystal's anger at her father. It was shocking to see her friend lose control like that, and so unlike her. Megan hoped Governor Chambers would at least give a proper apology after putting his daughter through so much.

"Surprise," a familiar voice whispered.

Chills trailed up her neck, and she spun around to see Kenneth smiling back at her, his expression adoring. Too adoring. Why hadn't she given him a call before now? But, if she'd known he was going to be in Seacrest, she would have.

His hand gently swept the hair away from her face, and he leaned in close. "My schedule freed up, so I thought I'd come say hello before I have to fly over the ocean and away from you." A smile tugged at his mouth. "How are you?"

His eyes roamed her face, and he leaned in alluringly close. The tension that had been winding through her suddenly rushed to the surface and she took a quick step back, her surprise turning strangely to angry. "Why didn't you call?" Cold wind whipped at her face, and she brushed her hair back. She hadn't meant for the anger to ring in her voice, but it must have because his smile fell.

"I'm, uh, sorry," He leaned back a little, "I should've known better than to surprise you like this. But I worried you'd had a hard weekend and"— He hesitated and moment and then leaned in, kissing her cheek—"it looks like I was right." His hands trailed down her arms, and he laced his fingers with hers, hugging her hands to his chest.

Feeling a little humiliated at her less than cold welcome, she looked into his eyes to see his confusion. She'd gathered up all her tension and used it like a weapon and now, somehow, she owed him an apology. If she were being honest, she still didn't know what kind of relationship she wanted with Kenneth. Or if she wanted one at all. That was at the heart of her struggles. But it wasn't his fault. After all, she'd never told him. Here he was, being kind and supportive with no idea how conflicted she was. It made her feel terrible, and on top of everything else, tears came to her eyes.

She swallowed hard, trying to fight off the emotion. Looking back at his kind face, she tried to get herself to feel more for him, but it just wouldn't come. Maybe it was because he'd be leaving soon and inwardly, she was protecting herself. Maybe they didn't know each other well enough yet and needed to spend more time together. Or perhaps her heart was already elsewhere.

Still, it stung to realize how much this weekend had affected her. And now, it was making things worse with Kenneth. She just needed to tell him she wasn't sure about their relationship, but it never seemed like the right time.

"You're right," she finally managed, although before she could explain, her eyes filled with tears. "This weekend was rough."

He scooped her into his arms and as much as she knew she should step away, her head rested gently on his chest as she struggled to catch her breath.

His arms stayed around her, and his head tilted down to hers, his words soft in her ear. "I understand. You've been under so much pressure. And besides that, you're out here managing this business and doing everything without much support or any family. I can't imagine doing everything on my own like that. It's..." His hand settled on her jawline, tracing it until she looked up at him. "It's okay to take a break now and then."

Voices reached them, and she flinched, glancing back to see a couple coming down the boardwalk. She stepped back quickly, brushing at her coat. "I need to open up the shop."

"I've got it." He held the door open and whistled for Fred, who'd taken to racing along the beach. He loped toward them, and Megan hurried through the doorway, anxious to be out of sight until she could dry her tears.

"Go ahead and take a moment," Kenneth said, waving at the couple who approached. "I'll handle the customers as long as you need."

Megan shook her head. What if one of them recognized him? What would they say to a billionaire waiting tables? "You don't have to do that—"

"I insist." He fairly pushed her through the room and down the hall until they were standing in the back office together. "Megan Henny," he said, giving her a mock-serious look, "take a moment for yourself, and let me help you. Okay?"

Megan's face slowly warmed into a smile as she gazed over his warm, dark eyes and easy grin. "Okay," she finally relented. He gave a satisfied nod and left the room. His voice could be heard greeting the couple cheerily, and she took a step back, collapsing into the office chair. She dropped her face into her hands. What was her problem?

Still, even with Kenneth's kind gestures and words, and the always perfect placement of his hands, he'd managed to have her feeling defensive instead of loved. Why did he bring up the fact that she was out here on her own? Her business was doing well, and she was more friends than ever.

In fact, she'd felt much more alone back in Seattle even though she'd been engaged and constantly attending parties.

But, on the other hand, look how he'd jumped in to help her.

Fred walked in quietly and sat in front of her. She peeked out from her hands, looking into his big, soulful eyes. "I don't know, buddy," she said, wiping under her eyes and combing her fingers through her hair. "I guess I've been under more stress than I thought?" She shrugged, still looking back at him. "You've never been a big fan of Kenneth, but what do you think? Could it possibly be that he's the one for... you know, me?" Fred's nose tipped down and his eyes appeared to grow larger as he looked up at her. It was an expression that said, *Can we hurry this along? Because it's breakfast time.* She searched his gaze for a while longer and then abandoned the conversation to find him some food.

Two cans of dog food and twenty minutes later, she glanced in the bathroom mirror. Satisfied that all signs of tears had faded, she went to take over for Kenneth. She found him serving up a tray with two perfectly made break-fast sandwiches. Grilled cheese, eggs, and bacon on an English muffin. It was a favorite in the small town. The couple thanked him and sat near the front window to enjoy their meal. Kenneth caught her eye and gave a quick wink as he walked back to her. Taking her hand, he led her down the back hall again, stopping just outside of the office. "Now tell me," he said, "what do you need?"

She took an easy breath, finally keeping her emotions in check. It was embarrassing to think of the way she'd returned his happy greeting only a few minutes ago. She shook her head, combing her fingers through her hair. "I'm fine, really. I'll get through the day, and then we'll see what we can do for Crystal." His gaze was so kind, but it only made her cheeks burn. "Honestly, I'm so sorry to have talked to you like that."

"No." He held a hand up, stopping her. "It's okay. I mean, we might have some things to talk about later, but let's just hold off for now." His eyes were asking questions as he spoke, showing he'd caught on quite well to her cold welcome might mean for them.

The shop door opened, ringing the bell with a delightful jingle. At least, normally it was delightful. At the moment, it was completely irritating. Megan straightened, ready to get back to work. "Thank you for stepping in for me," she said. Touched by his kindness, she gave him what she planned to be a quick kiss. But turmoil was quickly stirred up inside as he pulled her close and she couldn't help lingering. She told herself to step back, but instead, she reached for him.

The counter bell chimed, and she jumped, stepping away from him. "I'll see you later," she rushed. Spinning around, she raced down the hall, telling herself that Kenneth really needed to get back on a plane. Whatever was bothering her, she needed to get a handle on it and make a decision one way or the other. She was balanced between telling Kenneth no and yes... and that wasn't okay. Still, her heart was racing, and she really did like Kenneth... a lot, apparently. But then, it just didn't feel right.

"Two breakfast sandwiches, please?"

Megan's eyes shot up from the cash register. She'd been lost in thought long enough for the couple in front of her to look a little concerned. "Yes," she said, typing it in.

Get it together.

At the back of the building, the door closed, and she sighed a breath of relief. Kenneth said he came out to

Seacrest just to visit with her, but likely he had work to get done as well. He was sure to be busy the rest of the day, and she could spend it giving herself lectures about how to behave. She was an adult, after all, and perfectly capable of having an honest conversation. But she'd never been this unsure of herself before, not even with her former fiancé. Maybe if he'd been there for her when she needed him, even once, she might have. But he was always so engaged with flashy events, he hardly noticed her. Kenneth, on the other hand... Kenneth was different.

The cafe stayed busy all morning, blending into afternoon. Before she realized it, customers were ordering club sandwiches instead of English muffins. When Desmond walked in, she glanced at the clock and panicked. She was nearly late for story time. Desmond pushed at his bushy brown hair, revealing a bit of his face. He was losing his more kid-like features and becoming quite a handsome young man.

"You still need me this afternoon, Miss Megan?" Desmond asked, pulling an apron from the wall. He tied it around his waist.

"Yes!" Megan dashed down the hall, meeting Fred halfway. "Thank you, Desmond!" She shouted. Fred held his leash in his mouth even though he knew quite well that his walk wasn't until after story time. "Sorry, Fred." She took the leash and looped it over the hook in her office again. "I promise I'll take you in one hour."

She ran back through the shop, waving at Desmond as she went. "Thanks again!"

"Yep."

She glanced back to see him actually smiling at the next customer in line. His transformation from glum teenager to pleasant teenager was astonishing. Out the door she went. The cold was a shock, and she wrapped her unzipped coat around herself. It was only two doors down to Margaret's bookstore, anyway.

She ran inside to see Margaret talking to a small group of three children. Each had a parent sitting behind them, and one mom wandered the shelves, flipping through titles. Megan caught Margaret's eye and smiled, ready to take over. She'd been hoping to see young Gabriel back from his winter camping trip, but he wasn't there. He usually wasn't late, but she assumed he'd wander in eventually.

Margaret was letting the kids select their first story, and they all agreed. Megan smiled as the Big Book of Mountain Trolls was handed to her. "Sorry I'm late," she whispered. But Margaret only swiped the apology away with one hand.

"Nonsense. You're here, aren't you?"

"Yes," Megan smiled. "I'm here." She hesitated a moment as she looked across Margaret's usually energetic face, noticing a bit of paleness to her skin. Her movements were tired and dragging as she went to her favorite cushioned rocking chair at the back. She liked to listen in on story time.

"Daddy," one of the little girls on the floor whispered, twisting around to look up at her father. "Is she gonna read it?"

Megan caught the man's eyes, and he gave a quick smile. "Yep," he assured. Leaning aside the young girl, he pointed to Megan. "Right now, see?"

"Hello, everyone," Megan began, loving the enraptured way the kids watched her. "It's so nice to see you again. I hope you all had a lovely weekend."

"Wait!" Gabriel raced in the door. His cheeks were flushed and his eyes full of energy. "I'm here!"

"Oh, good," Megan gestured to the other kids. "Come sit down. Find a spot where you can see."

"I went camping," he said proudly, sitting with the other kids. "And I started the fire both nights all by myself."

"Wow, that sounds like so much fun." Megan saw his mother and gave her a quick smile. "You're learning some great skills. I'd love to hear more about it right after this story, okay?"

"M-kay," he promised, nodding. His lips were pressed tightly together, as if it was the only way to keep from going on about his exciting camping trip. Megan smiled.

The kids wriggled impatiently, but just as she was about to start, Megan caught voices from outside. A police car was parked just within view and a policeman was talking rather loudly. She tried her best to ignore it and held up the book, hoping the scene outside wouldn't be too distracting. But there was no need to worry. Four pairs of eager young eyes were trained on the cartoon trolls on the cover. She read the title in her best, most mysterious and exciting voice and then turned the page. The book was sweet and yet a wonderful adventure. She usually took the time to read through the books on her own before story time began, but today, she was hooked on every page as much as the children were.

"Excuse me, ma'am?"

Megan paused midsentence, glancing back at the door to see a policeman holding his hat in his hands. He looked slightly apologetic but not enough that she thought he might let her finish.

"May I speak to you for a moment?" he asked, giving a stiff attempt at a smile.

"Um," Megan glanced back to see Margaret had fallen asleep in the rocking chair. She turned back at her tiny audience, unsure of what to do.

"I can finish it for you if you need," said the father from earlier as got to his feet to the delight of his daughter.

"Yay, Daddy!" she cheered, clapping.

"Thank you," Megan said, hoping the police had news about Crystal's father. She stepped outside the shop with the police officer, following him down the boardwalk a short distance. He had gray threaded throughout his black hair, and his shoulders were strong but not overly built. Still, he was a striking man with bold blue eyes, deep brown skin, and a gentle jawline. She noticed his name on the front pocket, and her eyes widened. "Officer Morel," she murmured, "What are you doing in Seacrest?"

He nodded, pursing his lips. "Yes, hello. It's nice to meet you, Miss Henny. I apologize for taking you away from your responsibilities so abruptly, but there has been a rather unusual development with Crystal Chambers's father." He crossed his arms around a thick bullet-proof vest. "I came down here to speak with her, but her shop is closed and she's not answering her phone. I was about to go down to her house, but then I remembered she mentioned you." His blue eyes settled deeply into hers. "Do you know where she might be?"

Megan was still repeating the words *unusual development* in her mind, but she shook her head. "I haven't heard from her either." Megan sighed. "But I know she occasionally needs to take some time for herself when she's feeling overwhelmed. And it was pretty tough on her this past weekend.

She was very worried about her father and then, when she realized he'd just gone on a spontaneous trip, she was even more upset."

His eyes were suddenly uncertain, and he hesitated a moment before nodding. "I see," He glanced away. "Yes, I can understand that. I heard she tried to get in contact with me as well, is that right?"

Megan nodded. "Yes." She paid attention to the way his eyes worked, glancing around them as if there were an investigation going on in his head as they spoke. "Officer Morel," she said, bringing his gaze back to her. "What unusual developments?"

"Well." He glanced up as a group of tourists passed by, giving them a curt nod of his head. His voice lowered, and he took a step closer. "Her father, from all accounts, did not travel to Hawaii. At least, I haven't been able to confirm that claim. But where he went, I don't know. He's just gone."

"Then why would Charlie Williamson say he did?" Megan crossed her arms, feeling irritated.

Morel shook his head. "It wasn't Williamson who said that... was it?"

Megan's arms uncrossed, falling to her sides. "Alyana. Do you think she was lying?" She felt a little uncomfortable with what she was about to say, but if Crystal was there, she was confident her friend would bring up the same thing. "He's done something like this before. Crystal spoke about it a little. When her parents were going through some difficulties, I guess."

"Yes, I know," Officer Morel nodded. "I'm good friends with the Chambers. I was assigned to them when he was in office, and we've kept in close contact from the time he left." He glanced down and then met Megan's eyes again, looking apprehensive for the first time. "Mrs. Chambers called me on several occasions, requesting that I look for her husband. But every time, I've been able to locate him easily. He wasn't really hiding; he was just taking a break... not that running away is an acceptable way to handle conflict. But, " He shrugged. "It's similar to what you said about Crystal."

It gave Megan a chill just watching him. Clearly, he had years of experience, and she could see it on his face that he didn't feel right about the situation. She hoped his next words would wipe her fears away. Little did she know, they were about to do the opposite.

"This time is different, Miss Henny. There's no trace of him. I can't find that he ever left his office. That's the last record we have of him. At 8 p.m. Friday evening, he used his thumbprint to unlock the office door and turn off the security system. After that, he just... vanished."

Chapter Eleven

✦❧

Megan reached across to the passenger's seat and rubbed under Fred's ears. He ignored her. She'd been later than usual picking him up from the shop and now, as they drove behind officer Morel's patrol car to Crystal's house, he turned his head away with a sniff. A burst of fog appeared on the window in front of him. It hadn't warmed up much in the little car. Megan cranked the heat up full blast.

"Sorry, Fred." She slowed and turned onto Crystal's street. "There was sort of an emergency, and I was late. But Crystal's dad might be in trouble. Wanna help us figure this out?"

His ears perked up a bit, but he didn't turn his head.

Megan smiled. "You wanna? Huh?" He knew the tone of voice that meant an adventure, and finally he looked at her. "There we go, buddy." She pulled up to the curb and turned the car off. Rubbing his neck with both hands, his tongue eventually lolled out, a sign of total contentment. "Good boy," she said. "Let's go see what we can do."

She didn't bother with a leash this time. Fred knew the area, and the neighbors had fallen in love with him quickly. He appeared eager to behave as well, walking up the drive calmly.

"Wow!" Officer Morel paused outside his police cruiser. "He's a big dog, isn't he?"

Megan smiled, but tension was beginning to wind its way through her middle. She just needed to see Crystal. The idea that her father had gone missing without even a plausible reason was disorienting. What if there was someone preying on the family? Anything felt possible in the political world.

"You said you tried contacting her?" Officer Morel walked beside her to the front door, where Fred sat waiting.

Megan nodded. "I have."

He hesitated for just a moment and then reached across the big canine to ring the doorbell. They waited through complete silence. No voices inside, no television, no sounds of movement or footsteps.

"I wonder if she's even home," Megan said, trying to think of where she would have gone. "I know she goes to the beach alone sometimes."

Fred stood and whined, transfixed on the door with his nose practically touching it. Megan smoothed her hand over his back. "Hey, I don't think she's home, Fred."

He continued staring.

"Maybe he can sense she's here," Officer Velasquez said. He leaned to the side, peering in the window. "Beautiful place. It looks a little too perfect. Maybe she ended up going out of town."

"No, it always looks like that," Megan smiled. "I know how to get in the side window... if you want me to?" She shrugged.

"Well, legally I have to say I don't think it's a good idea to break in." A smile flickered on his lips. "But as a concerned friend, you have every right."

"Understood," Megan said. She patted Fred's back. "C'mon, boy, maybe she's around this way."

They rounded the house and came to the faulty window Crystal had told her about. She'd shown her how the lock could easily be disengaged if the window were tilted slightly and then lifted. Megan lifted one side, hoping she hadn't fixed the window yet. It clicked and gave way, sliding up. She snatched a stick from the ground and wedged it in one side, propping the window up. Pushing off the ground, she got her torso through, hanging by her middle.

Fred gave a shrill, sudden whine.

"It's okay," she whispered, sure the neighbors would call the police if they saw her. Then again, she was with the police. She wriggled until she was through and landed on her hands and feet.

A sudden burst of barking echoed through the house. Fred placed his front two feet on the windowsill in a panic.

"Fred!" she shouted, glancing around the house. Surely, Crystal would be racing out from one of the rooms any moment. But Fred wasn't listening. Finally, the barking paused, and Megan heaved a sigh of relief. Suddenly, Fred sailed through the window, landing with a slide that brought him halfway across the room.

"Oh boy," Megan knelt down, running her hand over the claw marks he'd just gouged into the beautiful hardwood flooring. "This isn't good." She hurried to close the window and let Officer Morel in. When she opened the door, his expression was suspicious enough that she was sure he'd heard every bit of the commotion.

"Everything all right in here?" he asked, walking inside.

"Yeah." Megan closed the front door. "Fred was just a little worried about me."

Officer Morel peered back at her. "I see." He gazed across the house. "She's not here?" He turned back to Megan.

"Er," Megan spun around. "Let me look in the back rooms and see if there's any trace of her. Maybe she was just in the shower."

"Ah." He rocked back on his feet. "Why don't you go take a look first."

Megan hurried down the hall. Fred's claws clicked on the floor as he trotted along behind. Her mind was spinning, trying to come up with a logical reason why Crystal would just disappear like this. As much as she was angry at her father for his actions, she wouldn't go and do the exact same thing, would she?

The door to the master bedroom was closed, and Megan knocked lightly before trying the handle. She eased the door open. "Hello? Crystal?" Across the room, the bathroom door was closed as well. There was a fan running from inside, and Megan walked slowly closer. She knocked on the bathroom door, placing her mouth close to the crack between the door and the frame. "Crystal?" She shouted. The sound continued humming, but there was no answer.

She tried the handle to find it locked. Tracing her finger across the small hole in the handle, she pulled a bobby pin from her hair and straightened it. Feeding one end into the hole, she felt contact and pressed. The lock popped. Her hands shook at the thought of what she might find inside. She took a deep breath and turned the handle.

There was a large, freestanding bathtub full to the top

with bubbles. A white noise speaker was turned full volume... and there was Crystal. Just her head was above water with headphones over her ears and a mask over her eyes.

Megan sighed, resting one hand on her chest. "Thank goodness," she whispered.

Fred dashed inside the room; there wasn't enough time to react before he was sailing through the air. He landed with an almighty splash. Bubbles and water cascaded across the tile floor, and an ear-splitting scream filled the air. Fred jumped out in the next instant with terror in his eyes. But this time, Megan was ready. She slammed the door, blocking his escape. He tried to stop, but only slid across the tile, catapulting into the door with a thud.

"What in the world?" Crystal ripped the mask from her face. "What's going on?" Her voice was angry, booming through the house.

Megan was sure Officer Morel could hear everything. She held her hands up. "I'm sorry, Crystal, but we were worried about you."

"What?" Crystal shouted. She shook her head and pulled the noise-canceling headphones from her ears.

"I said, we were worried." Megan could feel the embarrassment in her cheeks. "We tried calling, and I saw your shop wasn't open—"

"Yeah," Crystal interrupted, still shouting. "I was trying to relax!" She covered her face with her hand, and her shoulders lifted in a breath. Then they lifted again, and again. A smile crept across her face and laughter suddenly bubbled out. She crossed her arms over the side of the tub, laughing uncontrollably. "What was—what was Fred thinking?"

Megan couldn't help but laugh. "I don't know," she said,

laughing harder. She nearly toppled over, trying to catch her breath.

Fred, however, wasn't amused. He stood with his tail curled between his legs, dripping all over the floor. After a few minutes, Megan managed to stifle the laughter. "Here you go, Fred." She crossed the room and pulled a towel from the cabinet. Draping it over him, she began rubbing.

Crystal finally silenced the noise machine, and the room stilled. "Could you throw me a towel too?" she asked. "You know, since you ruined my moment of Zen and all."

"Crystal, I'm so sorry." Megan had to choke back another wave of laughter, but she retrieved the towel quickly and tossed it to her friend. She turned around. "Do you want me to leave?"

"No, just let me dry off," Crystal said. Water swished, and her feet patted on the tile. "There we go." Wrapped in her towel, she crossed the bathroom floor carefully, stepping through puddles. When she reached Fred, she rubbed his wet fur. "Sorry to be so unwelcoming, Fred." She laughed. "I just really wasn't expecting you." She stood a moment as if she were still trying to recover. "So, you couldn't get hold of me for a few hours and panicked or what?"

Megan shook her head, her mood sobering. "It's more than that," she said, wishing she had good news to share after such a rude welcome. "Officer Morel is here."

Crystal's eyes widened. "Here, like in my house?"

"Yes." Megan took Fred's collar. "I'll take Fred out to the living room and get him dried off. We'll wait for you there."

"Wait," Crystal took her arm, stopping her. Her face was overcome with fear. "What's the news?"

Megan took her friend's hand, squeezing it. "No bad news yet. He just said he believes the information you got about your father going to Hawaii with Williamson was incorrect."

Crystal's arm dropped, and she nodded quietly, taking a step back. She glanced around the room. "Okay, just let me get dressed, and I'll meet you out there in a few minutes."

"M-kay." Megan left, bringing Fred and the towel with her. When they got back to the living area, Officer Morel started at the sight of them.

"I'd wondered what in the world could be going on. I didn't dare go back there, but now it all makes sense." He was holding back a grin, Megan could tell. But the moment passed quickly, and then he was all business, glancing down the hall often, eagerly awaiting Crystal's appearance. Fred curled up on the rug by the door, licking his wet fur. Apparently, he wasn't satisfied with Megan's drying job.

After only a few minutes, she came quietly into the room, dressed in soft joggers and a long-sleeved T-shirt. Her eyes wandered from Fred, to Megan, to Officer Morel, where they stayed. "Okay," she said quietly. "Tell me what you know."

"Right," Officer Morel pulled something from his pocket. "I haven't mentioned this to anyone yet, Crystal." In his palm was a small camera. "This was in your father's office. Have you seen it before? Did you know it was there?"

Crystal took it from his hand. "It's a nanny cam. But no. I've never seen it. Why was it in his office?"

Morel pulled his phone out next. "I don't know the answer to that, but I believe your father was the one who placed it there. I'm just not sure why. If he had concerns about his safety, it's strange that he never mentioned it to me."

Crystal was leaning in, looking at his phone. "Is this the video?"

He nodded, and Megan leaned in too, trying not to let her heart race. But it was inevitable. She imagined a number of terrifying things as they watched Crystal's father walk across his office and sit at his desk. He set a briefcase down, scribbled on a calendar, and then set a small bag on top of his desk. His head turned slowly, looking directly into the camera. He rubbed a hand across his chin and then stood, walking closer. His hand reached out to the camera, and the video cut out.

"He turned it off," Crystal said.

Megan nodded, feeling that Crystal's voice wasn't alarmed enough. Warning bells were ringing in her head and her heart thumped in her chest. Why would he turn it off? What was in the bag?

"You have no idea why he would do that?" Morel asked.

His voice, too, was very calm.

Crystal shook her head.

"And you have no idea what might have been in that bag?" Morel tucked his phone and the camera away.

"No." There was a slight tremor in Crystal's voice. She stared back at Morel, waiting. Just as Megan did. He was the officer. This was his case. So, why wasn't he telling them everything was going to be okay?

"Here's what I'm thinking." Morel shifted his weight and crossed his arms. "The department isn't going to officially make a move for at least another few days, even with this video. But I can't just sit here while a friend of mine could possibly be in danger. So, I plan on digging around as much as I can here. If you wanted... you could go out to your mom's place in Hawaii just to visit for a week or so. You might be able to dig up some information. Maybe even chat with Mr. Williamson if you can find him. I have the address of his condo out there. It's only a half-hour drive from your mom's place."

"Uh." Crystal looked a little lost. Her eyes trailed across her home, and she tucked her hands in her pockets. "I don't know. I suppose that would be fine. I mean, I just got back from a trip but..."

Morel's two-way radio beeped, and a female voice came on, rattling away so quickly Megan couldn't catch what she was saying.

Morel lifted the radio to his mouth, stopping the chatter. "Ten-four. I'm on my way back. Be there in five." He turned again to Crystal, bringing his hand to her shoulder. "You're stressed and on-edge. Just go to your mom's. There's a good chance she knows something and just wasn't ready to talk about it yet. If you find anything out, it will help the case before it even starts and will give you some peace of mind. If not," He shrugged, and his hand fell away from her shoulder," At least you'll get away from it all for a little while. What do you think?"

She looked back at him for a moment and then nodded. "Okay... I will. Thanks."

"My pleasure." He gave her a quick smile and turned to go, stepping over Fred who'd stretched out to the full extent of his body and was now fast asleep. At the door, he turned around again. "If by chance I hear from him, I'll let you know right away."

"I'd appreciate that." Crystal sighed, staring at the door even after it had closed, and the police cruiser drove away. Megan watched it through the window until it turned out of view. Fred yawned, lifting up on his long legs and sitting next to Crystal. She rubbed his head and looked back at Megan. "How do you two feel about Hawaii?" She gave a tentative smile. "It's beautiful this time of year."

"Sorry, but I won't be going if it means Fred will have to ride in the cargo hold." Megan watched Crystal's face, wondering if her friend would think she was overreacting. "I read an article just last week on the number of dogs that are injured every year on flights, and I just wouldn't be able to do it. If anything, I'd find a really good kennel to leave him with. But..." But she wasn't going to do that either. Not to Fred. She was sure there were a great many kennels that were well run and treated their animals wonderfully... but Fred felt more like a family member than a pet.

Crystal only looked down at Fred and continued stroking behind his ears. "Let me see what I can do," she said, giving Megan a sly smile. "It would be a shame to leave him behind."

Chapter Twelve

✦✦✦

Megan had the feeling Fred was more thrilled than he was letting on. He sat looking out the airplane window and taking up two full seats. Across the aisle, Megan was quite comfortable in her own soft, wide chair. The private jet Crystal's mother had chartered for their trip was incredible. Roomy and chic.

"Only about an hour until we touch down," Crystal said, returning with a tall glass in each hand. Ice clinked together as she handed Megan a glass. "Strawberry lemonade?"

Megan took a quick sip. "Thank you."

Crystal sat across from her. The chairs were arranged in groups of four, with two on either side of a small round table. She crossed her legs and looked out the window, sipping her drink. "I'm glad Officer Morel suggested this," she said. "And it was nice of my mom to call in a favor and get us this jet." She smiled, looking across the aisle. "This way, Fred was able to come."

"I think he's having a great time." Megan couldn't help grinning at the way he was obviously trying to ignore them.

"Although he's trying to keep it low-key." She winked back at Crystal.

"He's a smart one," Crystal laughed. Her eyes wandered back to the window. "You know... I kissed a boy on this plane the first time I rode in it." A grin pulled at her lips, but her gaze remained on the sky outside their window. "A whole group of my friends were here, and I was madly in love with my best friend Isaac. He'd been my friend since grade school, so I just didn't know how to tell him. Then his friend came up to me, acting all sweet and wrapping me in his arms, and before I knew it, we were kissing."

She turned back to Megan. "But I wasn't even into him. The whole time I was thinking of Isaac. That kiss was amazing, but only because it was like I was kissing my best friend. Like a strange sort of transference." She smiled, on the edge of laughing, but then it vanished. "Isaac saw us, and he got pretty upset about it. I never understood why. He's married now, with two little kids." She sighed and looked out the window again. "I guess it's pretty common to transfer feelings about someone you can't have to someone you can. It seems strange to me now, though. I kinda always regretted that."

"Huh." Megan wasn't sure what to say. Visions of her kiss with Kenneth were assailing her mind, making her feel sick with guilt. That wasn't what had happened, was it? Besides, who would she really have feelings for? The only other man she knew at Seacrest was Santiago...

"You okay?"

Megan's eyes flickered back to Crystal, who watched her with concern. "Do you think I'm a total jerk now?" Crystal asked, biting her lip.

"No, not at all," Megan assured her, setting her empty

glass down on the table between them. "I've just never heard of that before."

"Yeah, I hadn't either." Crystal stood and picked up Megan's empty glass. "I read about it years later and everything kinda just fell into place. Wish I would have realized it sooner." She shrugged and wandered back to the front of the plane. She returned carrying a few snack bags. She handed two to Megan. "One for Fred, if you want."

"Thanks." Megan took the bag of snacks Crystal handed her, still lost in her thoughts and becoming more worried by the second. Is that what she'd done with Kenneth? Was it transference? Did she really, honestly, have feelings for Santiago? She eyed Crystal tossing a frosted cookie into her mouth. "Speaking of guys," she ventured, "have you asked Santiago out yet?"

Crystal's mouth was full of cookie, and she chewed quickly, holding a hand up in the meantime. "Well," she said, reaching for a water bottle. She took a quick swig. "I left him a message before all this craziness started with my dad." She shrugged. "He hasn't called me back yet."

"Oh." Megan opened a bag of snacks. "I'm sure he'll get back to you soon."

"Yeah," Crystal sounded a little unsure. "Does he usually take a few days to respond?"

Megan nodded, although Santiago always responded right away when she would text or call. Still, that would make Crystal feel bad, and her friend was already dealing with enough. On the other hand, she was tempted to send him a text as soon as they landed, just to check. Maybe he really was avoiding Crystal, but she couldn't be sure why he would do that. He was young and single after all. He probably went out with someone new every weekend.

They landed quite gently for such a small plane, which Megan appreciated. Especially when it was Fred's first time on a plane... at least, that she knew of. He seemed very excited the moment they walked down the steps of the aircraft and out onto the tarmac. Palm trees and warm, sunny weather greeted them, and Megan had to hold tight to the leash. "Whoa," she said, wrapping it around her wrist. "Fred, hold on."

"My mom had a car left for us in short-term parking," Crystal said, leading the way. "She said it was on the first floor... section A... fifth row down..." Crystal was gesturing from one car to the next and Megan's gaze skipped ahead to a nice BMW convertible. For some reason, it seemed to match. Sure enough, Crystal stopped right in front of it. "Here we are," she said, reaching into the front wheel well. Keys jangled, and she lifted out a keychain looped around her finger. "Not the most secure way to do it, but it works."

They hopped in and, while Crystal was rearranging their luggage in the trunk, Megan sent Santiago a quick text telling him the shop would be closed the next few days until Friday and asked if he could just check in on it now and then.

Crystal sank into the driver's seat and exhaled. "Well, I can't believe we're here. I'm feeling better already." She backed out, and they took the winding exit ramp. "I'm glad we came."

Megan glanced back at Fred, who was slobbering up the window as he looked this way and that, full of excitement. She faced front as they turned onto the main road, gazing over palm trees and happy people in bright colors and sandals. A swell of excitement and relaxation blended to give her a wonderful traveler's high. "Me too," she said, letting all the questions of Crystal's dad settle for a moment. They could wait. Hawaii was passing by in a blur, and she didn't want to miss it.

They turned onto a side road, and the car slowed considerably. "Here," Crystal said, rolling their windows down. "Smell that ocean mist and all the flowers and vegetation." She took a deep breath. "Nothing smells quite like Hawaii. This is my favorite part of the drive."

It was beautiful and green, with ferns and palm trees crowding the road. Big, open blooms of white and pink spotted the undergrowth. Megan leaned her head out and took a breath, realizing that Crystal was right. She really could smell the flowers in the air. It was incredible. Heady and delicious; she wondered for a moment why she lived in a place that insisted on being chilly the entire winter. It didn't seem like a fair trade.

But oh, how it made her appreciate the feel of the sun on her skin. She leaned back in her seat and closed her eyes in the warm sunshine. It was glorious. Her skin tingled happily.

The car slowed. "Well... this is my mom's house," Crystal said. "I mean, technically she's renting. She says she wanted to be self-sufficient on her own salary and not use my *dad's money*." She said the last part with air quotes. "Even though he'd be the first to tell you it's because of her that he was ever successful. He's always saying stuff like that, but I'm pretty sure my mom thinks it's all just politician talk."

It was beautiful and quaint, not quite the mansion Megan had expected. The shutters and windows were open, and the front doors had long windows set into them, giving an inviting view of a spacious, clean house. It was beautiful, and closer to something Megan would want than she would have imagined. Crystal's family house in Seattle was sprawling and built to impress, but this felt more like a native house. Small and loved. "It's beautiful," she murmured.

"Yeah."

There was a smile in Crystal's voice, and Megan turned to see the real thing on her face. But it faltered quickly.

Crystal shrugged. "I wish things were different, but there's something to be said for both of them finding happiness... together or not."

Megan gave a sympathetic smile. "Very well said."

They made their way down the small walk. The front door was open, and Crystal walked in. "Mom?" Megan followed with Fred on a leash this time, just in case. His energy levels were palpable, and she worried he might get carried away. Plus, she couldn't remember if Crystal had mentioned her mom having any pets. The last thing she wanted was for Fred to go tearing through the house chasing a cat.

"Anyone home? Hello?" Crystal wandered down one hallway and returned only to head in the hallway opposite. The house had appeared smaller from the front than it really was. It split off in two separate wings on either side, and directly ahead was an open view to a beautiful backyard patio space and pool. Palm trees leaned against the stone perimeter wall, framing it in tropical perfection. Megan walked to the back windows, mesmerized. She'd never been to Hawaii, and even if their trip wasn't under the best circumstances, she still couldn't believe she was finally there.

Crystal returned from the hallway, lifting a paper in her hand. "She'll be back tonight. I guess she had to help with a few rescues. She works in sea life preservation and awareness."

"Wow." Megan's eyebrows lifted. "That sounds incredible."

"Yeah, she loves it." Crystal's eyebrows furrowed. "I was really hoping to talk to her, but I guess it'll have to wait." She gestured to the backyard. "You two can explore a little bit if you want. If Fred needs to get out. There's a gate along the back wall with a pathway to the beach." She smiled. "I can meet you there, I just need to make a phone call first."

"Okay." Megan kicked her shoes off and grabbed her sandals from her duffel bag. "Do you need any help?"

Crystal had her phone to her ear, but she waved away the offer, giving a quick smile and mouthing the word no.

Megan waved and went outside, following an eager Fred. The peaceful sound of ocean breeze through the palms was supremely relaxing. She reached a charming back gate and lifted the latch, letting it swing open. A small, sandy trail led through bushes and patches of sand dunes with tall grasses escaping here and there. It was beautiful. Megan gave a happy sigh, and they started on the trail.

The ocean wasn't in view yet, but she could hear it. Seagulls called and waves were crashing. There were no sounds of voices, though, and she began to anticipate a secret beach where she could sit alone without the distractions of anything but nature. It sounded like heaven. Fred was excited, and he pulled hard on the leash, but she didn't let him loose. There was still the chance the beach would be full of people, and she didn't want to scare anyone.

When the landscape parted in front of her, a small cove lay ahead. The waves crashed to her left, along a rocky hill-side, but the cove was calm. Turquoise blue, the water was gorgeous. From one side to the other, the beach was empty. No footprints or tracks besides that of seagulls.

She let Fred off the leash, and he raced ahead, leaping through the shallow water along the sand. He raced down the beach while Megan settled in the sand. She planned to take her sandals off and walk through the water, but not yet. For a moment, she only wanted to close her eyes and listen.

Her phone vibrated in her pocket, and her lips twisted in irritation. She snatched it up and saw Santiago's picture on the front. Glancing behind her, she answered quickly.

"Megan," he rushed, "I've been wanting to call you but just wasn't sure if it would be a good idea, but then you texted me, and I decided to just let you know what's been going on."

Megan sat up a little. "What is it?" she asked, remembering when her shop was vandalized, and before that, her home had been almost completely destroyed by a flash flood. It was how they met. But right now, she really wasn't anxious to repeat any of those things. "Is everything all right?" she urged, anxious for an answer.

"Yes... I mean..." He sighed. "I don't know. Have you found Crystal's father? Have you spoken to him? Because I need his help with something."

"Oh." That wasn't quite what she'd been expecting. "No, we haven't. But Crystal mentioned she was trying to get hold of you and..." She paused. And what? Crystal's reason for contacting Santiago had nothing to do with business or her father. Megan glanced back at the trail again, anxious to avoid Crystal sneaking up behind her. "Did you get her text?" she finally asked, unused to such a quiet conversation with Santiago. Why wasn't he talking? If he needed something, why didn't he just say it?

"I got her text, but I haven't answered yet," he said. He sighed again. "I was looking into the funding for the trails.

No one ever questions what they get from the state, they just wait for it to arrive in the account and then go from there. But it never arrived this year. Like, nothing. That doesn't sound right, does it?"

"Well, no," Megan agreed, "but Santiago, Crystal's father has gone missing. I doubt she's going to appreciate the talk about funding right now. She's pretty worried."

"Oh," Santiago cleared his throat. "He hasn't done something like this for a while now, has he? It seems strange he'd do something like that now..."

"But even if he did return, he's basically retired." Megan glanced over to see Fred sniffing in a patch of dune grass. "I don't think he would know anything about it. Have you talked to the city council at Seacrest?"

He sighed yet again. "I have. They just said it's a rough year for everyone, and the funding probably got cut. They've been looking into it as well but haven't gotten any answers. But at the city building, they were talking about Mr. Chambers possibly having financial problems. They said he was putting his Seattle home up for sale and that his teaching job wasn't paying half as much as the salary he was used to. They..."

He paused again and Megan stood, sliding her feet out of her sandals. She walked to the water as she waited for him to continue.

"Well, what if he took the money and ran? He'd know how to do something like that, and if he needs the money... I don't know."

Megan's feet submerged in the warm ocean water as she tried to process what he was saying.

His breath gusted into the phone. "I don't know what to

think. I just wish we could talk to him or that he'd at least give Crystal a call."

"That seems like a pretty huge assumption on their part. Why would they say something like that?" Megan swished her feet through the water, making her way over to Fred, who was sniffing at a starfish stuck to a rock. "Listen, why don't you give Crystal a call. She's been pretty stressed, so I wouldn't mention all this about her father. Maybe just see if she can get a message to him and then don't worry about it."

"Don't worry about it?" He was practically shouting. Megan pulled the phone away from her ear a little. "But Megan, I haven't even told you why I called—"

"Megan!"

Santiago's question was cut off as Crystal appeared, running down to the beach.

"Just give Crystal a call, please," Megan whispered. "I have to go. I'll call you later."

There was no goodbye, but there was no time to wait for one either. She hung up the phone and tucked it away, wishing they'd had one minute more. But there was no time to worry about what Santiago was going to say. Crystal caught up with her, out of breath.

"I talked to my mom." She swiped her hand through the air. "She doesn't know anything about where my dad could have gone. She said she doesn't care." She took a few breaths and then her finger lifted. "But she said she's seen Charlie Williamson here on the island! He's right here, and she said he usually has a late dinner at one of the restaurants along the beach. We can ask him about my dad the night of the field trip."

"So..." Megan looked out along the horizon, where the sun was low in the sky.

"So, right now," Crystal said, linking her arm with Megan's. "Let's go!"

Megan only had time to call Fred as she was whisked away. But the thought that she'd missed something important persisted. What was it Santiago had been trying to say?

Chapter Thirteen

✦✦✦

"I'm sorry, but we're booked tonight," a young, well-dressed gentleman said. He studied them for a moment and then looked away.

"For the whole night?" Crystal asked, leaning to the side to look behind him. "But it's barely six o'clock, and you're practically empty. There are open tables everywhere."

"Ma'am, the building was rented out for a private event. I'm sorry for any inconvenience."

He didn't sound sorry.

Megan stepped forward a little, catching the man's eye as he glanced down at Fred. "Can you tell us if a man named Charlie Williamson is here?" she asked. "He's a friend of ours."

"I'm sorry, but I can't say."

"Thanks anyway," Crystal said, grumbling as they made their way back to her car.

When they were out of view of the restaurant, Megan slowed. Eyeing a small alley between the buildings, she grabbed Crystal's arm and towed her behind a row of parked cars.

"What are you doing?" she complained.

"Shh," Megan crouched down. "Let's just go around to the back of the building and see if he's out on the patio."

"That's crazy." Crystal glanced back nervously. "He just told us to leave."

"He didn't really tell us to leave, exactly. He just said we couldn't come in. But what if Fred ran off, and we were just trying to catch him?" Megan asked. Crystal's head swung around, and Megan smiled. "No harm in that, is there?"

"I don't know."

"It's strange." Megan snuck closer to the alley, leading Fred with her. "For someone who grew up in politics, you sure have a hard time bending the rules."

"Hey." Crystal hurried to catch up to her. "There's nothing wrong with respecting rules."

Megan's lips slanted as she thought a moment. "Sometimes," she finally conceded.

"Sometimes?" Crystal whispered.

They stood at the edge of the building, looking into the alley. Megan took the leash off and swung her arm forward. "Go, Fred! Go on."

His tail wagged and his ears perked up, but he didn't move. Megan dug into her pockets and then looked in her purse. "Do you have any crackers or anything?"

Crystal checked her pockets when suddenly, barking came from the end of the alley. They looked up to see a small white dog running along the sand. It was in view for only a moment, but a moment was enough.

Megan reached for Fred's collar, but he took off in a blur,

racing after the little dog. "Fred, come!" she yelled, running after him.

He didn't slow. His big, heavy bark echoed between the brick walls around them. "Isn't this what we wanted?" Crystal asked behind her, breathing hard.

"Well." Megan was pretty sure this was not what they wanted. She only meant to get Fred onto the sand, then she could hook the leash on and have a good excuse to take a look around. Now there was no telling when he would stop. Besides that, catching him when he was excited was nearly impossible.

They emerged on a long, flat stretch of sand to find Fred nearly at the water's edge. The beach seemed to go on forever. "Fred!" Megan shouted. The waves crashing right behind him must have drowned her voice out. The sun was huge above the horizon, just about to set. It was beautiful, but blinding. Megan turned her head... and there he was. Charlie Williamson sat alone at a table on the patio only a few yards away. She recognized him from the class presentation video. Same heavy build. Same dark hair and eyes. The restaurant was chic and elegantly lit. People wandered onto the patio with him and his face brightened as he greeted them.

"Crystal," she whispered, turning her back to him. Crystal was watching the ocean, but she turned to Megan, and then her eyes flickered back to the patio. They widened, and she sidestepped a tiny bit, hiding her face from his view. Her hand came to her mouth, covering a silent gasp.

"It's him," she said. "What do we do?"

"Here," Megan handed her the leash. "Why don't you go get Fred, and I'll talk to him."

"You're sure?" Crystal took the leash, glancing back at the paito.

"Don't worry," Megan assured, giving her a steady smile. "It'll be fine."

"Okay," Crystal said. Megan couldn't tell if she was referring to the plan or the intimidating thought of wrangling Fred. Either way, she started off in the right direction.

Megan didn't waste a second and hurried over to where Charlie Williamson sat. There was a quaint bamboo fence around the tables and gas fire pits scattered about. His back was to her but the other guests around the table glanced up as she approached. He must have noticed because he turned in his seat just before she reached him.

She froze for a moment and then moved in a little closer, speaking quietly. Although it wasn't as private a conversation as she would have liked. "Are you Charlie Williamson?" She recieved only a nod in reply. No smile, no hello. But what had she been expecting? "Good. Okay." She quickly straightened out her thoughts. "I'm here with Crystal Chambers, and we really need to speak with you sometime, if we could."

His eyebrows lifted at Crystal's name. Unfortunately, at the same time, Crystal's voice rose over the sounds of the ocean, screaming Fred's name. Mr. Williamson glanced back at the beach. "I see," he said, his expression cool. Megan forced herself not to look. She was sure she only had a few minutes before the guard at the front door would notice her and shoo her away.

"Sir." She gained his attention back from whatever was happening on the beach. "I'm sorry to bother you during dinner, but if we could speak with you privately? We're very concerned about Crystal's father. We were first told he traveled here with you."

A look of surprise broke through his polished face, then hardened. "Well, as you can see, that's not the case."

"I know it's not," Megan said. "But my point is, no one knows where he is, and in a few more days, an investigation will start. We'd love to avoid having things go that far. Did you—" She noticed his companions leaning a bit closer, and she lowered her voice even more. "Did you see him at all that night of the field trip? Someone told me a group got together for dinner."

He looked back at her for a moment and then gave a quick smile and a nod of his head. "A crowded party is not the place to talk," he said. "Why don't you meet me at this address tomorrow morning between ten and noon. Here." He fished a business card from his front coat pocket. "I'll speak with you then."

"Thank you so much." Megan tucked the card away just as the guard from the front door appeared on the patio. He spotted her immediately and changed directions, coming for her. "Miss, I've asked you to leave—"

"Fred, no!"

Megan spun around to see Crystal running with all her might, dripping wet with sand caked in her hair. Fred was ten feet in front of her and sailed over the bamboo fence, landing in the middle of the patio tables. Guests gasped, and a woman cried out, startled. But when he lowered his head, Megan knew it was only the beginning of their misfortune.

"Fred!"

It was too late. He twisted his head side to side, wringing his coat out and shaking so hard, the seawater and sand reached all the way to Megan. She closed her eyes to the sound of screaming and chairs toppling over. "Fred, come!" she shouted, turning and running for it. "Come!"

Crystal was ahead of her in no time, likely cursing her name and vowing never to listen to her again. Megan glanced back to see Fred close behind, frolicking along as if it were a wonderful evening. Voices continued to ring out from the restaurant, but he didn't even glance back, unaware of the utter chaos he'd caused.

They made it to the car and Crystal was inside before Megan could even get her door open. She let Fred leap through the front and make his way to the back. Then she jumped in, closing the door as Crystal floored it.

"I'm soaked," Crystal said, speeding through the town. Megan kept an eye out for cops, sure if she asked Crystal to slow down, she'd get an ear full. She tried to glance over without her friend noticing.

"I'm sorry about Fred," Megan ventured.

There was only cold silence as an answer.

Megan took the business card from her pocket. "But he told us to meet with him tomorrow morning."

Crystal gasped, snatching the card from her hand. "He did? Oh my gosh." The car slowed, and she turned onto her street. "That's such good news." She sighed and her shoulders lowered. She sank back into her seat. "Oh, I'm so glad."

"Me too." Megan glanced back to see Fred stretching his head forward, about to shake again. They stopped at the house, and she grabbed his collar, hauling him out the door. "C'mon, Fred," she urged. But it only managed to place him directly beside Crystal, who'd just come around the car. He shook magnificently while Crystal squeezed her eyes closed, otherwise unmoving as she was showered again. He finished and trotted toward the steps.

Megan cringed. She was sure Crystal would never speak to her again. But to her surprise, Crystal smiled. An honest, unrestrained smile. "What does it matter now?" She broke into laughter.

Megan couldn't help laughing with her. "Oh, Fred," she said between laughs. "Sailing through the air and landing right in the middle of all those well-dressed people! Let's go get you cleaned up." She reached for his collar, but before she could get to it, he sneezed, catching her hand in the process.

"Ugh." She gave up and made for the door. "You know what? Me first."

By the time everyone was washed, dried, and ready for the night, it was nearly 10 p.m. The gas fireplace flickered gently, and Megan began to wonder where Crystal's mother was. It seemed a long time to spend rescuing animals. Fred was curled up at her feet, and she reached down to pet his silky coat. They'd spent extra time to condition and blow-dry it so Crystal's mother wouldn't come home to the smell of wet dog. Megan was just about to ask when to expect Mrs. Chambers when headlights flashed past the window.

"Finally," Crystal jumped to her feet, "I was wondering what in the world was taking her—" She peered out the window and then dodged to the side, out of view. "It's the guy," she whispered.

"What guy?" Megan went to the window, but Crystal flapped her hand frantically.

"The Williamson guy. Don't let him see you!"

Megan stopped, looking back at Crystal's frantic face. Relenting, she sidestepped until she was standing against the wall. "Well, is he coming to the door?" Megan asked, feeling ridiculous. Hadn't they wanted to talk to him anyway? And, in that case, why were they hiding? She could hear their voices, but it was too muted to make out the words.

"He's with my mom." Crystal leaned ever so slightly toward the window. "They're talking. Looks like they each drove their own car here, so that's good."

"We should just go say hello, don't you think?" Megan dropped her arms to her sides.

"No, let's just wait a little while and see what's going on..."

Fred yawned loudly and got to his feet, trotting over. He looked at Crystal and back at Megan and then sat in the direct center of the window with his nose practically pressed against it.

Crystal was so focused on her mother and Williamson, she didn't seem to even notice. Megan couldn't help rolling her eyes. "Well, when your mother looks in her house, all she's going to see is a huge dog sitting there."

"Oh—Fred, go," Crystal said, attempting a whispered scolding. "Go lie down, Fred. Go!"

Fred didn't move. Instead, he flattened his ears and barked.

From outside, the voices were suddenly clear with Crystal's mother's voice ringing out first. "Oh my gosh, a dog is in my house!"

"It's not yours?" Williamson sounded even more shocked than Mrs. Chambers. "How'd he get in there? Wait—I know that dog."

"You do?" Crystal's mom asked.

"Crystal." Megan couldn't help laughing. "Face it, the gig is up."

Crystal groaned and abandoned her hiding place to open the front door. Her shoulders sagged, and she tromped outside. Megan managed to catch hold of Fred's collar before he could dash off after her. "Wait here, Fred," she said, scooting ahead of him and through the door. "We'll just be a minute. Stay."

His haunches plopped to the floor with a snort. He was clearly irritated. But with this opportunity to talk to Charlie Williamson, Megan didn't want to take any chances. She hurried to meet with the small group in the driveway. But when she came closer, she noticed the affectionate way Charlie was looking back at Crystal's mother. It had her steps slowing. And when he spoke to her, his hand came to her back.

Megan joined the group, and he smiled. "Hello again," he said, reaching his hand out. "I don't think I ever caught your name."

Megan took his hand, wondering where this comfortable, everyman attitude had come from. He'd been a different person at the restaurant. Still, she didn't know his circumstances. "I'm Megan." She glanced back at the window to see Fred had taken up his post again. "That's my dog."

Mrs. Chambers smiled, reaching her hand out as well. "Hello, Megan. Glad you could come out for a visit."

"Yes," Mr. Williamson said, although the timbre of his voice had deepened. "You visited my office at Natural Resources, I'm told. My secretary said you had something urgent to talk about?"

Crystal's mother gave a quiet gasp. "Is that why you came out?" She folded her arms dramatically, although her smile remained. "Well, now I'm offended. I thought it was just for a visit."

"It *is* just for a visit," Crystal said quietly. She glanced at Megan, hesitating. To Megan, it was clear she wanted to talk about her father but wasn't sure what she should say in front of Mr. Williamson. "We just..." Crystal's eyes scanned the group timidly. "We—wanted to ask why Sandy had to take down the tansy ragwort display."

"Sandy?" Mr. Williamson asked, raising one eyebrow.

"The girl at the gift shop," Carmen encouraged.

There was a moment of awkward silence.

"The what?" Crystal's mother laughed, but it died out quickly as she waited for an explanation. Mr. Williamson waited as well. He looked back at her not so much with confusion, but more a mild curiosity as to what she might say next.

"The, uh..." Crystal glanced back at Megan, and she nodded encouragingly. "It was the display at the Natural Resources building of all the invasive species and noxious weeds." Her eyes darted between her mother and Williamson. "It was supposed to raise money for the farmers and stuff. I guess they've had a difficult year."

"Yes, I know they have." Mr. Williamson sighed. "These fluctuations in invasive species in the forests and even along the coastline are sometimes erratic. They behave almost the same way as flu season every year. Doctors try to predict the flu shot as best they can, but some years are just worse than others." His hands sank into his pockets, and he frowned. "This is just one of those years, I guess. But next year should ease up. It always does." He gave a comforting smile. "As for the display, I didn't think it set the right tone for a gift shop. We want to inspire visitors with the charm of native Washington critters. Not depress them with the gloom of infestation."

"Oh, I see," Crystal said quietly. She glanced around, but no one else seemed to have anything to say. Megan waited for an explanation from her mother or Mr. Williamson as to why they were meeting at her house so late at night, but neither of them offered one. They just looked back silently.

"I'd better get going," Mr. Williamson finally said, backing away. "You all have a nice weekend."

"Wait," Megan still had so much to say. "We're still meeting with you tomorrow, right?"

He paused for just a fraction of a second and then nodded. "Yes, I'll see you then. Goodnight." His gaze flickered back to Crystal's mother. "Goodnight, Cassidy."

She waved quickly. "'Night, Charlie."

It was dark outside, even under the glow of the house lights. But Megan thought she could see a tint of red gracing Mrs. Chambers cheeks. She hoped she was wrong, but suddenly, she wondered if an interview with Mr. Williamson would be a complete waste of time. If he was lobbying for Mrs. Chamber's affections, odds were, he wouldn't be so keen on helping them locate Mr. Chambers. Maybe he was glad to have him out of the picture.

Chapter Fourteen

❧❧❧

"**B**ut Mom, why didn't you say anything?" Crystal argued. "Why didn't you tell him about Dad? Tell him he's missing, and then he would really believe something might be wrong. What if you go missing too? What do I do then?" Crystal's voice shook and her mother quickly wrapped her in a hug.

"Oh Crystal." Her words were filled with sadness. "I would have told him..." She leaned away, still holding her daughter by the shoulders. "If I thought your father was in danger."

Her words settled uncomfortably in the quiet house. Megan wished she'd gone to bed earlier so they could have their time together. It was awkward standing there, listening to something so personal. Because, if Mrs. Chambers didn't think her husband was in danger, she must believe he left on purpose. And the thought had Megan's heart breaking for Crystal. She didn't deserve to go through this.

"What are you saying?" Crystal's voice hardened, having

lost the desperation from only seconds earlier. "You believe the ridiculous rumors that he ran off with someone?"

Her mother sighed, and her arms dropped to her sides. She walked to the couch and fell onto the cushions, looking completely exhausted. "Running off would mean he was here in the first place." She looked back at her daughter with compassion and shook her head. "But he hasn't been back here for nearly three months. I'm sorry I didn't tell you. Honestly, I thought you knew. It was only a matter of time before we finalized it."

Crystal exhaled sharply, as if she would argue, but it never came. There was only the quiet of the house and the ticking of a clock somewhere down the hall. Fred lifted his head, as if he sensed the unease. The jingling of the tag on his collar felt too loud when he got to his feet.

Mrs. Chambers glanced over at him, and a smile found its way onto her face. "Hello," she said, reaching her hand out to him. He crossed the room and his big tail wagged, smacking the coffee table and sitting chair as he walked. He sat at Mrs. Chambers's feet and closed his eyes as she ran her hand over his head gently. "And who are you, gentle soul?" She leaned to the side to get a better look at his face. "What a handsome boy you are." Fred's mouth hung open, and his tongue lolled to one side as he panted happily. "You surprised me in the window, you know."

She looked back at Megan, smiling. "And this beautiful guy is yours, you said?"

"Yes, that's Fred." Megan walked a little closer. "I hope it's okay that we brought him."

"Oh, of course." She patted his head again and stood, crossing the room. "I'm Cassidy, by the way." She took

Megan's hand firmly, holding it longer than most handshakes. "And you're Megan."

"That's right." Megan smiled back at Crystal, but her friend still looked a little withdrawn. "Have you heard about me?"

"I have, and all of it good." She glanced back at her daughter.

Megan shuffled her feet in the quiet. "You, uh, rescue animals?" she asked, curious but mostly hoping to fill the silence.

"I do," Crystal's mother tucked her arms behind her back, folding them together. It was a stance Megan had seen Crystal take often. It seemed a peaceful, calm position.

"I've loved the sea for as long as I can remember. I even majored in marine biology... but I never had the chance to use my degree until moving out here full time."

Megan smiled at the genuine happiness on her face.

"We never had as much time as I wanted to be near the ocean. I spent twenty-five years raising a family and supporting my husband, and I wouldn't change a thing. But this, now. I love being involved with sea life and conservation. Even educating the community and just spending time in the water." She smiled. "It's incredible."

"Sounds like it," Megan said. "I'd love to see where you work sometime."

She smiled, giving a gentle nod. Her eyes strayed back to Crystal and then she straightened a bit. "The guest rooms are made up, and you're welcome to anything in the kitchen, if you're hungry."

"Thanks Mrs. Chambers," Megan said, glancing back at Crystal again.

Crystal gave a quick smile. "Thank you," she said.

"Goodnight, ladies." She gave Crystal a last, tender glance and disappeared down the far hall. A bedroom door closed, and it was quiet again.

Fred snorted and trotted past them, wandering into the kitchen where he began sniffing at every cupboard and shelf.

"I think he's hungry," Crystal said. She went to the kitchen but only walked to the window and crossed her arms, looking out at the darkness.

Megan wondered if she could see through the glass from that close or if her view was the same as Megan's. Just a sad reflection of her unsettled face. She unzipped her bag and pulled out four portions of dog food. They were triple-sealed in Ziplock bags to avoid permeating her clothes with the smell. After managing to get through all the layers, she poured a bowl for Fred and set it on the floor, where he eagerly began gobbling it up.

Megan walked up behind Crystal, spotting her tear-streaked cheeks in the reflection. There wasn't much she could say to ease her pain. She took a heavy breath. "You did say their relationship had been strained for a long time, right?" She placed her hand on Crystal's back. "Maybe this is for the best."

"I know." Crystal wiped at her cheeks. "I know it's for the best, and it's been coming a long time now, and... I know everything. But it still hurts." She turned from the window, looking watery eyed back at Megan. "I'd just built up this crazy hope that maybe they were working things out this last year or so. I don't know why I believed that. But for some stupid reason, I did." She hugged herself, running her hands along her arms. "Anyway, let's get our bags back there and get some sleep. Maybe we can meet with Williamson a little early tomorrow."

"Sounds great," Megan said. She'd expected to talk to her about Williamson and all the implications of him visiting her mother, but now she knew she couldn't be the one to bring it up. If they were going to broach that subject, it would have to come from Crystal.

Megan set her bag in the guest room across the hall from Crystal's and when she returned, Crystal stood outside her door. "My mom isn't even worried about where my dad went," she said quietly. Her mother was at the other end of the house, so there was really no need to whisper, but it felt appropriate. "I doubt he ever came out here."

"Who knows," Megan said, although from her perspective now, it didn't seem like her parents would voluntarily spend time together no matter the circumstances. "Let's just chat with him tomorrow, and maybe we can get an idea of what your father did after that field trip."

Crystal nodded, looking relieved. "Yeah, that's the best place to start. Maybe everything's fine."

Megan wanted to agree, but she had a reliable sense of intuition... and her skin was tingling ominously. She went to bed early enough that night, but only lay still, listening, and staring at the ceiling. Fred snuck onto the foot of the bed at some point, and it helped ease her mind. Eventually, her eyelids relented and slowly, the night had passed.

"ARE YOU SURE THIS IS THE PLACE?" CRYSTAL HESITATED AT the gate, looking back to where her mother's house was, just around the bend in the road. "They're practically neighbors."

Megan couldn't help thinking of the affectionate way Crystal's mother and Charlie Williamson had interacted.

And to find out he lived right down the street? It was concerning to say the least.

"Let's go see," Megan said, giving an encouraging smile. Fred seemed pleased with their activity, striding out ahead with his ears lifted. They walked past a row of tropical flowers Megan had never seen before, except maybe on postcards of Hawaii. Fred turned his nose to the big, large-petaled blooms, sniffing so deeply that his middle expanded.

But Crystal's gaze was locked on the front door. Her tension was palpable, from the crease between her brows to the quick, short pace of her steps. When they got to the door, however, she froze in front of it.

This time, Megan didn't want to take the lead. Crystal was clearly struggling with the entire situation they were in, and above all, she wanted to see her friend gain enough strength to get through it. She couldn't keep jumping in and handling the tough stuff. So, even though her finger was itching to ring the doorbell, she stayed back and pretended to be admiring the potted flowers along each side of the patio.

She heard Mr. Williamson take a breath and turned to see her slender fist rap on the door. After only a short wait, it swung open.

"Hello, hello." Mr. Williamson stood grinning back at them, apparently much happier to see them than he'd been back at the beach café. "Come in, let's sit on the back deck if you don't mind. It's a beautiful day today."

They took turns shaking his hand and Megan pressed her lips together, again allowing Crystal a chance to respond. She agreed, albeit hesitantly, and they started through the house.

"But then, every day is beautiful here," Mr. Williamson

continued. "Rain or shine, wind, or hail. Hawaii is a beautiful place."

"Yes, it is," Megan agreed, keeping an eye out for any family pets as they went. So far, Fred was wandering quietly beside her, almost bored. She doubted there were any indoor animals, or Fred would have smelled them.

The backyard was sprawling, surrounded by palm trees and short palm plants as well as bright pink and white flowers and glossy-smooth shrubs. In the middle was a big patch of what Megan liked to call island grass. It was short and thick and always looked healthy, but if she were to roll around in it, the stuff cut like razors. Regardless, it worked perfectly to provide a pleasant view. The deck was clearly the entertainment space; wide and multi-leveled, there was a section with an outdoor kitchen and another with a massive fire pit. Another still was lined with lounge chairs, likely for sunning. Megan, Crystal, and Mr. Williamson sat in the shadiest portion where there was the largest group of furniture.

"Now," Mr. Williamson gained back their attention and sat in a patio chair with thick red cushions. Megan and Crystal sat opposite him on a matching couch. His expression softened as his gaze fell on Crystal. "What's this about your father?"

Crystal twisted her hands together and glanced at Megan. "Well," she turned back to him. "He had that field trip on Friday, and he hasn't been seen since. We heard he went to dinner with some colleagues and thought maybe you were there?" She bit her lip, looking anxious.

He rolled his jaw to one side. "Yes, there was a fairly large group. All the NR employees plus him. He used to work closely with our department, so he knew almost everyone there."

He paused and Megan glanced at Crystal, seeing that she sat just as anxiously as before, waiting for him to continue. "And what happened at dinner?"

"Nothing out of the ordinary." Mr. Williamson rocked back in his chair, crossing his arms. "We talked for a little while about finances." His gaze flickered to Crystal and then away again. "The last time I spoke with him about a year ago, he was worried. I guess he was struggling for quite some time, but he assured me things were okay."

Megan waited through a few seconds of silence before she couldn't wait any longer. "And what happened after that? Did you see him talk to anyone else? Did you see him leave?"

He leaned forward again, smiling a bit before he became serious again. "Let me see here, he spoke with everyone there, but mostly it was just me and my secretary, Alyana. They're very good friends. She knows him probably better than I do."

Crossing her fingers, Megan hoped he wouldn't say what she was thinking.

"They left together but got into separate cars," Charlie said. "Alyana in her sedan and Stephen in an Uber."

"When you spoke with my father last year"—Crystal's foot was bouncing on the stone in front of her, making her knee hop—"what did he say? He never talked to me about any money problems."

"Oh yes, he thought he'd have to sell the house for half its worth for a while there." Mr. Williamson nodded. "The market wasn't doing well, but he needed the money. I can't remember if he told me what had happened to make things so difficult for him. Might just have been the transition from career to mostly retired life. Sometimes it's hard to cut expensive things out when you're used to them."

"I see," Crystal sounded glum. She didn't offer any other conversation and only stared at the ground.

"So, he left in an Uber?" Megan steered the conversation back, wanting to make the most of their time. "Did he say if he was staying the night in a hotel or if he was flying home? Anything?"

Mr. Williamson began to shake his head and then stopped. "Now wait a minute," he mused, rubbing his chin. "He didn't say anything, exactly. But when Alyana said good-bye, she followed with, *Have a good night*." He shrugged. "Not something you tell someone who's about to get on a plane."

"I suppose," Megan said, feeling like this conversation wasn't quite the miracle they needed. "And that was it?" She peered back at him hopefully. "That was the last time he was seen?"

Mr. Williamson crossed his legs, taking a slow breath. His eyes wandered back to Crystal. "Honestly, I suspected they were going to meet up that night."

Crystal's gaze jumped from the ground to meet with his, alarmed. "What makes you say that?" she asked, sounding hurt in so many ways.

But Mr. Williamson didn't answer right away. He only looked back at her, as if mulling it all over. "Just a feeling, I guess. But I found it strange that when I spoke to your mom just yesterday, she didn't say anything about Stephen going missing. We've spoken over the years quite often, yet she never mentioned money trouble or the possibility that they might sell their place in Seattle."

Crystal shook her head, looking confused. "Yeah." A

gentle shrug lifted her shoulders. "She's a private person, much more so than he is. What are you getting at?"

"Oh, it's just something I've been meaning to ask her but haven't gathered up quite enough courage." Mr. Williamson leaned forward, resting his elbows on his knees and clasping his hands. "Your mother is a wonderful person. Very kind and selfless from what I've seen. A joy to be with. And your father seems equally kind... although perhaps not as selfless. I just can't help wondering." His head tilted a little. "What are the chances of him leading at least a semi double life?"

His question hung in the silence, and his expression was unchanging as he looked back at her. Megan couldn't decide if he was simply inquiring and trying to help or if this question was just a lead in to something more. What else was hiding behind his calm exterior? She tingled with anticipation as the silence lingered on.

Crystal, however, suddenly appeared to be struggling to keep back the daggers in her eyes. After a moment of rather frozen contemplation, she leaned forward, staring intensely back. "And what do you mean by that?"

"Are you refusing to answer?" Mr. Willamson answered quite quickly.

"I'm clarifying first," Crystal's voice had hardened some, and it seemed to put an end to the stalling.

He nodded. "Right. Well, all I'm saying is what I've noticed over the years. I've been around through his political career and, although I'm not in Hawaii as often as I'd like, I vacation enough to know they're not spending time together. Here he goes missing after struggling financially, and I have to wonder if he's making a significant shift in his life. You know, from one thing to another."

"You mean from one person to another?" Crystal asked.

"Like Alayna? Have you spoken to her about this?"

Mr. Williamson got to his feet but didn't walk away. "Not yet, but I believe I should." He looked out at the view and sunk his hands into his pockets. "I understand why the police wouldn't open a search in this circumstance. I'm sorry to say it, but with the timing of all this... it doesn't look good for Stephen."

Crystal stood slowly; her lips parted as she stared back at him. "You're..." She stepped around him so they were facing each other. "You're not talking about him running off with someone, are you?"

Mr. Williamson released a long breath and looked like he'd rather not say what was hovering behind his parted lips. But Crystal stared back silently, waiting.

Finally, he shook his head. "I've been trying to give you pieces of the puzzle, hoping you'd put it together yourself. But if you're really going to make me spell it out for you, then I will."

"Spell what out?" Crystal stepped slowly closer to him.

Mr. Williamson's eyes lifted to hers, settling quietly. "Your father needed the money. He also had access to that funding before anyone else. Did he tell you he got permission to evaluate the NR budget coming in for the year long before he'd even told his class about that field trip? He even went over my head to do it."

"But that's not..." Crystal's voice trailed off.

"Proof?" Charlie shook his head, looking sympathetic. "No, it's not. But it sure is suspicious... don't you think?"

There was no answer. Crystal only shifted from one foot to the next, as if trying to work out how she could argue his point. But in the end, she remained silent.

And for Megan... it felt like proof enough.

Chapter Fifteen

✿

They got out of the car at Crystal's mother's house. Mrs. Chambers had gone to work and was going to be away most of the day. Megan followed her friend to the front door, wondering how they were going to find out one way or the other if her father stole hundreds of thousands of dollars.

But before she could deliberate further, Fred jerked on the leash so suddenly, Megan wished she hadn't wrapped it around her hand. "Ouch! Fred—"

The front door swung open.

Crystal gasped. A man stood in the doorway, tall and boxy. His blue eyes were similar to Crystal's except a little grayer. He broke into a smile at the sight of her.

"Daddy!" She raced forward and nearly knocked him off his feet in a hug.

"Hey honey." He wrapped her in a hug. "How are you—"

Fred growled. His teeth bared and the hair on his back stuck up rigidly. Mr. Chambers hesitated, backing into the house a little. "Whoa there, boy," he said.

"Fred." Megan managed to enter the house while keeping him away from Mr. Chambers. "It's okay, Fred. He's a friend." She rubbed his head, surprised when Crystal's father came closer and lowered down, holding his hand out.

"Hey, boy," he said, although his hand shook slightly.

Fred was completely still except for one side of his lip that twitched, revealing a long, sharp canine tooth. Mr. Chambers waited half a second and then stood, wiping the back of his hand across his forehead. "Well, we should get going then." He still had Crystal under one arm and his free arm for Megan. "C'mon."

Fred barked, but Mr. Chambers didn't back away this time. He spun his hand like a pinwheel, urging Megan with him. Crystal stepped out of his grip, and he began to beckon to both of them. "C'mon now, let's get going. I'm sorry to disappear on you, but I'll explain everything on the way."

"On the way where?" Crystal ducked under his arm a second time. "Why are you acting like this?"

Mr. Chambers's eyes darted around the room. "We need to get going," he repeated, whispering now. "I can't urge this enough. Let's go."

Megan felt her pulse begin to rise. Whatever the former governor was afraid of, she couldn't argue that it might be something formidable. Besides that, if they went with him, he would likely start talking. And they needed answers. She wrapped the leash tightly around her wrist again, despite the risks, and nodded. "Okay," she said.

"This way." He stood behind them, holding his arms out like a mother hen shepherding her chicks. His head was on a swivel as they went.

"Can you tell us why you're running us out of here?" Crystal complained, stumbling as they hurried out to his car.

"I can't," he whispered back. "Just get in."

It was a small, but luxurious sedan, and they all climbed in, filling the white leather seats quickly. As soon as Mr. Chambers got in the driver's seat, the car shot forward, skidding a little as it peeled out.

"Daddy!" Crystal shouted. "What's going on?"

"I'm probably being followed," he said, turning onto the main road without checking for traffic. A car swerved into the other lane, laying on the horn. "I stumbled across something and didn't even..." He held on to the wheel as they flew around a corner. "I didn't even know what I'd found. But it's big. I just hope my assumptions are wrong. By the way, do you know where your mother is?"

"And what are your assumptions?" Crystal asked. "We came out here to speak with Charlie Williamson because we thought he might know something about where you'd gone. No one knew a thing!" Her voice rose, shaking hard. "How could you just disappear and not tell me or Mom? What were you thinking?"

"I was trying to save your life, Crys!" He glanced over, shaking his head. "I'm sorry, hun... I'm sorry."

They took a dirt road so fast that the back tires began to fishtail. Megan held her breath, worried they would lose control. Rocks and gravel ricocheted inside the wheel wells, landing on the windshield from time to time. But Crystal's father didn't speak again. Megan could see sweat along the back of his neck, and she couldn't help worrying what they'd just gotten themselves into. A simple meeting with a state employee, and suddenly, it felt like they were criminals on the run.

"Here we are," Mr. Chambers said, pulling into an open shed. It wasn't exactly a garage, but the car fit well inside.

"This is an old fishing lodge. You remember when we came here?" He turned to Crystal.

"I was six," she said, irritated. "But yeah, I remember. What, have you been hiding out here or something?"

Mr. Chambers took a deep breath, letting his shoulders lift and fall with it. "I didn't know where else to go. It's the only place I could think of that was hidden well enough. You know, off the beaten path." He turned in his seat, looking behind them. "I've never seen anyone else out here, so I figured it would work. So far, it has. But today..." He shook his head. "Who knows."

"Can you tell us exactly what is going on?" Megan asked, taking hold of Fred's collar when he growled.

Mr. Chambers looked at the dog and then tilted his head. "Let's go inside first. We can talk in there."

Crystal didn't respond and only stepped out of the car.

Megan followed behind them.

"I never imagined things would elevate like this." Mr. Chambers sat down in a folding chair. There were a few others placed around a fake leather card table. It was just one small room with a couch on one side that had a blanket and pillow strewn across the cushions, and cabinets and a sink along the other side. It didn't look like there was even any electricity. A red metal lantern was lit and sat on the card table.

"So what's going on, Dad?" Crystal asked, the irritation still ringing clearly in her voice.

Mr. Chambers sighed, running one hand through his hair. "I'm not even sure of it myself, honey." He folded his arms, narrowing his eyes as he stared across the room at the wall. "All I know is, a whole lot of money has gone missing, and there was someone keeping tabs on me."

"What do you mean by keeping tabs?" Megan asked. Fred was practically sitting on her feet, his body pressed against her legs. It was clear he didn't feel comfortable in the little lodge, but at least he'd stopped growling. She ran one hand along his back, but he didn't look at her. He kept a steady gaze on Mr. Chambers.

"Well, it all started just before that class trip," he said, standing. He paced back and forth in the tiny space. "Someone called me, claiming to be from Charlie Williamson's office. I was fairly sure Charlie only worked with Alyana, but at the time, I didn't question it. Who's to say he didn't hire a new assistant? Maybe he had a heavy workload." He shrugged. "Anyway, the man claimed Charlie had asked him to gather an itinerary for our class trip. They wanted to know when, where, and what we planned to do."

He stopped pacing, turning to Megan and then Crystal. "So I told him, and we ended the call. But then, I began to rethink our conversation throughout the day. I mean, I'm a former governor of Washington State, and I just gave my full itinerary to a complete stranger over the phone. What kind of an idiot does something like that? The more I thought about it, the more I worried someone was planning to come for me. I set up a camera just in case. I'm no stranger to things like this, and I've learned to go off my gut and take action quickly. But I didn't tell officer Morel about it, although I probably should have." He glanced at Megan. "He's been our family's unofficial security detail since I left the governor's office."

"Yes, I've met him," Megan said, hoping to hurry him along. "So, you set up a camera and went on the trip. Then what happened? Did you notice anything during the trip?"

"And where did you go if you didn't ride the bus home

with the class?" Crystal's question was softly spoken, but it rang with irritation.

"About that," Mr. Chambers said. "I admit I made a rather poor choice that night."

Crystal shot to her feet. "Ugh, I knew it! Why aren't you even trying to patch things up with Mom?"

"Hold on, Crystal." He took a step toward his daughter. "I wish I could patch things up, but your mother... well, I don't think she's interested in that option. She's never been happier than she is now. At least, not with me."

"It wasn't because of you, though," Crystal argued, flicking one hand in the air. "It was politics. And what if both of you could be happier than you've ever been, together?"

He sighed, gazing back at her quietly. "It's painful to hope for impossible things. But I adore your optimism, and I promise that I haven't given up completely, okay?"

Crystal looked rejected, but she nodded. "So, what was the poor choice you made? Did it have to do with Alyana?"

"Well, partly." Her father hesitated and then returned to his seat. "When I left office, it was a relief to create some space between Alyana and me. She was always very... well, forward. Flirty. It was a little obvious that she at least had a crush on me. She'd gone through a tough divorce, and I was her listening ear a lot of the time. We became quite close, spending a lot of time together. There was even a moment where I considered a future with her."

He looked deeply into Crystal's eyes, appearing a bit devastated. But clearly, he was still on edge and rushing through the backstory as quickly as he could. He glanced down at the floor. "Nothing ever happened between us. However, when I came back with the class on this trip, she picked up right where we'd left off. Except she was unusually blunt about it, even for her. She mentioned hearing that I'd split up with your mother and that she would like to give us a chance." He pulled in a deep breath. "We spoke about it briefly after dinner that night with everyone. When she brought up your mother, I told her she was mistaken and... well, she fell apart a little. I thought maybe if we could just talk a little more, it would help. She's my friend, after all..."

"I can't believe this," Crystal said, her eyes narrowed at her father.

He held his hand up. "But she didn't come that night."

"What?" Crystal's voice was tinged with anger.

He shrugged. "I don't know why. Charlie mentioned he asked her to print up the budget to give to me. He was getting some heat from his constituents and wanted me to see firsthand where the funds had gone. I guess he didn't like our estimates of the budget."

Megan glanced at Crystal, but neither of them spoke up. This didn't quite match Charlie's narrative to them. So, which one of the two was lying?

"I stayed the night at a hotel and then drove back to Harvard in the morning," Mr. Chambers continued. "I went to my office early enough that I had to use my key to get in the building. But there was only time to walk in and set my things down before I heard voices. It became clear that whoever it was, they'd broken into the building. So, I hid. There's a passageway behind the bookshelf wall. I turned off my camera and ducked inside."

"And why did you turn off the camera?" Megan asked.

"It was in too obvious a location. I knew if they found it, and it was recording, they'd suspect that I knew more than I do."

"Then what?" Crystal asked. "How did you get out here?" She threw her hands up, still obviously frustrated.

"Well, they came into my office." Mr. Chambers leaned forward, folding his arms and resting them atop his knees. "I could hear them, but just barely. They were talking about the job they had to do, and my name came up. They mentioned keeping tabs on me in case I figured out what they'd done." His eyes stilled, settling intently on Crystal. "They talked about the budget. They talked about watching my family." He cleared his throat. "Then, one of them said, *She would do anything to keep this from the public. He's gone missing before*. They said, *We'll just make it so he doesn't come back this time*."

"Wait," Crystal held her hand up. Her voice had gone very soft. "So, who were they talking about?"

Mr. Chambers stood, pacing a single step. "I can't be certain, but it could be your mother."

Crystal stood as well. "No way."

He sighed, facing her. "What has she been up to since you arrived?" His eyes searched her face. "Was she worried about me? Has she been looking for me or even tried to contact me at all?"

"But why would she need the money?" Crystal shook her head. "It doesn't match up. She's never been a big spender."

"No," Mr. Chambers hesitated, looking at Megan and then back at his daughter. "Not for herself maybe, but there are foundations she never got the chance to fund while I was in office. She was very passionate about them, and I can't say for certain that she wouldn't take matters into her own hands and place the funding where she believed it belonged. She would see it more as a Robinhood move than theft."

"Dad!" Crystal's cheeks were pink with anger, but her father held a hand up, stopping her from going further.

"I know how it sounds, but your mother can be very determined. She's a hero among underdogs and will resort to questionable means to do what she believes is right."

Megan's stomach twisted, with Charlie Williamson's claims fresh in her mind. She wondered if Crystal was coming to the conclusions she was because it felt very much like her father was trying to win their favor. Possibly to mask his own guilt? She couldn't be certain that the answer was no.

"And what about you?"

Crystal was still facing off with her father, although he didn't seem to grasp where she was going with her question. His eyes were narrowed, and he shook his head. "What do you mean?"

"I mean, we were told you were going to sell the house in Seattle?" She shrugged. "Are you in trouble? Because it has come to our attention that you had access to the budget and possibly even the transfer of funds." Crystal crossed her arms, although Megan caught a slight slight tremble of her chin. "Is that true?"

There was no visible reaction. Mr. Chambers only stared back. Tension wound through the room until Megan felt nearly rigid with it as she awaited his answer.

Finally, his expression changed. His eyes widened, and his head tipped slightly. "Did Charlie Williamson tell you that?" he asked, sounding a touch threatening.

Crystal confirmed it with a simple yes, clearly still waiting for more. But it was silent around them.

When Crystal's phone rang, all three of them jumped. Megan kneaded the tight muscles along the back of her neck as she watched her friend take out her phone. Crystal's expression lifted with surprise, and she answered quickly.

"Hello Santiago," she said, her gaze connecting with Megan's. "How are—"

Her question cut off, and there was silence again. Megan couldn't help feeling a pinch of jealousy that he'd called Crystal instead of her. It was childish and ridiculous, but it couldn't be helped. Because she *was* jealous.

Crystal's gaze returned to Megan, and she forced her face into as pleasant an expression as she could manage. But her heart dropped as she saw Crystal grimace. The few seconds that passed had Megan's insides feeling hollow with fear as she observed her friend's widening eyes and downturned lips. Panic tingled on Megan's face, leaving her nearly faint.

"I think her phone must be dead," Crystal said, her voice weak.

Megan snatched her phone from her pocket to see the screen was black. How long had it been dead? How long was Santiago trying to get hold of her before he ended up calling Crystal?

"Yes, we found him," Crystal continued. "Or, he found us." Her eyes flickered up to her father and then fell to the floor. "Okay, hold on." She held her phone out and tapped a button on the screen. "Okay, you're on speaker."

"Hello, Governor Chambers. It's Santiago Fitch. Do you remember me?"

Megan's emotions nearly overwhelmed her at the sound of his voice. She blinked back a sudden wave of moisture in her eyes and took a quick breath, steadying herself. But the desire to feel his comforting arms around her was so strong, it was almost paralyzing.

"Yes, Santiago. I remember you."

Mr. Chambers' strong baritone voice woke Megan just enough that she was able to recover from her almost breakdown. She took another breath, chasing away the heady emotions, at least for now.

"It's about the boy that went missing," Santiago said. "I've been searching for him for over thirty hours, and I don't believe he just wandered off. I think he saw something he wasn't supposed to. I finally got the chance to speak with the vet who treated his dog, and he said what I've been fearing. That the wounds on the dog appear to be afflicted by a person with a weapon, like a knife. I think..."

Crystal glanced nervously back at Megan as he paused.

"Well, I think he was taken."

"What boy?" Megan was surprised her voice had carried as well as it did, especially with how her entire body was trembling. There was a brief pause where she felt entirely consumed by the thought that Santiago was focusing on her, thinking of her. Maybe his wishes to begin a cautious relationship had vanished, but she couldn't help wondering if he was anxious to see her again, if only a little.

"You haven't heard, Megan?"

His voice was so cautious, it had her fears expanding in seconds. She swallowed hard, assuring her voice would be strong. "Heard about what?"

Again, there was a pause, and again, Megan was working to chase off her fears.

"It's Gabriel," he said. "He's gone missing."

Crystal gasped, but Megan was frozen, unable to find her voice. She could only think of the young boy and his mother, Amanda. She pulled her phone from her pocket and tapped the screen desperately, unsure if she'd saved her number. But she'd already forgotten it was dead. The screen remained black.

Chapter Sixteen

"I can't understand why anyone would do this," Santiago said. "But it doesn't change the fact that I think he was taken, although he might not have been taken out of the forest. And I was hoping, Governor Chambers, that you could help."

Megan's head was spinning so hard, she could barely concentrate on what Santiago was saying. She glanced at Governor Chambers to see him step closer to the phone, his brows set determinedly.

"What did you have in mind?" he asked.

"These trails haven't been maintained, and I need to know why. Like *really* know," Santiago's voice was clear and deep. "Who had the final say on that decision? Because I learned today that it wasn't just trail maintenance that was left unfunded for the year. There are stories from farmers in Washington of an uptick in blight and invasive pests. Things that the state usually keeps up on. Even marine habitats are suffering."

"We know," Mr. Chambers said. "It's a problem I believe

we're close to solving." He cleared his throat. "Although, I'm worried my wife, Celeste, may have had something to do with it. I have our security detail searching for any transactions she might've made."

"Dad," Crystal sounded just as irritated as before. "It can't be her. It just can't."

"It's not impossible, hun." Mr. Chambers sighed. "And with the way she's gotten so close to the head of NR, I wonder if all she wanted was access to that funding."

There was silence around the room with this new information. Megan thought back to Celeste and Charlie, wishing they'd known this earlier. She could've asked much more direct questions. But maybe they could get back to Charlie's house somehow...

"It amounts to well over twenty million dollars," Santiago's voice seemed to blare through the room with his sudden announcement. Megan couldn't help catching her breath at a number as high as that. What would a person do for financial freedom for the rest of their life? Would Crystal's mother really take that much money from such a worthy cause? Would her father take it for himself? He seemed to be relentlessly pushing this narrative of his wife being the one responsible.

Megan steadied her voice, her thoughts returning to Santiago. "How did you find that out?" she asked, managing to keep her voice from shaking.

"I spoke with a girl at NR. She runs the gift shop there," Santiago said. "Sandy, I think her name was. Her father travels around quite a bit for work, and he knows the numbers."

"Yeah, we spoke to her too," Megan sighed. "But what does any of this have to do with Gabriel?" There was a pause, and she began to feel antsy, wishing they were on the plane already, on their way back to Seacrest. What if Santiago was wrong and Gabriel really was lost in the woods? If only Fred could get on that trail, she felt sure they could find him. How cold had the temperatures been dropping at night? What would he eat?

"I don't know," Santiago finally answered.

"How long has he been missing?" Crystal asked.

"Two days," Santiago said.

"Two days?" Megan echoed; her breath pulled from her lungs.

"I've been trying to reach you," Santiago's voice was soft and sincere, as if he spoke only to her. It had Megan's cheeks warming, even through her shock.

"We're starting up another search party in a few hours," Santiago continued, "and they have helicopters running the area non-stop. Kenneth Bradburn even paid for two personal choppers to scan the area as well, so it's being covered."

Megan caught Crystal's eye at that news.

"Santiago," Mr. Chambers said, "I'd like to help. But if people were to make a big deal out of me being found, it might detract from the search for this little boy. And besides that..." He hesitated, glancing across at Megan and Crystal's faces. "It's not entirely safe for me or my family to be out in public."

"I'm fine with it," Crystal interrupted, her voice strong. She eyed her father, and Megan caught the look of distrust on her face.

"I see," Mr. Chambers said, appearing to have noticed the same thing. He looked back at his daughter, seemingly with distaste. "I suppose I should just stay out of this whole thing then?"

"It would probably be best," Crystal said.

Megan couldn't hold back her surprise. It seemed as if a flip had switched on Crystal's opinion of her father, but she couldn't understand why.

Governor Chambers shuffled his feet under him, fidgeting with his hands. "I'll, uh, see what I can dig up regarding who handled the funding."

"Thank you," Santiago said, although a touch of disappointment laced the words, as if he'd expected more.

"Megan and I will head back, Santiago," Crystal said, glancing back at Megan.

She wasn't sure what had changed Crystal so suddenly, but she was absolutely certain that returning to Seacrest to search for Gabriel was the right thing to do. "As soon as possible." she added.

Santiago sighed heavily. "Thank you both," he said. "I'll be in touch. And, Megan?"

Megan's pulse pounded in her ears. "Yes?"

"Charge your phone."

He hung up, and the three looked back at each other. Megan waited for Crystal to explain herself... but she didn't.

Fred began growling again.

"Now, Fred." Mr. Chambers knelt down in front of him.

Megan tightened her grip on the leash, cringing at how close the former governor's face had come to a sharp set of teeth. "I don't know why he keeps growling at you," she warned. "He's usually not like this."

"No, I understand." Mr. Chambers held both his hands out, palms up, and allowed Fred to sniff him. "Dogs don't trust politicians." He smiled. "They can see right through the bologna, so I'm used to it. Besides," He reached out and rubbed Fred's neck, "He has no reason to trust me yet."

He stood, and Megan breathed a sigh of relief.

"Although," Governor Chambers's gaze wandered back to his daughter. "I would hope both of you have reasons enough."

Crystal's gaze didn't return to his, although he was clearly waiting for it to. She made for the door instead. "We'd better be going. Can you drive us back to Mom's since you're planning to, what, stay in hiding?"

Her father's head tilted, and his jaw firmed, as if there was a sharp reply waiting. "I'm reaching out to those I feel I can trust. If things get sorted out, I'll be on the plane right behind you." After a moment, he sighed and pushed a button on his keys. The car outside chirped, and Crystal headed out the door.

Megan studied them both, aware that it was possible he committed the theft and believed he'd gotten away with it. It seemed to be what Crystal thought now, after all. And she was very anxious to hear how she'd come to that conclusion. She gave the governor a final glance before following her friend out to the car.

☙✺❧

"WHAT'S GOING ON, CRYSTAL?" MEGAN WAITED ONLY until Governor Chambers's sedan drove off. They entered Mrs. Chambers's house, and Crystal hadn't made eye contact once. "What happened?"

Finally, Crystal turned around. She pulled out her phone and held the screen up. "Just as I got the phone call from Santiago, this text came in from my mom."

Megan glanced down at it.

I checked with Morel. He says your father made a significant deposit into a private account just last month.

Megan's heart dropped. Her eyes lifted to Crystal's. "So, he did take the money?"

"It looks that way," Crystal said. "I think he's just trying to find a way around it, a way to pin it on someone else. Even if it means his own wife takes the blame."

"So why didn't you confront him?" Megan asked. Again, Crystal turned the phone to her, scrolling down to the second text.

Don't mention a word of this.

"I see," Megan sighed. "I thought Morel wasn't taking the case yet."

"I guess my mom found out otherwise," Crystal said glumly. She tucked her phone into a pocket and rubbed Fred's head. "I'll go check on getting a flight. Let's just leave this to the police and go see how we can help with Gabriel."

Megan swallowed away her concern for Crystal's family life and attempted to give her a smile. "Good idea," she said. "He needs us most right now."

Crystal only nodded and disappeared into her room. It was barely five o'clock and still, Megan doubted she would see her friend for the rest of the evening. She was the type that needed to process and recharge in solitude.

Megan sat at a small bench near the front door with Fred at her feet. She stroked his head rhythmically as her thoughts wandered. Her gaze turned to one side until she was seemingly staring through the wall and down the street, around the bend in the road... and right into Charlie Williamson's house.

She leaned to the other side and checked down the hall to find Crystal's bedroom door still closed. There was plenty of time left in the day, and right down the street was a man who might know much more than he claimed. Maybe he knew about the theft, but he'd fallen in love with Crystal's mother and didn't want to rat her husband out while they were still technically married.

Megan stood and slipped her feet into her sandals. Fred danced around her feet, excited to go out, and she took his leash from a hook by the front door. He barked excitedly, spinning in a circle in front of her.

"Shh, Fred," Megan whispered, kneeling. She hooked his leash on. "We're just going for a quick walk."

His excited panting stopped for a moment as he looked back at her with his lip caught on an upper tooth, clearly communicating that he couldn't be so easily fooled. She rubbed his head with a sigh. "Yeah, I know." Her neglected hair fell forward, the natural waves more pronounced than usual. It had been awhile since she'd brushed it out, and with all the rainstorms lately, her curls were properly encouraged.

She tucked a few strands behind her ear and ran her fingers through it, vowing to take a little time for herself as soon as possible. Traveling had her feeling too much like a vagabond.

But walking helped.

She hurried Fred along, trying to look casual while moving so fast that she was practically running. They made it down the street and around the corner without encountering a single person or car, which was a relief. Megan was sure Crystal's mother would pull up at any moment, and she'd be forced to make up a reason why she was sprinting down the street.

They hurried up Charlie Williamson's drive, and Megan hopped up the steps before she could think herself out of it.

She knocked and took a step back, waiting. Fred whined impatiently, refusing to sit. He sniffed at the window beside the front door, and Megan knocked again. When no one answered, she peered through the window with Fred. It appeared empty.

"You looking for Charlie?"

Megan spun around, her scream barely choked off. A surprised squeak came from her lips instead. A tiny Hawaiian woman scooted past them. She wore a bright green Mumu patterned with huge white hibiscus and had a large coil of dark hair wound into a bun at the top of her head. Her face was very pleasant, with a cheerful smile and blue eyes that glinted with humor. She held a small plastic bucket by the handle that was loaded with cleaning supplies.

"Uh, yes," Megan said. "I talked to him earlier and just wanted to discuss a few more things. Is he around?"

"Oh no," she shook her head, unlocking the door. She pushed it open and went inside. "He leave on plane." She waved her hand through the air between them. "I'm sure he'll be home in a few days though. He love this place."

"Yes, I'm sure he does." Megan swallowed a sudden wave of nerves. "Uh, do you mind if I look around a little bit? I left... a few papers here. He was supposed to give them back, but I guess he forgot with all the excitement of going out of town."

The woman set her bucket down at her feet and crossed her arms, peering back at Megan for a time. "Sure." She finally smiled and waved them through, giving Fred a pat. "Hello there." Her eyes flickered back to Megan. "In the office?"

"Yeah," Megan smiled back at her, afraid to look around

the room for fear she'd give away the fact that she had no idea where the office might be located.

The woman pointed a long, polished finger down the hall. "That way. I'm sure you remember." She gave a subtle wink as if to let Megan know that she, too, wasn't so easily fooled.

Megan sighed with a small laugh. "Thank you." She escaped down the hall with Fred's claws clicking on the hardwood floor as they went. The office was the first open door she came to, but after a sweep of the desk and shelves, she found nothing. Almost as if it were merely decorated as an office and not actually used as one.

She stepped back out into the hall. Glancing behind them first, she continued checking each room. The place was immaculate, cleaner than any house she'd ever seen. She peered into the last, largest room to find a sunroom with a couch and flat screen. An antique desk sat in one corner and, after another glance into the hall, she went to investigate. It was where she'd hide a secret document if she ever found the need.

Fred got to work inspecting every inch of the piece. No doubt there were ancient smells that were very unique. Megan dropped the leash and left him to it as she searched through one tiny drawer after the other. While there was a lot of dust and a tack or two, there wasn't much in the way of clues. She even attempted to discover any hidden compartments that might be detailed in, but with no luck.

"Mmm."

Again, Megan spun around, and again, she choked off a startled scream. The cleaning woman was back, now with bright yellow rubber gloves on her hands. She had a spray bottle in one hand and a white rag in the other. "A lovely piece, you think?"

Megan tried to release her nervous breath as subtly as possible. "Yes." She turned around and looked at the desk again, although she'd already inspected every corner of it. "I didn't find the papers though."

"No, no." The woman shook her head, swirling the rag in her hand so it whipped toward the other side of the room. "He would put there."

She turned back to Megan.

"Uh..." Megan glanced across the room. "Where?"

The woman smiled, displaying glimmering eyes again. She walked quickly across the room in her short steps and lifted the bench seat that sat under the window. "Here. Old papers, notes, other things. I throw away every month." She shrugged.

Megan joined her, peering down at an organized collection of boxes and files.

"If you no find—" She shrugged. "Then I'm sorry."

"It's quite all right," Megan assured. "Thank you so much for your help."

The woman smiled again and made her way out. Megan could hear the spritzing of her spray bottle in the other room as she got to work again. If these papers were something the cleaning lady knew about and cleaned out often, it wasn't likely she'd find anything important here. Still, she couldn't help digging around a little.

And apparently, neither could Fred. His entire front end sank into the bench's interior as he scratched and searched, seeming to only care about getting to the bottom. Megan tugged on his leash, encouraging him back. But before she was able to dissuade him, his feet sunk and the opposite side lifted up. Startled, Fred jumped back, his ears perked. There was a quiet thud, and the papers settled again.

Megan was frozen, looking into the bench with wide eyes. She turned to Fred and smiled, leaning in close and whispering just for him, "Good boy, Fred."

Keeping still for a few seconds, she heard cheerful whistling from somewhere at the other end of the house. She turned back to the bench and hurriedly pulled out one box and file after the other. There were random community fliers, scribbled notes on stray sheets of paper, and lots and lots of junk mail.

When she'd removed it all, she surveyed the bottom. It appeared to be a simple wood panel except for a small leather loop along one side. She took a deep breath and looked at Fred. He turned to her so quickly, his ears flapped in his eyes. Then Megan slid her finger through the piece of leather and pulled.

The entire bottom of the bench lifted until it rested against the frame, revealing a single manilla envelope. She reached down cautiously and took it. Opening the clasp, she pulled out a half dozen pages. Keeping her ear tuned to the cleaning woman's whistling, she rifled through them anxiously. A bank note was on top for a deposit of just over two million dollars. Her gaze flickered to see the name, *Stephen Alexander Chambers*. But there were no other bank slips. If he did take as much money as they claimed, maybe they were still on the search for other bank accounts.

Still, two million was nothing to sniff at. Behind the note was an article from almost a year earlier that detailed the former governor's fall from luxury succeeding his leaving the office. It painted a picture of a man eager to stay relevant in the public eyes. The next page was an official legal letter detailing a timeline of events from the time he left the office to current dates. All in all, it appeared to be an entire case against Mr. Chambers.

Megan sat on her heels, wondering if all this time perhaps Morel had been working with Charlie Williamson to prove the case against Crystal's father.

Fred's cold nose touched her cheek, and she jumped, coming back to the present. She recognized the sound of footsteps approaching and quickly slid the papers inside the envelope and tucked it away. She closed the hidden compartment and stacked the contents on top quickly, managing to close the bench and stand just as the woman walked in.

"You find?" she asked, beginning to wipe down a leather chair.

Megan released a monumental amount of breath as quietly as possible. "No," she said, working to sound dejected. "I'll just have to give him a call."

"I'm sure that would be best." She moved from the chair to the desk in the corner. "He's out looking for a boy he says is missing in... Washington state?"

Megan nodded. "Yes, I'm headed there too." She sighed as her nerves for Gabriel ignited. "He's a special kid."

For the first time in their conversation, the woman stopped cleaning. She turned around with deep creases between her eyebrows. "You go too?"

"Yes." Megan watched closely as darkness shadowed the woman's abundant cheer. She was frowning properly by the time her gaze returned to Megan.

The woman shook her head, pointing at Megan with the white rag that was now tinged with dirt. "You be careful, Miss."

She took a step toward Megan and leaned closer, whispering, "Dangerous."

Chills shivered through Megan from head to toe. She already knew it would be dangerous to go out in the woods, but somehow, she knew... the woman's warning had nothing to do with Gabriel.

Chapter Seventeen

When Megan returned, Mrs. Chambers hadn't come home yet, and when Crystal finally emerged from her room an hour later, she'd found the pilot couldn't fit their flight into his schedule until the next morning. So again, Crystal retreated to her rooms. The house was luxurious with that distinct vacation feel. But it didn't stop the tension from coiling in Megan's mind so tight, she felt about ready to snap. The more she let herself think of Gabriel, the more it tortured her.

Later that night, sitting in her bed, it felt like hours had passed. It had to be getting close to morning. She glanced at the clock to see it was almost midnight. Her head rested on a soft, luxurious pillow, and Fred was curled up at the foot of her bed. But she couldn't sleep. All she could do was picture how dark and cold the forest was at that moment and hope that Gabriel was warm. Her heart ached to think of him. And, as for Mr. Chambers, who knew why he was blatantly lying to their faces. She'd given up trying to figure it out. Soon, he was going to have to face the consequences of his actions. It was frustrating to know how thoroughly they'd been lied to, but at least Morel was finding some answers.

Her thoughts often turned to Santiago. At every spare moment, she pictured him and wished he was there with her. But even thoughts of him couldn't keep away the worry over Gabriel. That young boy had tunneled deep into her heart, and it hurt to think of him in real trouble.

Finally, she sat up in bed, frustrated. Sleep wasn't going to come, and she was tired of trying. Santiago had mentioned he was going on another search, so maybe that meant he was still awake? She bit her lip and took her phone from the nightstand. Hesitating only a moment, she found his number and pushed call.

He answered on the second ring with his voice full of energy. "Megan?"

Thank goodness.

"Hi, Santiago," she said quietly, not wanting to be overheard by Crystal or her mother... if she'd come home. "How's everything going? Are you on a search?"

"Well, yeah," he said hesitantly. "But it's after midnight. Are you okay? What's wrong?"

"I'm fine," she said, feeling better now that she'd heard his voice. "I'm just so worried about Gabriel." Her voice cracked, and she fought hard to keep everything back. The worry for this sweet boy. How was his mother surviving? "Do you think he's all right?" Her voice shook, and tears began their ascent down her cheeks, ignoring her struggle to hold them back.

"Honey, it's okay," Santiago said sweetly. "I wish I was there with you. It kills me to hear you hurting. But I promise we're doing absolutely everything that can be done. Honestly, I'm not positive he's even out here. But that doesn't mean I'm going to stop searching. If there's even the slightest chance he's camped out somewhere in this forest, we'll find him."

He paused a moment, as if giving her a chance to respond. But the tears were still trailing down her cheeks, and she didn't trust her voice enough. Falling apart would only make things worse for both of them.

"If he's not in this forest... and someone did take him," Santiago continued, "then it's likely he's being taken care of. I'm sure his basic needs are being met. But that doesn't mean we're going to have the least bit of sympathy for whoever took him once we find them. They better hope it's not me."

The threat in his voice only made her heart throb more. She couldn't think of anyone else she'd want on their side, out there looking for Gabriel. He was the most incredible person she'd ever met.

"Are you feeling better now?"

His voice was so tender, her panic finally eased. She closed her eyes. "I am," she whispered, "Thank you."

A man's voice called out in the background.

"I need to get going, Megan." Each word was gently spoken. He paused a moment. "I love you."

Megan's chest throbbed, and she took a deep breath, trying to calm her racing pulse. The words she whispered back came from deep inside. Hadn't she known them all along? "I love you too."

He said goodbye, and the line ended with her eyes wide and the phone pressed to her chest. She loved him. Santiago. She loved him so deeply, it made her weak.

Her door creaked, and she sat up with a gasp, switching on the bedside lamp. Fred lifted, and both of them looked back at Crystal standing in the doorway with her mouth dropped open. Megan wiped her cheeks quickly, panicking. She put her phone on the bedside table. Had Crystal heard everything? Was their friendship ruined?

She tried to remain calm as Crystal came forward quickly, sitting next to Fred on the end of her bed. "Was that Kenneth?" she whispered excitedly, patting his head. "I'm sorry, I didn't mean to overhear but... I had no idea you two were in love, Megan!"

Megan wiped at her wet cheeks, shocked. "Uh." She fumbled with her blanket, twisting it in her hands. Her eyes flickered back to Crystal's. "Yes... it was." She felt instantly drowned in shame. What was she doing lying to her best friend?

Crystal set her hand over Megan's, giving a wide smile. "I'm so glad," she said. "I know I said some things based on our past together, but I can see that he's changed. He really is a great man."

Megan was partially frozen, and her thoughts were spinning. She wanted to take it back and set Crystal straight right then and there. But how could she when she'd only just discovered her feelings for Santiago? The words had burned on her lips the moment she'd spoken them, truer than anything she'd ever felt. They burned inside her still, making her dizzy.

"I'm sorry. I'm sure you're tired." Crystal slid off the bed. "We can talk tomorrow, okay?"

"No, it's all right," Megan said, but Crystal had already taken hold of the door, about to step through. "I..." Megan's voice faded away. I what? I lied? I said you could have him, but I didn't mean it? I'm an idiot?

Any of those would work, but she found herself unable to

respond. Crystal gave her a little wave, and she only lifted her hand in return, watching as the door closed behind her.

"Oh no," she whispered, falling back on her pillow. But even with her confusion, she was surrounded by Santiago's voice. His concern for her; his reassurance. The moment he'd called her honey, she'd melted, although she hadn't even noticed at the time. The deep, smooth way he'd said he loved her repeated in her mind, chasing away the sleepiness until most of the night passed. She stared up at the ceiling, thinking of him. But as Fred snored away, in the back of her mind, she worried about the next morning.

How was she ever going to make this right? It was humiliating to even think through the words; her cheeks turned hot imagining it. If only Crystal hadn't walked in on her conversation.

Light was barely showing in the sky, and she probably only got a couple good hours of sleep, but Megan didn't care. She needed to clear her conscience. She threw the covers back and went about her morning routine.

Showering quickly, she reviewed the apology in her head, nearly crying a couple of times before she managed to quell the emotion. If Crystal wasn't her very best friend at Seacrest, it wouldn't be so imperative that things be smoothed over. But she was her best friend... practically her only friend. So, it mattered. A lot. If there was a rift between them, and Crystal became avoidant or even just a touch bitter, she would notice. She didn't even want to think about the pain and guilt it would cause her.

By the time she was dressed and standing outside Crystal's bedroom door, the sky was at least bright enough to glow through the windows. It lit the house softly. She tapped her knuckles on the door. Fred had been lounging on the bed, but now he emerged from her bedroom with a large, tongue-curling yawn and sat beside her.

"You might not want to see this," Megan said, although when her hand rested on the big dog's head, she felt infinitesimally better, and she was glad he'd come.

She lifted her hand, about to knock again, when the door suddenly opened. Crystal stood with her head tilted, holding a warm curler in her hand.

"Come in, come in," Crystal said, returning to her bathroom. Megan followed her through the bedroom where her bed was already neatly made, and her clothing was folded in a small pile at the bottom of it. Fred sniffed around and then lay down, clearly appreciating the tranquility of Crystal's room.

"So, how are things going?" Crystal said, taking the curling wand to the last straight section of hair. She smoothed the strand of hair through the hot tool, turning it as she went. Then she set it aside on the counter as she held the last curl in her hand. She turned around, facing Megan, who had yet to think of a way to start this conversation.

"Um." Megan glanced around the room, working a smile onto her face, and trying to remember how she acted when she was at ease. "I guess I just needed to talk to you."

"Yes, of course." Crystal ran her fingers through the curl, blending it with the rest of her hair. "Is your stuff packed and ready? We should leave in the next fifteen minutes."

"Oh," Megan said and glanced back through the room, "almost."

"Well, go on," Crystal smiled. "We can talk about things on the flight."

Megan hesitated for just a moment and then simply turned and trudged back through the room. She caught sight of Fred as he lifted his head from the floor for just a moment. The dry squint of his eyes said it all.

"I know," Megan mumbled. "I'm being ridiculous."

"What was that?" Crystal's voice came from the bathroom.

"Oh, nothing!" Megan called back. "I'll be ready in a few minutes."

◈◈◈

THE FLIGHT, AGAIN, WAS QUIET AND COMFORTABLE. IT took a considerable amount of self-encouragement before Megan was able to turn to Crystal, poised to spill the truth. But by then, her friend's chair was reclined, and she was fast asleep. Maybe Megan wasn't the only one who hadn't slept well.

Megan took out her phone instead. She'd made sure to charge it fully overnight and now she surfed the local Seacrest news coverage of missing Gabriel. There was more talk of the lost boy than she'd realized. It sounded frightening and foreign the way they referred to him, especially the way they constantly reiterated how much time had passed and how dire the situation was. It was difficult to read, but she couldn't stop herself. Maybe there'd been some clue discovered, or some tip called in. But even after reading every article she could find, there wasn't anything new.

Nothing.

He was just gone. Megan rubbed at her arms, realizing they were covered in goosebumps as chills radiated through her body. She suddenly felt even worse for where her attention had been. Here was a little boy who was supposed to be coming to story time and running around with his yellow lab. He should be going to get ice cream with his mom or out exploring the coastline and collecting shells.

Megan shook off her worry over Crystal. They were good friends, and Crystal was a reasonable person. They would get through it.

There. Enough. She'd think nothing more on that subject until they'd found Gabriel. When he was back with his mother, then she'd find a way to break the news to Crystal that she'd been a complete coward. But until that time, she was going to focus on Gabriel. If what the news channel and weather person were saying was true, they had a tight window of time before a decent storm surged through the area. They had to find him before that.

They had to.

Chapter Eighteen

The toe of Santiago's hiking boot caught on a log, and he nearly ended up with a face full of dirt. He managed to regain his balance. The log was small, but he hadn't been paying attention.

"You all right, man?" The rescue volunteer called Big Jim was eyeing him suspiciously. "I've never seen you trip before. You get enough sleep? We can't use you if you can't even walk."

"I'm fine," Santiago assured. "Just didn't see that one."

It wasn't a lie, but it wasn't exactly the truth either. Since talking to Megan, he was stirred up inside, caught in a whirlpool of emotions like the tide. It rushed over him relentlessly, never giving him a chance to catch his breath. He'd loved Megan for a long time now, but he hadn't let himself feel it. From the very beginning, she was clear on where she stood, and so he'd held back. He might've teased her every now and then, but tonight... listening to her struggle. He'd been so overcome that he didn't even think twice before telling her he loved her.

And he did. So much it was breaking him apart inside.

He stopped a moment, resting his hands on his hips and taking some time to breathe. He needed to get hold of himself and focus. Gabriel was counting on him.

Finally, the thought of that little boy did the trick.

"Hey!" Big Jim shouted from farther down the trail. It was the first time in the whole three days that Santiago had fallen behind. "Come take a look at this!"

Santiago held fast to his newfound clarity and ran down the trail, catching up quickly. Jim was holding something in his hand with his flashlight shining down on it. Santiago looked down at a tiny paper book. "What's that?" he asked.

"It's the kid's library card." Jim handed it over. "Here, look."

Santiago took it. The front was made to look like a book cover with *Marg's Books* as the title. Inside, there was a list of membership deals with a line at the bottom and an uneven, hand-scrawled name.

Gabriel.

"It's his," Santiago said. "Where did you find this?"

Jim took a step into the brush and leaned down, pointing his flashlight at the ground. "Right there. I thought maybe the kid really was caught out here, wandering around. But then." He shuffled to the side, aiming his flashlight at another spot in the brush, just up from the first. "I saw this."

On the ground, pressed against a patch of thin, tender grass, were tire marks. Skinny and lightweight, Santiago already knew what they belonged to. "A dirt bike," he said. "But how would no one have heard it?"

"Well, there's a lotta country out here." Jim nodded, agreeing with him. "The sound doesn't carry as far as you'd think. And they're fast, so it wouldn't take long to get far enough away."

"I see." Santiago was sure the big man was right. Someone had raced through and scooped up Gabriel as they went. But why take him? If the boy was merely out hiking, what did they have to fear? Unless...

Santiago spun around, looking back at the trail. Gabriel must've come from back down the trail, so he must've encountered his kidnapper there first and then ran off the trail. "Let's backtrack a little," he suggested, zipping the library card securely in a chest pocket of his coat. "He might've dropped something else."

They paid closer attention to the trail as they went, scanning the ground slowly with their flashlights. Santiago caught a glimpse of the tire tracks again and pointed them out. Jim nodded, frowning. "Where do you think he was when they spotted him?"

"I don't know," Santiago answered. "I'm wondering if it was the other way around. Maybe Gabriel spotted them first. Maybe he saw something he wasn't supposed to."

"Like what?" Jim had stopped and was scanning the trees now. "What would they even be doing way out here on these damaged trails?" Santiago didn't know what to say. What could the answer possibly be?

They came to an open area hikers used quite often for camping. At least, in the summer months. Santiago tucked his flashlight under his arm and rubbed his hands together, fighting off the cold. They were beginning to go numb. He cupped his gloves and exhaled a gust of hot air into them. His flashlight was shining on a pile of rocks just off the trail near his feet. They hadn't been used for a fire pit, but someone had stacked them. Maybe they'd just wanted to get the ankle-breakers off the trail, but between the dark rocks, there was something shining underneath.

He took hold of his flashlight and lowered down, aiming it into a hole between the rocks. A leather case shone back at him.

"Jim!" he called, digging away the rocks at the top and letting them thud to the ground next to him. "There's something hidden here." The next rock fell away, and he pulled out a leather-bound book like a journal. Two strips of leather hung down from the spine, as if they were normally used to tie the book closed.

He opened it, finding plain white pages inside. Gabriel's name was written at the top of the first page and underneath it was *scientist and explorer*. There were pencil sketches of a variety of leaves and a few bugs. Each drawing had a description below it, and Santiago couldn't help smiling at the description below a little black beetle.

Slow but stinky, so it doesn't matter. Nothing will eat it.

"What's that?" Jim shone his flashlight down on the book. He looked at the page silently until Santiago turned to the next and the next. There were a dozen pages at least. Drawings of pine trees and wildflowers, tadpoles and minnows in the stream. Sketches of his dog took up a few pages on their own.

Then Santiago turned to a page that was different. No drawings at all, just scribbled notes.

Found two cameras on the trail.

People are hiding out here. They talked about Governor Chambers and Santiago. They talked about lies and money. These aren't good people. I want to go back, but they might hear Tank. He might bark.

Mom will be worried if I'm not back before dark. I don't know what to do.

"Do you have any idea who these people mighta been?" Jim took the journal, flipping through the pages again and stopping at the notes. "Why would they be talking about you?"

"I don't know," Santiago said. His fingers were still numb, but now he hardly noticed them. He shook his head, dazed. "I have no idea who would do this. But if..." He walked down the trail even more, shining his light along the trunks of trees and into the branches. "What if those cameras he wrote about are still here?"

"Bet they took 'em." Jim began shining his light around at the trees as well. "But we haven't been looking up in the trees much, just calling around and searching through the brush. We could've walked right past 'em."

"Right," Santiago said. "Let's look around. If Gabriel saw cameras, they were probably close by. I bet he stayed on the trail until these people scared him off, whoever they were."

Jim agreed, and they searched the trees, scanning their lights up and down each one. They moved farther down the trail and then farther again. They circled back and searched in the other direction; in case they were wrong about which way Gabriel was going. One hour passed and then two... but there was nothing. Not even any ropes or equipment were left behind.

When Santiago met up with Jim again, after combing the trail one last time in both directions, he held up a walkie talkie.

"Time to check back in at the camp," he said. "They wanna see what we found."

"Okay." Santiago's mood had fallen. He didn't want to

waste time talking about where Gabriel had been, he wanted to find the boy now. Tonight.

Suddenly, a headlight appeared directly in front of him. Santiago dove to one side before he could be hit. The bike zipped by, and then its tires slid in the dirt. Santiago looked up to find Jim on the ground on the other side of the trial. "Did it hit you?" he called.

Jim grunted as he got up. "No," he growled, sounding furious. He started toward the bike that was circling back around.

The driver raised one hand up. "Sorry!" he yelled, returning to them. "I didn't even see you." He was breathing hard, as if the moment had shaken him as much as it had them. His bike was electric and nearly silent. "I'm really sorry about that. I didn't realize anyone was searching out in this direction. I rode all over this trail the past few hours but never found anything."

He pulled off his helmet, showing he was older than Santiago had assumed. His brown eyes were narrow and his brown hair messy from being under the helmet.

"Hello," he said, extending his hand. "I'm Charlie Williamson."

Santiago froze. "From Natural Resources?" he asked. Megan had mentioned him but only briefly.

Charlie's eyebrows lifted. "That's right, although I had no idea my title reached this far. How do I know you?"

"No," Santiago said, "you don't know me." He shook his head. "I'm fairly surprised to see you out here though. You guys can't send funding, but you send people?"

"Well." Charlie stepped off the bike and set the kickstand. To Santiago, his expression wasn't nearly sorry enough. Still, he constantly glanced around, as if anxious to find the boy. Maybe Santiago was jumping to conclusions.

"It's a sad deal," Williamson said. "I heard about it and just couldn't rest. I knew you guys would need help in a small town like this, so I came right out. These missing kids' cases... you gotta find 'em fast, especially in the cold."

"And you've been riding around on that?" Jim asked, still sounding gruff. "All over this trail?"

"On and off the trail," Charlie nodded.

"Great." Jim turned around and trudged off. "C'mon, we gotta meet up with the group."

"I don't understand," Charlie said, putting his helmet on again. "Is that wrong?"

"It's nothing," Santiago said, following Jim. He couldn't help but feel devastated. If Gabriel wasn't taken out of the forest on a dirt bike, maybe he really was lost and wandering. Or worse, maybe they'd disposed of him somewhere. They had cadaver dogs coming in a day or two, but that wasn't soon enough.

They walked back to the campsite where a fire was going, and a group of volunteers and policemen gathered. When they spotted Santiago and Jim, they waved them over. Charlie Williamson followed behind, although he seemed content to watch from the edges. Jim's boss Tate was the one in charge, but Santiago figured it was just because he had a voice like a bull horn. Tate's name seemed to match him as much as a butterfly matched a forest fire. He was burly and hairy and reminded Santiago somewhat of a gorilla. Just as intimidating too.

"Didn't hear much on the talkies," Tate said. "You guys find anything?"

Santiago took out the bookstore card while Jim handed over the journal, pointing out the messages on the last page.

"Well, well," Tate said, scratching his forearm as he turned to the group. He read the message aloud and excited chatter started up. "Even with this"—He held up a hand and the voices quieted—"We don't know for sure that he was taken." His voice echoed around them. "The police will do their part, and we still need to do ours. A storm is moving in tomorrow night, and we don't want to have to call off the search because of a storm. We want to call it off because we found the boy. We're going to rotate through the morning and afternoon." He pointed to the volunteers standing opposite Santiago. "You all, if you're comfortable doing so, I need you to take the morning shift." He pointed to the other side of the group. "This side, get some sleep and rotate in at 1 p.m. sharp."

Everyone mumbled their agreement and began to disperse.

"I'll see you all at one," Jim said, heading back toward the vehicles. But beside him, Charlie didn't move. He only gazed back into the trees.

"Do you have a place to stay?" Santiago asked.

Charlie swung around, taking a moment to answer. "I didn't come out here to sleep," he finally said, putting his helmet on again. "I came here to find a missing boy, and that's what I'm going to do."

"How long have you been looking?" Santiago wanted to keep looking too, but he'd been wandering in the forest for two days and nights, and he was feeling it. The last thing rescuers needed was another person to rescue. He'd seen it happen firsthand. It could quickly become a dangerous situation, especially with the storm moving in. No, he really needed to get at least a few hours of sleep.

"I started as soon as I got here, around midnight last night." Charlie straddled his bike. "I'm fine for a while longer. You look a little rough around the edges though. Might want to take a break."

Santiago felt a wave of irritation. But he knew it was mostly the lack of sleep talking. Charlie was right, after all. He needed sleep bad. "Yeah," he agreed grudgingly. "I'll be back here as soon as I can."

"I'll see you then." Charlie started his bike up and turned around, heading down the trail again.

Santiago felt like he'd walked every inch of the forest himself, but maybe Charlie would find him. Maybe someone would. Anyone. He'd only met young Gabriel twice, but he was a special kid. Happiness and a love of the wilderness were obvious with the little guy. It reminded Santiago so much of himself. He'd always been in love with the wild.

When he finally made it back to his tiny apartment, his eyes would barely open, his lids so very heavy. But after a hot shower and lying in his bed, his thoughts managed to keep him awake. He'd never told Megan where he lived. She probably wondered if he lived anywhere at all or just propped himself up against the base of a tree at night. A smile pulled at his mouth just thinking of her. But what would she say walking into his apartment? What would she think?

He rolled to his side, looking out at a simple table, chair, and lamp. It was fine for now, when he was a lonely bachelor. But what if she really meant it when she said *I love you*? He already knew he wouldn't want them spending time together in a tiny, bare-bones apartment. It wasn't what he'd planned in the first place, after all. He was well accustomed to fine living and knew how to arrange a space. He knew design. He knew structure. He knew what would impress her. Maybe it was time he did just that.

As his eyes drifted closed and exhaustion fell across his body like a heavy blanket, he felt it was time to make some changes in his life. Create a home and carve out a living for himself right there in Seacrest. The thought of a relationship with Megan brought a whole new wave of motivation. He'd taken enough of a break from the world; it was time to start living again.

Chapter Nineteen

They could see the storm clouds rolling in from way out at sea. Big, dark plumes of precipitation. Megan caught Crystal looking out at the horizon from time to time, and she knew they were both thinking the same thing. It would be a bad one. It felt like too much time had passed and here it was Saturday morning already. If Gabriel was out in the woods one more night, especially in a storm like this one...

She took a shaky breath, wrapping her arms around Fred's neck. He had his legs over her lap, and she tried to relax at least a little. He laid his big head against her chest, and it was nice to have his warmth.

Megan's stomach was already in knots, but seeing the worry for young Gabriel on Crystal's face made it even worse. She took a slow, steady breath.

"I texted Velasquez, and he said they're gathered just behind the boardwalk," Crystal said, scrolling through her phone. "There's a campsite they're using as a kind of base, right at the head of the trails."

"Yeah," Megan said, "I know where that's at."

They passed the boardwalk, and Megan was surprised to see all the shops were closed up. It warmed her heart to realize the shop owners must all be out looking. Seacrest really was an incredible town.

"We have to find him," Crystal said, craning her neck as they rounded the back of the shops. There were over a dozen cars parked alongside the pathway, and they pulled up at the end of them. "Well." Crystal looked back at Megan. "Let's go see what we can do." Her eyes fell to Fred. "I'm putting a lot of hope in you, Fred." She rubbed the Great Dane's big, silky ears.

"So am I," Megan said. Fred had only met the boy once. She crossed her fingers that maybe it would be enough to recognize his scent.

They'd hardly begun walking when Megan spotted a tall, dark, familiar face. Kenneth turned toward them... and right next to him stood Santiago. Her gaze stalled on the shorter of the two, on his simmering eyes and perfect face. His long hair was pulled back, and he looked at her with complete adoration on his features.

"Megan!" Kenneth strode toward her.

Megan's heart nearly stopped beating. Why hadn't she sent Kenneth a text at the very least? Now, once again, here he was, with a smile stretched across his face. In the background, Santiago's expression fell.

"Oooh, Megan," Crystal practically whispered, entirely too loud. "It's Kenneth!"

Megan's gaze shot back to Santiago one last time. She was sure he'd heard; it was plain enough on his face. There was only a shocked, frozen stare that tore at her heart.

What was she going to do?

She wanted to stop Kenneth before he greeted her too intimately, but it was too late. His arms were around her and he swept her into a kiss. She had to hold on to him to keep from falling backwards, but her heart was racing with devastation.

Finally, Kenneth released her. "I've missed you," he breathed, standing too close. Megan took a quick step backward, hardly able to speak. She glanced at Crystal, who smiled at them in a way that communicated far too much. She couldn't bring herself to look at Santiago again.

What a mess she'd made.

"Hi, Santiago," Crystal said. Megan's gaze shot over to see Crystal pull him into a hug. "You look so tired," she said, keeping one hand on his arm tenderly as she spoke. "How can we help?"

Santiago didn't answer at first. He appeared too stunned. But then he cleared his throat. "We're searching one last area before tonight, and then they're afraid the storm will call us off." His gaze flickered from Crystal to Megan, but it didn't stay.

Megan felt like she would burst into tears at any second. But explaining everything to them would be utterly humiliating, and it would delay their search for Gabriel. But maybe, if she could just find a time to speak with Santiago first... he deserved a good sincere explanation.

"Uh." Santiago turned back to the group in the distance. People were starting off on the trails. "We're not going to stop until we have to. C'mon." He didn't look back and walked well ahead of them. Crystal skipped to his side, close enough that Megan glanced down to see their arms brush together. She waited for Crystal to take his hand.

"Megan?"

Kenneth touched her back, and she whipped around. He was frozen awkwardly. "Everything all right?" he asked.

"Sorry." She tugged on Fred's leash. "I'm just worried, I suppose. Let's get Fred out on that trail."

"Good idea," Kenneth said. Megan hurried along, but Kenneth's long legs had him keeping up easily enough. She busied both hands with Fred's leash before he could reach for her. And while Kenneth glanced at her from time to time, his silence had her wondering if she'd hurt him too. It felt terrible, but what else could she say? There was no time to fix anything until they found Gabriel.

"Dad?" Crystal gawked at a man approaching their group. She stepped away from Santiago for the first time, and Megan was ashamed at how much relief flowed through her. She tried to shake the thought away and focus on Crystal as she met with her father.

"Hey, hun." He looked around them. "I wanted to help out."

Megan couldn't help wondering just what Crystal's father was up to. But if he wanted to use his last days of freedom to help search for Gabriel, she wasn't going to stop him.

"Okay," Santiago said. All eyes returned to him as he scanned the group.

Megan's heart cramped when he scanned past her without stopping. But what did she expect? Kenneth's arm came around her shoulders, and she resisted the urge to shrug it off. Besides, the last he knew, they were in a relationship. It was just that, the second she'd given Santiago a chance in her heart, everything had changed. She could hardly think straight anymore.

It had never been that way with Kenneth.

"Megan?"

Her gaze shot up to see Santiago paused, looking back at her expectantly.

She faltered. "I'm sorry, my mind was somewhere else. What did you say?" The following silence sent her pulse spiking, especially with the way his eyes stayed locked onto hers, resonant pools of turquoise melting her soul away.

"I only asked if you wanted to start off first," Santiago gestured down the trail. "Before too many other scents fill the air." A few volunteers had joined their group and were looking back at her, waiting.

"Oh." Megan wrapped the leash around her arm, glancing around the broken little group. The man she'd crushed on, the man she was in love with, the friend who wanted to date him, and her father who was possibly a felon. It was a tumult of sorrow and longing, and she was eager to leave it all behind as quickly as possible.

"I'll start us off," she said, starting. She planned to continue right past Santiago without stopping.

"Hey." He grabbed her arm, and it sent electricity straight through her skin. She flinched, facing him, and suddenly felt completely terrified. "How are you doing?" he asked. He stepped forward slowly and brought his arm around her, taking her into a warm hug.

She couldn't stop herself from closing her eyes. Her head swam, and she rested her hands on his back. But she could feel her emotions gripping her throat, threatening to release the tears.

She practically pushed him away, stepping out of his arms so suddenly it had her feeling slightly off balance. An artificial smile flashed across her face. "I'm good, thanks." She'd meant for the words to come out strong, but they'd wheezed through her throat in shambles. Still, she pretended everything was perfectly normal and hurried along, starting off the rescue party.

Her thoughts both cleared and darkened as she looked into the face of each volunteer she passed. Men and women, young and old. They were out of time and looked at her as if she were their last hope. Her and, of course, Fred. People patted his back and rubbed his head. They uttered their thanks and wished him well. His tail wagged and his head was high. But when they passed the group and started into the woods alone, he walked slower, looking up at Megan often.

"Ma'am?"

She turned around to see a big man wearing the typical orange reflective vest of the volunteers. He had a little red T-shirt in his hands. "My name's Jim. People call me Big Jim," he said, taking her hand briefly. "This is one of Gabriel's shirts, if maybe your dog can track the scent." He shrugged. "It's worth a try."

"Yes, thank you." Megan led Fred to the fabric, allowing him time to take in the scent. At first, he wasn't very interested, giving it one quick sniff. But then, as they led him to it again and again, he appeared to understand. He buried his nose in the fabric and stayed there, breathing in deep. This time when he backed away, he kept his gaze on Megan and Jim, waiting.

"Looks like he's got it," Jim said. "I'll take this back to camp, so it doesn't confuse him. And, Megan?" He set his heavy hand on her shoulder, and she could see dirt, exhaustion, and strain on his face. "Good luck."

She tried to smile, but there was too much weighing on her. There was no telling whether Fred would be able to actually follow the scent or if he even knew that was what he was supposed to do. Regret began to gnaw at her until she was sure she'd made the wrong choice. Now, if he wasn't successful, it would be the thing everyone in town thought of when they saw him.

They had to find Gabriel.

She waited until Jim was well out of sight and then knelt down in front of Fred. "We have to find him, boy," she said, rubbing under his ears. "Okay? Where's Gabriel?" Her voice caught, and she forced the emotions down. "Where is he, boy? Can you find him? Where's Gabriel?" She stood and swung her arm out. "Let's go!"

He jumped to his feet and shot forward. The leash jerked hard on her arm. She tried to go at his speed, but it was fast. Her feet were sailing above the trail as the leash practically dragged her on. But she managed to keep on her toes.

He stopped suddenly, sniffing to one side and then the other. Megan wasn't sure if he was really following the scent, but if he was, she kept reminding him of the goal. "Where's Gabriel, boy? Where is he?"

They circled back and started down the way they'd come, and she worried he'd caught the scent of the T-shirt again. Maybe they were just following big Jim back to the camp. But then, he stopped, lifting his head. He turned right. Then left. Then right again.

And then Fred shot into the brush.

"Whoa." Megan held her arm up, protecting her face from the branch of a pine tree. It scraped against her forearm, but she kept running. Kept encouraging him. Kept hoping, praying, and running some more.

After nearly an hour, she needed a break. Her heart was going to beat out of her chest. She pulled back on the leash. "Hold on, Fred," she said between breaths. There were granite rocks scattered through the area and she sat down, propping her hands on her knees. "I need a break. Just for a second."

He stilled, but he didn't stop. His head snapped this way and that, intense and ready. She was sure the second she got to her feet again, he'd take off. And she was glad, but... she wasn't quite ready.

They'd gone off the trail by a considerable amount, their stopping place positioned on a rounded peak. She could see over the treetops on one side, spying the steep shale slope she'd nearly tumbled down before. It looked beautiful from a distance. But the entire view had become shadowed, covered in clouds and gray. The first signs of the storm.

Suddenly, birds called, and wings fluttered in the tree-tops. Megan shot to her feet, watching and waiting. She wasn't sure what to expect, but something had obviously frightened the birds from their perch. There was a pile of boulders between her and where the birds had come from, and she started around it slowly. Fred stayed by her side. He seemed to be walking quieter than before, which she appreciated, but the silence around them meant every step felt too loud.

Gradually, the other side came into view. The redwoods were more spaced out here, allowing a good view of the downward slope of the mountain. It was gradual and easy to traverse, so she kept going. But it was clear that whatever had startled the birds was gone now. More than likely, it was just an energetic squirrel or a fox that had gone unseen.

Fred tugged on the leash, diverting them to the right, and she let him lead. He picked up the pace gradually. Soon enough, they were running again. She kept an eye on the ground, watching for pine cones and sticks and any other forest debris that could roll her ankle. As much as she wanted to slow, she could feel the wind picking up and the temperature dropping. It could hardly be past two in the afternoon, but the sky had darkened considerably. Ahead, the cloud cover was thick.

She nearly ran into Fred as he skidded to a halt. She quickly hobbled to the side. "What the—" She stopped, taking in his erect posture and ears. His tail didn't wag. He didn't turn to her. He only stared ahead.

They faced a wall of trees, thicker than they'd traveled through all day. It was where she would go if the rain really started getting bad. What if Gabriel could tell the storm was coming and had the same idea? She moved closer cautiously, taking her cues from Fred. He remained rigid but crept forward, staying just ahead of her.

They ducked into the cover of the trees, and the wind whistled overhead. Although in the cover of the dense forest, it stilled considerably, offering protection. But it was dark and difficult to see through. Even on a sunny day, she imagined it would be that way.

A voice reached her, and Megan froze, listening. Her heart pounded as she waited to hear it again. Fred had his head lowered, and it sent chills through her. It was the position he took when he felt threatened, and she doubted the boy's scent would have him acting that way.

The voice reached her again as if it were being pushed about by the wind, floating past her ears at random. This time, she could tell it was a man speaking.

Fred growled low and deep, and then his head lifted suddenly. His ears relaxed, and he shot forward.

Megan held on, following him through the trees and back onto the trail. She pulled him to a stop, listening. She could still hear the man's voice, and it was getting closer. Fred was digging at the ground, whining to move. But she held him back, going more slowly down the trail. She needed to hear what this mysterious person was saying. She hoped beyond anything that he was talking to Gabriel, but she couldn't be sure.

"I wasn't surprised to find you out here doing so well," the voice rang through the trees as if turned in their direction. "It's clear you're a smart boy. You know these woods, don't you? You decided to explore farther than usual and became a little lost. There's nothing wrong with that. I admire you for being so brave."

Fred tugged hard so suddenly that it pulled the leash from her hands. He loped down the trail and out of view. Megan ran behind him, panicking at the thought of Fred surprising someone. But when she came around the corner, what she saw had her stumbling to a stop. She sank to her knees.

Fred licked at Gabriel, wagging his tail and whining. The young boy laughed and wiped his face, wrapping his arms around Fred's neck. Megan sighed, overcome with relief. She rested a hand against her chest and turned a grateful eye to none other than Charlie Williamson. He stood next to a dirt bike, walking it beside him as he approached her. The smile was cautious on his face.

"You found us," he said, holding his hand out.

She hesitated, feeling a strange thrill of fear. But then she took his hand, allowing him to help her to her feet. "And you found Gabriel." She gave the boy a smile. The young boy took Fred's leash and met up with them. "Hi, Ms. Henny!"

She lowered down, giving him a hug. Her eyes clouded.

"Gabriel!" She smoothed down his wild hair. "Have you been out here all this time?"

The boy didn't answer. Instead, he looked back at Charlie Williamson, and the smile waned on his face.

"He found the safest part of the forest," Charlie Williamson said, patting him on the back. "A smart one, this boy. His dog ran off, but he didn't panic. Just made a camp and kept himself safe until help arrived. We're proud of you, Gabriel."

Megan smiled, feeling a little off-balance at the story Mr. Williamson was essentially feeding them. It felt strangely forced. She reached out to Gabriel, and he took her hand, keeping a hold of Fred's leash in the other. They started down the trail. "Is that right?" she finally asked him, trying to sound impressed although her insides screamed with suspicion. "You made a little camp and just hung out here waiting for us to find you?"

"Uh... yeah," Gabriel said, fiddling with the leash. He reached down to rub Fred's ears.

Megan studied him as they walked. Charlie Williamson was just behind them, but she didn't look back. She only watched Gabriel's face, reading a few expressions she knew quite well. Confusion, relief... and the one that had her stomach rolling into a knot.

Fear.

Chapter Twenty

Santiago knew what Crystal wanted. Her arm brushed his so often that he was surprised she didn't just grab his hand on her own. But as much as she was vying for Santiago's romantic attention, it wasn't going to happen. She was beautiful. A wonderful person. But he looked at her the way he would look at a good friend. Or his sister. There simply wasn't any desire in him. No longing or admiring. Nothing like how he felt for Megan. She'd turned his world around the second he met her. He couldn't help thinking back to that moment. Her eyes alight with the fear that her home would be swept off the mountainside by a flash flood. But he was the one swept away instead.

He praised the day he signed up as a rescue volunteer.

It had only taken a few minutes to get to know her, and then he was hopelessly drowned in his feelings for her. And then today, watching as she'd run into Kenneth's arms... it was devastating. His chest had nearly cracked in two at the sight.

He paused on the trail. But, now that he thought back to

it, she hadn't been the one running. In fact, she'd only stood there looking more surprised than she should have. And when her eyes had settled on his, he could have sworn—

"What is it?" Crystal whispered, peering into the trees where Santiago's gaze lingered.

But he wasn't even paying attention. Here, a little boy was lost, and he was ignoring everything around him. A fine rescue volunteer he was turning out to be.

"I..." He glanced around, gathering his bearings. Trying to become the man Gabriel needed him to be. The boy's life might very well depend on it. "I think we should head down a little farther."

"Good idea," Crystal said, walking beside him again.

How they'd ended up alone together, he wasn't quite sure. Maybe she was just crafty. He snuck a glance in her direction to see her eyes were on him. A smile flashed across her face.

Definitely crafty.

He focused again at the task ahead, pushing the turmoil of his feelings aside. He was becoming increasingly worried. And if Gabriel was taken, but not taken out of the woods, where would they go? He thought back to a cave he'd explored far to the east, but it was easily a ten-mile walk. Someone couldn't have dragged him all the way out there.

Thunder rolled through the sky overhead, and he glanced up. The storm wouldn't wait much longer, and the weather was something humans and animals alike had to respect. So, if there was a kidnapper, they would also be looking for cover. Or for a way out of the woods. And with the way out being heavily traveled by a slew of rescuers, they were likely hunkered down somewhere.

He stopped again, gesturing into the trees, "There's a

place we should check out," he said, avoiding eye contact as he scooted past her on the trail. "The trees are really thick, and the granite rocks would provide a good barrier against the wind and rain."

"Yeah, that sounds like a great idea. Let's go," Crystal said.

And this time, she did it. Her hand laced with his from behind and her grip tightened. Santiago's breath caught in his throat. He wanted to pull his hand away, but he couldn't just shake her hand off like a jerk... could he? She wasn't someone he wanted to get involved with, but he didn't want her hating him either. They were friends, after all.

His heart was pounding with nerves, but he didn't want to lead her on. He glanced back with a smile and took his hand from hers, patting her back as he stepped aside. "Why don't you go first?" He gestured ahead. "Just around those rocks."

She faltered a little, but a smile quickly spread across her pretty face. "Okay, thanks." It was clear she enjoyed being the leader, as she charged ahead. Her pace was quite a bit faster than his had been, and he was wishing he'd set her out front in the first place. He'd been too worried about leaving her behind, but clearly she wasn't a stranger to hiking.

They made their way up a hill littered with so many granite boulders, it was easier to step from rock to rock than to try to make their way around. Crystal hopped ahead of him, and he followed, scanning the area as he hoped he was taking them in the right direction.

A raindrop landed on his face and another quickly followed.

"It's raining," Crystal said, pointing to the raindrops spattering down on the dry granite.

Santiago nodded. "I think we're about there." They scrambled over the last of the rocks to meet with a dense section of forest. He took the lead again, pointing to the west and covering ground swiftly. The rain was beginning to fall with energy now, and the wind blew hard across the tree-tops. If they didn't find Gabriel soon, they'd have to call it a night. But Santiago was sure the trail looped around just ahead of them.

"Hey."

Crystal grabbed his arm, and for one dreadful second, he imagined her kissing him. But when he turned his head, she had her finger to her lips.

"Listen," she whispered. "Do you hear that?"

He turned to the wind and caught a voice. His eyes widened, and he made his way forward, listening as hard as he could. Crystal stuck next to him, still clutching his arm, but for the moment, he didn't care. The voice grew louder, and suddenly, he recognized it was Megan's. He looked back at Crystal, and she nodded.

"It's Megan," she whispered. "But who's she talking to?"

"I don't know." Santiago was caught between the urge to call out to her or to sneak closer. Then her voice rang out clearly, as if turned in their direction.

"You made a little camp and just hung out here waiting for us to find you?" she asked.

She was talking to the boy. But her voice was a bit off, even from a distance. She was speaking a little too loudly, and he could hear the thread of tension in her voice.

"Something's wrong," Crystal whispered beside him.

He nodded.

They began moving together, pausing between steps to listen. But there was no more conversation. They came to a clearing, and Santiago scanned it quickly, eager to see Megan and the boy. Eager to make sure they were okay. On the floor of the trail, already damp from the rain, he could still make out prints of both animal and humans. Tire tracks were along one side, and he lowered down, tracing one hand gently over the top. "Charlie Williamson is with them," he said, feeling a wave of relief.

But when he turned to Crystal, she wasn't pleased. "The Natural Resources guy?" she asked. "What's he doing here?"

"He said he heard about Gabriel," Santiago explained, "and felt so strong about it, he knew he had to come out and help."

They looked at each other for a moment, and Santiago reviewed his explanation in his mind. It hadn't felt wrong until he spoke it out loud. Now, combined with her obvious mistrust of the man, he felt a jolt of real fear. "C'mon," he said, "let's just catch up to them."

They both started to jog. Then as they rounded a curve, and the empty trail opened up in front of them, Santiago ran. How had they gotten so far ahead? He blinked back the rain pouring down his face, paying it no attention.

"Right behind you," Crystal puffed behind him, her feet splashing down the trail just as quickly.

He tried not to let his imagination get the better of him, but he couldn't help it. Why hadn't he challenged Williamson's reasons even a little? He'd been working in rescue for so long, he'd seen people fake injuries and propagate stories of their near-death experiences just to gain attention. Why should this be any different?

Except this time, it was more serious than that. Much more.

He ran harder.

MEGAN'S HEAD WAS SPINNING THE LONGER THEY WALKED. Mr. Williamson wasn't exactly the chatty type, and in her mind, she was reasoning all sorts of things. It had nothing to do with the storm overhead, or the thunder they heard that seemed to be growing louder. She didn't care about the rain that was now falling hard, soaking her hair and clothes, and trailing down her face. What she worried about was Williamson. A thought that sent shivers down her back that had nothing to do with being cold and wet. Was there any chance he'd been the one to kidnap the boy? Or maybe he found him and threatened him not to talk about... about what? What kind of danger was a little boy?

She kept a good hold on Gabriel's hand, walking as swiftly as possible. Gabriel seemed happy to walk fast as well, especially with Fred out front, pulling him along. He had a cheerful expression even in the rain.

"I let the group know we're returning to the camp with you, Gabriel," Mr. Williamson said. "Your mom will be there and maybe some news channels. They'll be so excited to hear about your smart thinking after being lost in the forest, and to see you home safe, of course."

Megan glanced back and smiled, although she noticed the way Williamson's eyes flickered quickly to her. He was watching them so closely.

"Your mother will be there too," he added.

Gabriel looked back at Megan, and she smiled at him through her nerves. "I bet she'll be so relieved to see you," she said.

"I don't know," Gabriel frowned.

He walked a little closer to Megan, giving her the feeling

he wanted to talk only to her, not Williamson. She squeezed his young hand. "Why would you say that?"

His lips twisted for a moment. "Well, we lost Daddy two years ago, and she might be mad that I was trying to do what he did when he died." He kicked a rock in the trail, splashing his jeans and sending it into the brush. "He would study all the plants and animals and be gone for two or three days without calling or anything. It was his job, but it always made her worried until he would call."

He looked up at the trail in silence for a moment. "He was supposed to take me with him the next time. But..."

Megan stopped. She knelt down in front of him, her heart breaking for his pain. The knees of her jeans squished in the muddy mess of a trail, but she didn't care. "Gabriel, listen to me." She paused, hoping her words would sink in. "Your mother won't be disappointed, or angry, or any of those things. The only thing she will feel when she sees you is happiness. More than she's ever felt before in her whole life. I promise."

A smile pushed at one side of his mouth. "Yeah?"

"Yeah." Megan stood again, rubbing his messy hair and walking a little slower. She still didn't know what to think of Williamson, but thankfully, he seemed to want the boy back with the group as much as she did. If he was a threat, at least they weren't in any danger... for now.

"Megan!"

She spun around to see Santiago running down the trail, splashing through mud and puddles with each step. Crystal appeared right behind him, waving with a big smile on her rain-soaked face. For a split second, Megan felt a pinch of irritation at seeing they'd been alone together, but she brushed it aside quickly. What was her problem anyway?

Still, she couldn't help watching Santiago intently as he met up with her.

He stopped right in front of her, ignoring Williamson. She wanted him to wrap her in his arms, but that wouldn't exactly meet the occasion, would it? She wasn't the one who'd gone missing.

"Everything all right?" he asked quietly, looking deeply into her eyes.

She wanted so badly to tell him what she was thinking. But with Williamson standing right there with them, it was impossible. Instead, she lifted the hand that held Gabriel's, turning to the young boy. "Everything's wonderful. Isn't it, Gabriel?"

Gabriel smiled at Santiago. "Hey, Santi," he said.

Santiago scrubbed his hand over the boy's head, making him giggle. Water sprayed all around, but it didn't matter. They were all soaked through, anyway. "Kid," he said, giving a tender smile. "You are the bravest person I know."

"What about you?" Gabriel pointed to Santiago. "You're braver than me."

"Nope," Santiago shook his head definitively. "I've never done what you did. I've never wandered in this forest for almost three days. Not like you."

Gabriel's smile faded a little.

"What's wrong?" Santiago asked, his voice growing softer. "I'm sorry, I'm sure you want to get out of here and get warm, right?"

Gabriel glanced up from beneath thick, dark lashes, but he didn't answer.

"And your mom and Tank are probably so anxious—"

"Tank?" Gabriel practically shouted. His face broke into a smile.

"Yes!" Santiago waved him on, taking the lead as the group started down the muddy path. "He was able to go home from the vet yesterday, and I would bet he's here waiting for you."

Gabriel walked faster, charging ahead. But the return trip seemed to be taking ten times longer than it had taken to walk out. Megan couldn't stop herself from shivering anymore. The thought of being warm and dry was taking over everything else.

And then she glanced back at Williamson. He followed behind, walking his dirt bike and watching. Gabriel was walking ahead with Santiago, so she slowed until she was walking next to Williamson. Her heart pounded. He looked over at her but didn't speak.

"So, Mr. Williamson," she began, feeling like her tongue had gone numb. The words were difficult to make out. "What was it like to find him? How did you know where to look?" She tried to give an expression of admiration, but it was difficult. Everything inside was telling her to get far away from this man.

His eyes trailed across her face and then stilled. "Well, it wasn't easy," he began, glancing ahead at the others. "I knew we needed to find him fast. It's always that way with lost kids. Time is your greatest threat."

She shivered but not from the rain. It was his voice, cold and calculated. There was no feeling involved with his story of finding a lost boy. Only reasoning.

"I went as far west as I thought he could possibly go and then just started combing up and down, moving east." His gaze shifted to the boy, and his voice rose as he continued, "It was when I was covering this last section of ground that I found him. He'd made a kind of shelter under a good, thick cover of trees. A smart move. There were remnants of a fire too."

Megan smiled. "I'm so relieved he's found." She peered ahead. They were close, just a little bit longer.

"Yes," Williamson agreed. "Everyone will be."

Crystal joined them, walking beside her. She glanced at Williamson with a noticeably dry expression. Maybe she didn't feel the level of fear over the man that Megan did. Something told her they were all walking a fine line when it came to Charlie Williamson, although she could be sure why.

Cheers broke out from far down the trail and Megan's attention turned. She peered through tree trunks to find a group of volunteers still huddled at the campsite. White smoke rose from the fire pit, signaling the fire's demise against the rainstorm. But the volunteers remained.

"Gabriel!"

Everyone stopped at the sight of Amanda with her dark hair flying behind her. A big yellow dog was at her side, but upon seeing Gabriel, he streaked out ahead. Mud splattered his legs and dripped from his belly; a big pink tongue trailed out of a wide, happy mouth.

"Tank! Mom!" Gabriel raced ahead. Laughing or crying, Megan couldn't tell. But when his arms came around the wet dog's neck, she couldn't hold back her own tears. His mother dropped to his side, hugging the dog and boy together. Then she scooped him into her arms, lifting him as she stood. "My boy," she cried, swinging him around. "My Gabriel."

"Well done, Williamson." Santiago held his hand out, smiling back at Mr. Williamson who gave a quick high-five.

"Thanks," Williamson said. "I knew I'd find him."

Santiago shook his head. "That's incredible. Fate must've been guiding you the whole way." He tilted his head, glancing at Gabriel walking down the trail with his mother. They all began to follow. "But what I don't get is, what happened to the dog?"

Santiago was looking down the trail, but Megan caught the quick turn of Williamson's head.

"I mean, if the boy just wandered off and was lost, how did his dog get all cut up?" Santiago shook his head.

"Probably an animal," Williamson answered. "Mountain lion or bear. Something like that. The kid is lucky he didn't stumble across a predator."

An eerie silence fell on the group, leaving only the sound of the storm and their feet slopping through the mud. Megan was shivering continually now, but something deep inside began to burn hot.

Whatever this man thought he was getting away with, he had another thing coming.

Chapter Twenty-One

egan felt shaky, but it wasn't from the cold. Not anymore. She studied the tendrils of steam rising from her cocoa in a slender trail. But her thoughts couldn't move on from the past hour. It was clear enough in Charlie Williamson's voice that he was lying. The reasons could vary, but she had a tendency to go for extremes in her assumptions. And unfortunately, she was often right.

"Hey you."

Her eyes flickered up from her paper cup. Kenneth smiled back at her, and suddenly she was overrun with a whole new kind of nerves. Just how had she planned to tell him that her feelings had changed? It was all organized in her head, but now it was like that section of her brain had vanished. Considering she needed to figure out what had really happened with Gabriel, maybe it was all for the best.

"Quite a day," Kenneth said. His voice was cautious, as if he knew there were things she needed to say but he wasn't anxious to hear them. "I'm told Gabriel checked out just fine. No health issues to worry about. That's a big relief."

"Yeah," Megan hesitated. She met Kenneth's eyes and knew she could place her trust in him. Turning her back to the group, she spotted Charlie Williamson, Santiago, and Crystal huddled around a heat lamp. She stepped in closer to Kenneth.

"About that," she said, gaining his attention quickly. Concern mixed with worry on his face. He was reading her well. "I don't think Charlie Williamson is telling the truth." She said, "Don't you think it's strange that his dog was cut up badly enough to deserve a few days at the vet while a ten-year-old boy walks out of the forest without so much as a touch of dehydration?"

Kenneth's head tilted. "Most would call that a miracle, but... What exactly are you saying?"

"I'm saying I don't think he's been in the forest all this time." Thunder rolled through the storm, and Megan glanced up at the clouds. People were heading for their vehicles, beginning to load up and pull away.

"But why wouldn't he tell us that?" Kenneth asked. He glanced back at where Gabriel stood beside his mother. She was holding his hand and began to walk with him toward their car.

Next to her, Fred shook his coat out. Megan glanced down to see his legs half-covered with mud. His head was lowered as if trying to avoid even one more raindrop. She smoothed her hand over his wet coat. "Sorry, boy." She turned to Kenneth. "I'm going to talk to him."

"Who, Charlie?"

She shook her head. "No, I'm going to talk to Gabriel."

Kenneth took her hand, stopping her. "I don't think

that's a good idea, Megan," he said quietly. "He's been through a lot already. Maybe you could just wait until morning."

Megan didn't want to wait. She felt injustice and deceit twisting away at her insides. But after taking a slow breath, her gaze went from the young boy to Fred, who had his eyes now squeezed closed in the rain.

She let her breath out and relented. Kenneth was right... but he was also still holding her hand. She turned back to him and caught Santiago's eye over his shoulder. He was stopped halfway to his car, watching. His lips pressed into a quick smile, and he gave her a gentle nod of his head, as if wishing her well. Panic turned in her chest, and she pulled her hand out of Kenneth's, but Santiago had already gotten into his car. He pulled away.

Kenneth glanced behind him, noticing her distraction. "I don't mean to stop you from doing something you feel strongly about." He turned to her again. "If you really believe Charlie Williamson is lying, we should go talk to the police."

"Yes," Megan said, still rolling with regret. Why hadn't she just picked up the phone and told Santiago how she felt? There had just been so many things going on, she hadn't had the time. Then, showing up to search for Gabriel and coming face-to-face with Kenneth when she'd expected him to be out of the country. Everything had turned her in circles until she wasn't even sure how she felt anymore. But one thing was for sure, she needed to set Kenneth straight. She admired him immensely, but a serious relationship with him wasn't the right thing for her. At least not right now. It would only mean pain for both of them if she let it continue.

"Kenneth," she said, facing him squarely. She could see in his eyes that he was preparing himself for the worst. He was ready, although it looked like he would rather run away than listen to anything more. "I'm sorry I didn't say anything earlier, before I met up with you today."

"Uh-oh," he said, dipping his head with a smile. "I'm pretty sure I know where this is going." He brought his hands to her arms, rubbing them gently. She really loved when he did that.

"I could tell when I kissed you," he said. His voice was tender and soft, and his eyes were so kind. She felt guilt beginning to pool in her chest, but being honest with him was the only way to ease both of their suffering.

He sighed. "I know I've been gone a lot, and I'm going to be away for quite a while on this next trip. I had hoped for you to come with me, but..." He gazed across her face tenderly. "I won't ask you to wait for me." A smile spread across his face. "I hope you will, but I won't ask it."

Megan fought against the pain in her chest. It would be so much easier to just kiss him, send him on his way, and then tell him the truth after he'd left. But that was a coward's approach to life, and she was no coward.

She steadied her nerves. "I think I just need some time to find myself again, before I commit to any one person..." As soon as she said the words, she realized how true they were. She really did need to find herself. "I wish I knew what the future held, but I honestly don't know. My time in Seacrest has mostly been spent trying to scrape up a life, and now that I have the bones of one, I need to live a little... on my own."

Wind blew her hair across her face, and he reached forward, brushing it back. His hand lingered at her neck and his gaze warmed. "I understand that," he said. "But I can't leave without letting you know how much I love you."

He leaned closer so slowly, she hardly realized it was happening. When he kissed her, she tried to decide what she really wanted. What was really in her heart? He held her so gently, leaning into a soft kiss that was growing steadily more passionate. Her heart raced as she kissed him back, no longer thinking her way through it. The ache in her heart was something she couldn't ignore. If there was a chance for them in the future, she couldn't just throw it away.

She touched his face, lingering close to him even after their kiss had ended. His arms came around her, and she relaxed against him, ever wondering. Maybe one day she would find a clarity that would make this decision so much easier. Or maybe this was their goodbye. Either way, it was both heartbreaking and healing to be in his arms, and she stayed there for a long time.

Eventually, although it felt like he was resisting it, he stepped back. He took a deep breath but didn't seem to be able to manage a smile again. He only looked back at her, scanning her features softly. "I'll go to the police station with you, if you want?"

She smiled, although she already knew staying with him much longer would be a mistake. Especially after a kiss like that one. "Thanks," she said, "but no. I'll just go talk to someone. I'm sure it'll be fine. Don't you have a flight to catch?"

"Yeah, a few days ago actually." He grinned. "But I couldn't just leave when there was a little boy out there lost."

Her smile deepened. "No," she said, quietly. "I guess not."

"Listen, Megan." He took her hands. "Don't do anything too crazy on your own. I know you're worried about this, but the boy's home. Everything's fine." He shrugged. "Maybe give it a day or two and then see how you feel. Could just be the stress talking."

She knew he was probably right. The past week alone was enough to give her heartburn for the rest of her life. She should just sit tight and let the events calm down. Let the police and media take the story over for a little while. Let it settle.

As Kenneth got in his car and drove away, she waved. There was no one left but her and Fred. He'd jumped in the car as soon as she'd opened the door, and he sat tall on the backseat watching her, clearly ready to get going. And they should go. Head back to the house and take a hot shower. Change into dry clothes and turn on the gas fireplace. Sit and relax.

She pulled the hood up on her raincoat and rolled the window down a crack. "I'll just be a minute," she said, closing the door. Fred perked his ears but didn't look particularly interested in going with her. She glanced around at the soggy, wet, empty forest... and started jogging. The trail was easy to follow, after all, and she had a good idea where Charlie had claimed Gabriel had a camp set up. It wouldn't hurt to go check it out. Maybe the press would even appreciate a few photographs.

All her justifications kept on rolling through her head, but she blocked the real one out. The one that had a hold on her so tight, she couldn't ignore it.

Charlie Williamson was lying, and she was going to prove it.

She followed the trail all the way to the point where she'd come across him and Gabriel. Thoroughly soaked now, she paid no attention to the additional rain pouring down. She followed the trail around a tight bend and trudged up the steepest part yet. Little streams of rainwater rushed down the trail, pooling into puddles. The wind was howling now, pelting her with rain no matter which way she turned.

When she spotted the thickest spot in the trees, she left the trail. The wind wasn't quite as bad under the cover of so many branches. She made her way across, then across again, slowly covering every inch of ground. If there was a little camp out there, she didn't want to miss it. When she was just coming out of the densest part, she flinched.

She could hear voices. Pulling her hood back quickly, she paused, listening with her breath held.

"Right here should be fine," a man's voice said. Megan glanced around and ducked behind the thickest tree trunk she could find. Peeking out one side, she spotted two men walking towards her. They stopped and began piling sticks and swiping debris from the area.

"I can't believe we even agreed to do this," the other man said. He kicked at a rock, and it ricocheted off the tree where Megan hid. She ducked behind it again.

"Well, it's not for free," the first man replied. "We're getting paid big time. Something like this is worth tens of thousands for a guy like him."

"What do you suppose a kid would use for a camp?"

The men spoke back and forth, debating on sticks and tools and how to make it look like it had been there awhile. Megan took her phone out and turned it to video. Recording, she moved the camera slowly until the men were in view. She hoped their voices were loud enough to pick up. Her hand was shaky with cold and fear, as she wondered how long it would be until she could get out of there and back to the car. But she'd been looking for the camp, and here she'd found it.

Her ringtone jingled loudly, and she gasped, dropping it to the ground. She snatched it up and ran for it without looking back.

"Right there!" one of the men shouted. "Get her!"

She ran as fast as she could, gasping for breath. She didn't turn back, and blood rushed so loudly in her ears, she couldn't have heard them even if they were shouting. She just kept running. There was no other choice, unless she wanted to be the next person listed as missing in the forest. This time, she doubted anyone would find her. She spotted her car and saw Fred's nose out the window. He barked fiercely, telling her that the man was likely still behind her. She jumped into the car and started it quickly. Just as she shifted into reverse, one of the men landed on her hood.

Fred erupted and Megan screamed, pressing the gas pedal down hard.. Fred was in the front seat, snarling viciously as Megan cranked the wheel. Finally, the man slid off. She gunned it, fishtailing before finally catching some traction. Her little car jetted away, and she looked in the rearview mirror to see one man helping the other to his feet. She exhaled a shaky breath. Even though they'd been chasing her, she was relieved that she hadn't run either one over. She glanced back again to see one of them hold a phone to his ear. She needed to act fast. They'd seen her and Fred clearly enough. Whoever they'd just called, and she had a good idea who, he'd be on her tail any minute.

The tires on the little red hatchback squealed as she turned a tight corner around the boardwalk and hit the old highway. She raced along the scenic road as the sky grew darker. Evening was settling in, and she needed to get somewhere safe. Maybe she'd just stay at the police station for the night.

Her phone rang again. It was sitting next to Fred on the passenger's seat, and she pressed the button on the front, turning it to speaker and holding it in one hand as she continued racing down the highway.

"Hello?" she said, glancing at the speedometer as it neared 60. She sailed around the next corner, glancing at the cliff on the other side.

"Megan, where are you?" Crystal asked. She sounded cheerful and unaware, which was a relief. The last thing Megan wanted was for any of her friends to be in danger. "Mr. Williamson is here at your house with me."

Megan felt suddenly dizzy, and she eased up on the gas pedal. "He's at my house?" she asked. "With you?"

"Yes," Crystal laughed. "That's what I said. He's here at your house with me. I came by to chat, and he was here too, waiting for you. I figured you'd be home any minute, so we just came in for some hot tea and—"

"Is he listening in on this call?" Megan asked, lowering her voice. Crystal didn't seem to catch any of the fear in her voice, as she answered just as loudly as before.

"Oh, no," she said. "He's on the phone. He got a call just as I was calling you."

Megan's throat went dry. She swallowed hard, frantically trying to come up with a way to get Crystal out of there.

"What was that?" Crystal's voice was directed away, but then she spoke into the phone again. "He wants to talk to you, I guess?" she said, sounding confused. But whether she handed the phone over, or Charlie snatched it out of her hand, his voice rang through on the heels of hers.

"Megan," he said.

He knew. He knew everything. Megan couldn't even respond. The turnoff to her house came, and she pulled off the highway, stopping the car. Far down the lane was the tiny glow of her porch light.

"I hadn't expected to wait this long," Williamson said. "If I'd known how much you had going on tonight, I never would've presumed to take up any more of your time. You've been pretty busy, it sounds like."

Megan could hardly breathe. She needed to hang up and call 911, but that would mean abandoning Crystal with this man. She couldn't do it. "What do you want?" she asked, fighting to keep her voice steady even as her hand trembled so hard that the phone shook. With a sudden thought, she turned it to speaker while she sent a text to the man she trusted most.

Williamson is at my house. Help. Call 911.

"What do I want..." Williamson sounded like he was simply musing. As if he were strolling down the street on a lazy day. "That's a very good question, actually. It's difficult to answer because I want so many things. Doesn't everyone?"

"Yes, but most people won't resort to kidnapping children to get it." Megan knew she needed to get Crystal out of there before she made Williamson angry, but she couldn't help it. He was infuriating. And worst of all, he sounded like he wasn't afraid. Like he fully expected to walk out of this unpunished.

"Well, that's not how things went at all," he replied. "I simply had to keep an eye on my investments. They're very valuable, and when you discover a risk to any investment, you need to act. I just didn't realize how much liberty my employees were going to take on the action-taking." He chuckled and Megan suddenly felt sick. She'd been completely blind to what a twisted, terrible person he was.

She glanced down at her phone, hoping to see a reply. But there was nothing. She shifted the car into drive and eased off the road, parking in the trees. Stopping the engine, she clipped Fred's leash on and snuck out into the night. The rain had ceased, thank goodness. But not the wind. It blustered around her as she walked, making her way towards the house.

"What are you guys even talking about?"

Crystal's voice in the background was so unaware. Megan hoped that the police would get there soon. But when Williamson's voice came again, her whole body began to tremble.

"Megan," he said, sounding disgustingly cheerful, "Crystal wants to know what we're talking about. It sounds like you've stepped outside for a little jaunt? Nice weather for it too. Although I would've thought you'd be finished with sneaking around in the forest. Perhaps you're coming to see us after all? That would be nice. We'd love to see you... wouldn't we, Crystal?"

"Megan?" Crystal said.

Megan's breath caught as she heard the terror in her friend's voice. There was a click as the line cut out. She wrapped her hand around the leash and ran.

Chapter Twenty-Two

Santiago wasn't sure what to think anymore. He'd driven away from the campsite, but then just before she was out of view, he'd waited. Watching Megan from his car, he'd hoped that Kenneth would leave so he could finally talk to her. He needed to. It was driving him crazy. But as he watched, Kenneth kissed her... and she kissed him back. It was then that he'd pulled away from the curb.

He tried not to think about that kiss, but it was a losing battle. It wasn't a goodbye; it was much more than that. So much more.

When he got to his apartment, he stepped inside and glared at the scene before him. His life felt like a ruinous dump. He tossed his phone on the chair and left it all behind. It was still raining, and the wind was blowing harder than before, but he needed to get outside. He needed to clear his head. All this time, he'd enjoyed teasing Megan and seeing her now and then. But since that phone call... he couldn't get her off his mind. Ever. She was all he ever thought about. He'd been so anxious to see her, he hadn't even realized what it might mean to have Kenneth standing right beside him. Not until the man had swept her into his arms the way Santiago had wanted to.

But obviously, he'd read her wrong on the phone. He never should have told her he loved her. It was stupid and reckless of him. He should have kept a stronger hold on his heart. Thinking back to the way she answered was always the hardest, when she'd told him she loved him too. It had caught him off guard, but at the same time, it was the answer he'd been waiting for. He adored that memory. But right now, it was torture.

The wind shook loose several strands of hair, and he pulled out his hair tie. He wrung out the water and wrapped it into a knot again, securing it back. His chest ached, but it was his own dumb fault. Why had he put that pressure on her? Why had he told her he loved her over the phone? It was an idiotic thing for him to do. He needed to whisper it to her over a candlelight dinner or sitting on the beach at sunset. Somewhere beautiful, where he could look deeply into her eyes and gauge her reaction. A place where he could hold her in his arms and kiss her. Touch her silky hair. Take in her beauty.

Not just blurted out over the phone like some stupid kid.

"Ugh!" He groaned, tipping his head back so the rain trailed across his face. No doubt she only returned his words because she felt pressured. What else was she supposed to say? Now here Kenneth comes and does everything just right. Of course he does. With a dozen years more experience, he knows how to do things. Whether he really means what he says, that's another story.

No. No, that wasn't fair.

He wiped a hand across his face, wiping away the water. Kenneth was a good man. He was a friend, even if Santiago wouldn't mind never seeing him again. That was only due to the fact that he was crazy in love with Megan. But obviously, he'd been too affected by her pain over the phone. It had set his chest on fire. He would've done anything to stop her tears.

Maybe he should just go talk to her. Set things straight so he could be sure to at least have her as a friend. Nothing would be worse than alienating her so completely that they couldn't even be that anymore.

Santiago turned back to his house, walking quicker now. He just needed to get their fragile relationship past this awkwardness that he'd so carelessly caused. Then things would be fine. When he got to his apartment, he stepped in quickly and snatched his keys, leaving his phone on the chair. They weren't needed anyway, since he was just going a short distance and wanted to talk to her in person. Not over the phone. Not with something this important. He wouldn't make that mistake again.

❧❧

"MA'AM? MA'AM, ARE YOU THERE?" THE POLICE dispatcher's voice blared from her phone.

"Yes," Megan answered, nearly whispering. "Please, have them hurry. I'm going to get my friend out."

"No, ma'am, I need you to wait there—"

Megan hung up and set her phone to silent, praying that Crystal was okay. If Williamson did one single thing to her... she had to pause for a moment to take a steadying breath.

"Okay, Fred," she whispered. They were around the side

of the house next to Megan's bedroom window. At the base of the foundation, there were new rosebushes planted that would bloom in the spring. It had been a long time since Fred dug up a note from the original owner of the house right where the roses now grew. The note that bequeathed Megan with a priceless black pearl necklace.

She brushed the memory aside and carefully stepped up to the house. Sneaking a glimpse in the window, she found the room dark. The door to the bedroom was closed, and it was empty. She sighed with relief. If she could just get inside, maybe her and Fred could surprise them and... and she didn't know what. But would she really be able to hoist Fred up and into the window without making a huge racket?

Decidedly not.

She turned around to see Fred dancing on his feet, anxious to get in. After all, they'd scrambled in through Crystal's window not too long ago. It was getting to be a regular thing. She grabbed Fred's collar and held her hand in front of him. "Sit," she whispered. "Fred, sit."

He shifted his eyes, and then his rump landed on the wet mulch.

"Good boy," Megan said, letting go. "You need to stay. Okay, Fred? Stay."

He froze, locked into an obedient sitting posture. She could tell he didn't appreciate the command, but she patted his head and repeated it a few more times. It was the one thing she wanted him to think about at that moment. It was his only job. Just stay.

She lifted the bedroom window slowly, inch by inch. Listening for any sound of Crystal or Williamson, she climbed up and reached one leg through, settling her foot carefully on the wood floor, then the other. When she was inside, she eased the window back down. She glanced at Fred, who was still frozen in his sitting position, staring intently at Megan. Her breath held, she walked gingerly around the bed, terrified her wet shoes would squeak.

When she made it to the door, she leaned close, listening. Williamson was talking, but it was impossible to make out. At least it didn't sound like he was yelling. Where was Crystal? Why wasn't she saying anything? Slowly, she gripped the door handle and twisted it. Williamson's voice continued, and she eased the door open just enough to see down the hall and into the living room. Crystal sat on the couch with her back to Megan, facing the fireplace. But Williamson's voice was coming from the kitchen. He talked about coffee creamer and sugar and then about the weather. Rambling.

Crystal didn't answer and only stared at the fire. Maybe she was annoyed that instead of hanging out with Megan, she was left to make conversation with Williamson. Maybe she still had no idea she was in danger.

Megan stepped out of the bedroom and into the hall, not sure what she would do if Williamson appeared. But if he was putting on a show of being a normal, sane person, then maybe that was what he wanted Crystal to believe. Maybe he had to convince everyone that he was just fine. Everyone except Megan. She already knew he was insane.

A knock came at the front door and Megan froze. Crystal turned her head, and for once, Megan caught sight of something on her face, just visible on her cheek. A strip of gray tape. Megan's breath stopped, and she could only stare at her friend.

"Maybe that's Megan?" Williamson said as he walked past the hallway. Megan pressed against the wall, but he didn't look her way. After he'd passed, she hurried down the hall and crouched down just behind the couch where Crystal sat.

She listened to the locks twist and the door open.

"Oh, Mr. Williamson..."

The sound of Santiago's voice had her panicking completely. What was he doing? Did he plan to rescue them on his own? It didn't seem the smartest way to respond to her text. She bit her lip and peeked out from behind the couch. The door was only open a tiny bit, blocking any view of Santiago. Williamson stood in the small opening with his hand on the door as if he would slam it closed at any second.

"Yes, hello Santiago," Williamson said. "Did you need something?"

"Yes, uh... is Megan home?"

Santiago sounded completely naive to the situation. It had Megan's hope crumbling apart. Somehow, he hadn't seen her text. He didn't know.

"No," Williamson answered. "I think she's out with Kenneth Bradburn. Do you know him?"

Megan fumed, but however terrible the conversation might be, at least it was buying her a little time. She could explain everything later. She reached up carefully and tapped Crystal's shoulder.

Her friend spun around, eyes wide. She shook her head at Megan, glancing frantically back at the door. Her wrists and ankles bound together with skinny strips of rope.

Megan crawled around the couch, keeping as low as possible. When she heard growling, she fumbled harder with the rope, trying to get her fingers to move faster. Fred must've come around the house. Maybe he didn't recognize Santiago, or perhaps he was growling at Williamson.

"Hey, boy," Santiago's voice came quietly, as if he'd turned his head. "Where's Megan—whoa!"

Fred's sharp barking filled the house. Earsplitting, There was a thud against the door just as Megan got the rope loose from Crystal's ankles. Crystal glanced at the door. Williamson was struggling to force it closed as Fred clawed and pushed against it.

"What's wrong with this dog?" he shouted, finally slamming the door closed.

Megan grabbed Crystal's arm, and they ran through the kitchen to the back door.

"Oh, here she is," Williamson shouted through the door. "Let me get her for you."

Megan flipped the lock and pulled with all her might. But it didn't budge. Then she spotted the piece of two-by-four nailed across it, sealing it shut.

Crystal jerked to the side and out of Megan's hands. She spun around... and then her world froze.

Williamson held a knife to Crystal's neck. Megan could see the pressure of the blade on her skin. He shook his head and stepped back, taking Crystal with him as she walked in short, panicked steps. Her wide eyes stared back at Megan.

"One movement, and it's all over very quickly," Williamson warned. "Her, you, even that dog. I'll go through every single one of you. Now go to the door." Williamson backed away with Crystal in his arms. "Santiago's waiting for you."

"Just let her go, and I'll do what you want," Megan said, following him.

He stepped behind the door and shook his head, whispering, "Answer it, then send him away. And make sure he believes you."

"You don't have to do this," Megan whispered. "Think about it. Leave now, and you get away before anyone knows you were even here."

"Oh, I plan on leaving soon, don't you worry." Williamson's eyes narrowed. "If I hadn't wasted so much of my time looking for old Mr. Chambers, I'd be out of the country already. Didn't seem to matter anyway, the guy doesn't have a clue about what he found in that budget. Now open it. Quickly."

Megan pulled the door open a tiny bit, the way Williamson had done. Santiago stood a few steps back from the door, holding Fred's collar. "Megan," he said, clearly startled. "What's going on?"

"I think I'm sick," she said quickly. Her voice was shaking, but she hoped he couldn't tell. "Can you take Fred for me, just for a little while?" Her words were so rushed, and her heart was pounding hard. She didn't even realize she was crying until a tear trailed down her cheek.

"What about Williamson?" Santiago asked, looking angry now. Fred was twisting in his hands and forcing him to grab his collar again and again. "He's staying, or what? What's going on, Megan? Where do we stand?"

"Hurry," Williamson whispered. There was a gasp, and Megan glanced over to find Crystal on her toes, straining to ease the pressure of the knife at her throat.

"He's leaving in just a minute," she choked the words out, praying Santiago would believe her. After all, Williamson just wanted to get away. If he was going to kill them, he would have done it by now.

Santiago hesitated, clearly hurt by her brush off. He took a small step forward, and Fred whined, digging at the wood planks of the deck and trying to get inside. "Megan, I was really hoping to talk to you. I... I need to apologize."

Megan heard Crystal gasp again, and she shook her head at him. "Not right now, Santiago. Just go, okay? I'll talk to you later. Can you take him?" She watched Santiago desperately, hating the pain in his eyes.

Finally, he nodded back at her. Then she slammed the door in his face. She twisted the lock but not all the way, hoping it hadn't engaged. Maybe Santiago would still be able to get in.

Fred lost it, barking wildly.

"There," she whispered, walking back from the door and holding her hands up. "It's done. He's leaving and you can go."

"Can I though?" Williamson asked, moving with Crystal back toward the kitchen. "Old Mr. Chambers might know how to lie low, but I find it very hard to believe that someone as loud-mouthed as you wouldn't have told anyone what was on your mind. In that case, I think it would be safer to just have you ladies come with me." He jerked his head toward the back door. "Hurry now, get that strip of wood off. There's a hammer on top of your fridge there." He smiled. "It came in handy."

Megan snatched the hammer from the fridge and began prying away as fast as she could manage. But the nails were deep, and it was at an awkward angle.

Suddenly, the front door burst open, sending splinters of wood flying. Santiago stumbled inside with Fred's collar still in one hand. He stopped cold at the sight of them, holding his hand up. "Williamson," he said, "just hold it right there. Put the knife down and let her go."

Fred struggled and dug his claws into the floor. He snarled and squirmed, but Santiago held him back.

When someone entered the room behind Santiago and Fred, Megan couldn't have been more shocked. Alyana strode through, dressed to the nines, as always. She sauntered past a struggling Great Dane and eyed down the situation. Megan felt a rush of relief to have so many people in one room against Charlie Williamson. But as Alyana walked toward them, her hopes slowly blackened. A dark truth that settled in her stomach like poison. "I trusted you," she whispered.

Alyana turned an uncaring eye to her. "No." She paused, crossing her arms. "You wanted to trust me. But never really did. To your credit though, because, well..." She walked up to Charlie Williamson and touched her face to his in a quick, passionate display, barely keeping from knocking heads with Crystal. Then she stood beside him, surveying the situation. "Police will be here soon," she said, with little to no concern in her voice.

"Keep going," Williamson demanded, glaring back at Megan.

She spun back around and pried harder, getting one side loose. Glancing back at Crystal, Megan started working on the other side. Working to pull the board off, she nearly had it when something slammed against the door from outside.

Megan jumped back, uttering a startled scream.

Someone pounded on it. "Police!" a voice shouted from outside. "Open up!"

Williamson turned quickly, startled. In that moment, Crystal ducked out of his arms. She fell to the floor and swung her leg hard. The toe of her shoe struck Williamson in the crotch, and he hunched forward. Crystal rolled away out of his reach. But Williamson still held the knife in his hand and his reddened face turned to Megan. He swung at her. Megan stumbled back, lifting the hammer just as the knife clashed against it.

Suddenly Santiago collided with him, slamming Williamson onto the door. Fred went for his legs, acquiring a mouthful of pants. He shook and twisted his head, growling and snarling. But Williamson wasn't going anywhere. Santiago had his wrist pinned up. He slammed it against the wall. "Drop it!" he shouted. "Now!" Again, he slammed his hand and finally, the knife dropped to the floor.

Alyana looked startled, but she didn't fight. She only stood to the side watching.

Megan's entire body shook. Williamson caught her eye, and the hatred she saw there sent chills down her spine. He was just waiting for the first chance to reach for her. To end it.

She grabbed the knife from the floor and kept his gaze, backing up to stand beside Crystal. They watched as police filed in, and Williamson was forced to the ground. His arms were handcuffed behind his back, all while Alyana watched.

"We've got testimony from the boy, Mr. Williamson," the sheriff said. Morel came behind them, approaching Alyana. He said something to her that Megan couldn't hear, but the surprise in Alyana's face was rewarding.

Suddenly, Alyana lunged forward. She hooked her arm with the sheriff's and twisted, rolling across his back and flipping him down hard. Charlie tucked his knees in and jumped to his feet, but Morel was there. Alyana made it to the door, pulling it open just as Morle kicked it shut again. He grabbed her wrist with one hand and slammed her against the door. With her arm twisted behind her, he pressed it to her back and reached for the other.

The sheriff had recovered quickly, and he held Charlie Williamson with one hand, massaging his jaw with the other; apparently where he'd landed.

Morel shot Megan a quick glance and winked. "We had proof these two were working together, but I kinda wanted to see it in action." A grin grew on his face. "It was worth it."

"As I was saying," the sheriff continued, clearing his throat in irritation. "Gabriel got hold of those cameras, didn't he? The ones where your illiterate goons recorded themselves bragging about the job you gave them and how much money they were making. Gabriel was kidnapped by those two you hired to make sure your theft was kept a secret. And now, as they say, it's all over."

They lifted Williamson to his feet, and the sheriff stood mere inches in front of him with a smile on his face. "We know you stole from the state. We know you had someone watching Governor Chambers's house. You didn't like how close his class got to the truth, did you? Wanted to make sure you got off clean, right? But it's going to cost you big time." They began to lead him away but stopped when the sheriff stepped in front of him again. "Oh, and Mr. Williamson?" He paused, tilting his head patronizingly. "You shoulda left these ladies alone. Maybe the courts could have questioned the testimony of a little boy but combined with two well-known and respected locals? Well, you'd better be ready for a nice long vacation in a very cold cell."

They led him out the door with his head low.

Crystal's arm came around Megan. Her neck was red, and there was a small welt where the knife had been, but she was okay. In Crystal's eyes was the expression of a woman who was strong and unafraid.

Megan smiled. "You got him," she said, wrapping her friend in a tight hug. Crystal laughed, although she was shaking. Megan squeezed her tight, feeling her throat tighten. "Thank you, Crystal," she said.

Fred squeezed between them, wagging his tail so hard, his backend was swinging. Crystal stepped back and rubbed Fred. "I got him good," she said.

Megan smoothed her hands over Fred's coat too, kneeling down. "You saved me," she said, looking into his big, soulful blue eyes. "You're my hero, buddy." He sobered in her hands and under her stare, and his nose touched her cheek. She kissed his head. "Thank you, Fred. Good boy."

Finally, she rose. Through the window, she could see a patrol car remained in the drive, but it was a relief to see the lights were off. They'd already driven Williamson away. She could hear the policemen's voices, but she hoped they didn't need to talk to her soon. Maybe they'd even wait until tomorrow. She could claim she was too traumatized and that she just needed some sleep to recover. Because there was something she needed to do first, before anything else.

Her gaze wandered over her house, the scattered splinters on the floor and the hammer lying there. The couch was disheveled, and the front door was in pretty bad shape. Then she came to Santiago. He stood just inside the doorway, looking back at her.

First things first.

Chapter Twenty-Three

Santiago's emotions had gone through so many turns in the past hour, he still felt dizzy. The moment he'd knocked on her door and Williamson had answered, he hadn't known what was happening. Maybe he'd never really known Megan like he thought he did. Because it seemed she was interested in every guy except for him. His thoughts had gone in a hundred different directions. He knew he was misjudging her even as he'd thought it, but what else was there to think?

Then, the way Fred had acted... it finally got through his tortured, lovesick head that something was wrong. The look on Megan's face had been completely confusing. He was so sure she was just trying to protect his feelings; let him down easy. But then she'd asked him to watch Fred. Twice she'd said it, and it made no sense. When the pieces came together, and he heard sounds inside the house, he'd gone crazy and kicked in the door in one go.

Now, standing there, looking back at Megan, he could

only be grateful. Grateful he hadn't walked away, giving into his feelings of rejection. Grateful he was strong enough to hold on to Williamson without killing him. Because he'd wanted to. And especially grateful she was okay and looking back at him with those beautiful green eyes. Crystal stood behind her, but she didn't chase Santiago down like she had in the forest. Maybe she saw something in Santiago's eyes that told her where his heart truly lay.

He was balanced on the next second, and the one after that, waiting for Megan to say something. Or move at all. Whatever she was going to do, he didn't want to rush her. There was no need anyway. They had all night.

She finally took a step closer, and then another. He held onto his heart, sealing it firmly in his chest. There was no call to go gushing all over her with all his big feelings. Not again. He would hold them steady and let things happen the way she wanted them to... however she wanted them to. His only wish was that they could stay friends. He hoped for it more than anything.

His eyes flickered down for just a second to where her shirt buttoned in the front. The top buttons were left undone, and the soft cotton material fell open just enough to reveal a necklace made of twine. His heart throbbed in his chest as he looked over a turquoise stone suspended at the bottom. Intricately woven knots held the rock like a net. It was a design he'd worked long and hard over, throwing away too many strands of twine to count before he'd gotten it right. The rock had been the easiest part. The second he'd seen it in the sand, he knew it was for Megan. It was the brightest turquoise he'd ever seen in the ocean, and the bold shimmering copper flecks throughout the stone reminded him of her gorgeous hair.

To see it now lying close to her heart, he felt a rush of hope. It was the proof he'd needed that their friendship would outlast this moment. The simple gift he'd given her weeks ago wasn't forgotten, and that meant something.

His gaze lifted to hers, and he smiled softly. Whatever she was about to say to him, he was ready.

❦

IT WASN'T THE TIME FOR MEGAN TO SPILL ALL THE feelings that were bursting inside of her; she knew that. Her hands were still shaking from the shock and fear of the last few moments. From watching Crystal with a knife at her neck. From fearing what Williamson was going to do to them. For a few seconds, she just looked back at Santiago with such a rush of relief and tenderness, she wasn't sure she could handle it.

She glanced back at Crystal, and it seemed her friend was putting the pieces together just now. Her eyebrows rose, and she smiled softly, giving a subtle nod of her head. But when Megan turned to Santiago once more, she knew it definitely wasn't the right time. Not with Crystal standing by, however supportive her sweet friend might be.

"How did you know?" she finally managed, although her eyes were asking other questions, tracing the lines of his face and sinking into the color of his eyes.

Fred wandered over to him, and Santiago knelt down to rub his ears. He knew all the favorites with Fred. A smile pulled at one side of his mouth, and he glanced up at Megan. "I didn't at first, I'm sorry to say. I really had no idea what was going on. But as I turned to leave, I thought over the way you were acting." He looked back at Fred. "And you." He stood again, pausing. His eyes were something she could read all day; the tenderness there was heartbreaking. "Without Fred giving me clues, I would've convinced myself that you just secretly hated me." He laughed, although it sounded pained.

"I'm sorry, Santiago," Megan let her breath out, running her fingers through her hair. The front door shut, and she glanced back to see Crystal was gone. Her heart suddenly felt like it would explode. She had to tell him now, before anything else could go wrong. She swallowed, suddenly abuzz with nerves. But the second she turned back to him, he stepped in close, holding her hands in his. She was frozen, looking into his vibrant eyes but not seeing what she'd expected. He was far too nervous.

"I hope I didn't ruin things," he whispered, holding her hands up and hugging them to his chest. "I didn't mean that. I'm sorry that I rushed it, and I was hoping that we could just... start again? Nothing is more important to me right now than our friendship. It would kill me to know I ruined it. Please tell me I didn't."

She could feel his heart pounding in his chest, but suddenly confessing her love for him felt like too much. He was willing to take a step back after all. Maybe that was what they both needed. She considered it, glancing across his face. But clearly, he was about to crumble if she didn't answer soon.

She took a slow breath and held tight to her emotions. Her lips slowly lifted into a smile, and she reached for the necklace he'd made her. Sliding her hand down the twine, she held the stone at the bottom and watched a smile light his face. "We're friends, Santiago," she assured, although her heart throbbed in her chest. Weren't they more than that? Her eyes were unsteady on his, and she let them drop, afraid she would say too much. "You didn't do anything to break that. I promise."

He exhaled slowly and brought her into a hug. "Thank goodness." His voice remained soft and sincere and deeper than usual. She closed her eyes and held on to him, feeling so much relief. Taking it slower was the way to go. With something so valuable, the last thing she wanted to do was risk breaking it.

After a time, he leaned back, but didn't break away. His fingertips touched her cheek and trailed through her hair. He looked back at her so tenderly, she couldn't stop herself.

She lifted on her toes and kissed him. At first, she could feel his surprise. His lips were frozen in place while she touched his jawline tentatively and then continued on to thread her fingers together at the back of his neck. She tilted her head, and he finally awoke... and suddenly her heart was racing. He kissed her with more emotion than she'd expected, but she could tell he was holding back at the same time.

They parted slowly, and she wanted to kiss him again. For a moment, she thought he would. He leaned closer, his eyes catching hers softly. Her hand came to his face again, she couldn't resist. He didn't tell her he loved her, but it was clear enough in his eyes. She could see it burning deep inside, and she hoped he could read her as well. Because she'd never fallen this hard for anyone. No high school crush, no college boy. Not even her former fiancé had ever had this much of her heart. If she were to tell the truth, it was terrifying.

"Do you kiss all your friends like that?" His voice was weak, and they broke into laughter. She knew she should step away, that the moment should be over. But she didn't want that, not yet. Being in his arms was the only thing keeping her together.

She could see the question in his eyes, and no doubt he was wondering if he should let go. But thankfully, he didn't. "I was kinda hoping..." She had to pause; her pulse was racing so fiercely. Looking into his eyes was a strange mix of euphoria and devastation. She wasn't sure which one hurt worse.

"What is it?" he asked, gazing back at her softly.

She smiled through the nerves. "I was hoping we could go out on that date sometime."

His smile returned, and this time, it reached his eyes. When he stepped back and his arms dropped away, she felt a sudden wave of panic. Confused, she only looked back at him, awaiting an answer, albeit impatiently.

"What about Kenneth?" he asked. Some of the softness left his face, but mostly he looked as confused as she felt.

She nodded and suddenly remembered how right it had seemed when she'd decided to focus on herself. On building up her broken soul. It was the right thing to do, she'd known it. But did she know it still? Did a relationship with Santiago change that? She looked back at him, considering. And hoping. But there was one thing he needed to know right away.

"I broke things off with Kenneth," she said, seeing his shoulders soften as if he'd been holding his breath. "He's going out of the country for a few months, and it just wasn't feeling right. And..." Her heart began to pound again as much as she tried to stop it. To stay calm and just get the words out. But it was no use, she was in too deep. Tears came to her eyes, and she tried to swallow the emotions away, but they remained. "Turns out—" Her voice shook, and she brushed away a wretched tear. "I think I'm in love with someone else."

When she looked into his eyes, he lost his composure, breathing a heavy sigh of relief. "Oh my gosh, Megan." He swept her into his arms, kissing her cheek and laughing. "You're kidding me. I can't believe it."

He leaned back, and she laughed with him, shaking her head. "I said I *think*," she teased, although she was partly serious. What was she doing jumping in so deep? But when she saw the shine in his eyes, she knew there was no thinking about it. She was in love with Santiago.

"I'm fine with that," he said, his voice softening again. "Take all the time you need. I'm just relieved you don't hate me."

"No." She leaned in close, touching his face again, tilting her head. "I don't hate you." Their lips brushed together just as the back door opened.

She jumped out of his arms, quickly kneeling beside Fred. Fumbling with his collar, she took a moment to adjust it and scratch his head just in case Crystal had been the one to walk in on them. Then, touching her cheeks to make sure they weren't red with heat, she stood. But the officer looking back at her appeared anything but convinced.

He smiled and gave a curt nod, as if acknowledging the act she'd just performed. "Yes, well..." He gave Santiago a glance. "We'll be needing statements from you both. We're taking Crystal Chambers to the emergency room to get checked out just as a precaution—"

"Oh, I'll go with her," Megan said, heading for the door.

Fred scrambled out ahead of her. But when Santiago caught her hand, she spun around. Looking back at him, the tears returned. Her heart felt like it would burn clean through her chest.

"Can I go too?" Santiago asked softly, his eyes locked onto hers. A moment of silence passed, and they only looked at each other.

"O—kay." The officer squeezed behind Megan and headed out the door. "Right this way, folks. I'll get your statements at the hospital."

She walked next to him, enjoying the slight swing of their arms together and especially enjoying the way he held hands. The pressure of his grip was purposeful, always communicating. The shift of his fingertips against her skin and the way his thumb slid gently atop hers took her breath away. It was all happening so fast. Suddenly her world revolved around him and their future together. It was the kind of relationship she'd always dreamed of, and she couldn't imagine things ever changing.

⋆⁂⋆

"I wasn't scared for me, just for Tank," Gabriel said, rubbing the big yellow lab by his side. He bent down and kissed Tank's head, and his shaggy dark hair fell forward. "He's my best friend. My dad brought him home when I was five, and we go on hikes and stuff. He really likes the beach too."

They sat at a small cafe next to Duthenger harbor two weeks after getting Gabriel back. To their left, were the docks with boats lined up, home for the evening. They tottered and swayed with the sea against a background of small colorful houses and shops very unique to the small town of mostly Irish emigrants. A sandy beach trailed up from the harbor, giving way to a rocky, green wilderness dense with moss, ferns, and trees cloaked with vegetation. Along the other side, stretching in front of them and far to the right, was a larger beach with finer sand. It was clearly a favorite hangout as there were still a few groups out enjoying the coastline.

Santiago sat next to Megan at the table with Gabriel and his mother across from them. But all their chairs faced the sea. Tank sat next to his boy, focused on the coastline as if awaiting his chance to explore. Fred lay at Megan's feet, perhaps anticipating quite a few more minutes of conversation. His ears perked up, however, at every movement from Tank. Megan knew she would have to let them off to play soon, but that would mean keeping an eye on him, and right now, she had so many more questions for Gabriel.

"So, what did you do all that time?" Megan asked. "Three days seems very long." She glanced at his mother in hopes she wasn't being too nosy. But Amanda gave her son an encouraging nod of her head.

"Well..." Gabriel tilted his head, and his dark eyes peered into the distance. "At first, I guess I was pretty scared. But then, I could tell they didn't really know what to do next. Like, we were in this little house, and they turned on cartoons and sat me on the couch and then"—he shrugged—"they just kinda watched me. Neither of them were mean really. And they would even joke about me being their guest."

Megan glanced at Amanda, seeing a completely different

emotion compared to the carefree expression of her son. Her jaw was set and her pretty, blue-gray eyes had turned to stone. She was fighting back her anger, there was no doubt. Likely she'd had a much worse time over those three days than her son. Megan wished she could take some of that pain from her but, at the same time, knew it was impossible. This was her burden and, as with all burdens, it would get lighter with time.

"But then, they started to get pretty upset that last day," Gabriel continued, talking quickly as if he were in a hurry to get out to the beach as well. "They talked on the phone a lot, and it sounded like they were in trouble." He pulled his gaze from the sea and turned back to Megan. "Then they drove me back out to the forest and dropped me off. Told me to stay there and that their friend was coming for me. Then the one with blond hair warned me to do just as I was told, or they'd come find me again, and next time, they wouldn't give me back."

Megan shook her head. "Santiago was right," she said. "You are one brave kid."

"You sure are," Santiago echoed.

"Thanks." Gabriel smiled and turned back to his mom. "Can I take Tank down the beach?" he asked. But Amanda's face tensed. She glanced around them and then, it seemed with considerable effort, she smiled. "Just to these rocks here. Wait for me to finish talking to our friends, and then I'll come with you."

"M-kay, Mom." He hopped up, and Tank practically dragged him down the beach in his eagerness. Gabriel's laughter filled the air. Fred sat up suddenly, watching the two with ears alert and tail swishing the concrete.

"Looks like he wouldn't mind playing on the beach too,"

Amanda said, although her voice was quieter than usual. She looked back at Santiago and then Megan, and her shoulders fell. "Please don't ask me questions just yet. I'm sorry but I can't... it's something I'm going to have to work on getting over, and it's going to take some time."

"I understand," Megan said, reaching across the table to take Amanda's hand. "I can't imagine what you've gone through."

Amanda's eyes shot out to the rocks often, checking on her son. She squeezed Megan's hand and offered a quick smile. "Yes, it's difficult, I'll admit." She shook her head slowly with her lips pressed together. "When I think of those men, all three of them, I just..." She took a slow breath. "All I want is revenge."

"Don't worry, Amanda," Santiago's voice had her gaze flickering up to meet his. "They're all behind bars. You're safe. Your son is safe. And we're here with you. If you ever feel worried or need anything, you can call me or Megan anytime. Day or night."

"Absolutely," Megan agreed. Fred took a few steps toward the beach, and she tightened her grip on the leash, just in case.

"Thank you both," Amanda's voice was louder now. She stood, taking a deep breath. "It's a beautiful sunset. Should we all walk the beach, or do you need to get going?"

"I'd love that," Megan said.

They headed down to the rocks where Gabriel and Tank explored. Fred scrambled to his feet and trotted along, barely able to hold back his excitement. Santiago walked close to Megan, but he didn't take her hand. It had been two weeks since their big step forward into relationship territory, and for whatever reason, it seemed he'd taken a big step back. Megan had chosen to feel relieved, even if she refused to admit the fear that gnawed away at her from deep inside. Fear that perhaps he regretted how quickly they'd jumped into it. She could hardly remember how it had all happened when she thought back to it. It was just a lot of emotions swirling around inside until she just couldn't handle them anymore. Then, being in his arms... that was the part she loved the most. The part that settled all her fears.

"Hey."

She glanced up, seeing Santiago lagging, waiting for her. "You coming?"

Amanda and Gabriel were already quite a way down the beach. His hand was held out, and his face was pulled into a question, as if giving her the choice to take it or not.

Megan's eyes trailed across his face, and she slid her hand into his, intertwining their fingers together. He looked back at her with a simmering smile that set her heart on fire. But as they walked, she couldn't help wondering just what was going on. She'd assumed they would be much more *together* than they actually were at the moment. They hadn't even kissed since that day. Had it all just been the emotions of the moment? Fearing she was in danger and then sweeping her up in a kiss? It seemed strange to think of his actions that way. She was most likely wrong. But then... what was it?

But it was a concern that didn't stick around. With the seagulls calling and the gorgeous deep colors of sunset blanketing the area, she couldn't hold onto the worry long enough. It drifted away with the salty breeze. Whatever his reasons for pulling back, he clearly wasn't going anywhere. His hand held hers confidently, and he walked close and contented beside her. If he wanted to take it slow... it only managed to make her love him more. Maybe that was his plan all along. Who knew?

Megan bumped him with her hip as they walked and he threw a teasing glance her way that sent her heart into frenzy.

Yep, things were fine between them. Better than fine, actually. Having someone like Santiago by her side was more than she'd ever dreamed she'd find in her lifetime. A true happily ever after. They paused a moment and faced the sea, and she ran her hand along his arm, leaning her head against him.

No more worries. Megan pushed them away. There was only the man beside her and this feeling in her heart that she wanted to think of. It was a moment that carried her away, and she couldn't be happier.

The End.

Sneak Peek of the next book in the Megan Henny series!

IT HAD BEEN A LONG DAY EXPLORING THE COASTLINE, AND Fred was already snoring away in the passenger's seat. For a Great Dane, he fit surprisingly well in the little bucket seat of her red hatchback... at least, when he was curled up. Megan kept a wary eye on the road. It was a difficult drive even in the daytime, but at night, it was critical to pay attention. A winding, beautiful stretch of scenic highway that had a wall of trees on one side and a cliff on the other. The moon was full, and she was grateful for that. It left an especially bright glow on the surface of the road.

Still, the curves seemed never-ending.

She'd never gone so far up the coastline since moving to the little seaside town of Seacrest, nestled among the redwoods of the Washington Coast. It was a gorgeous place to explore, although she hadn't expected to be going it alone. She'd invited Santiago, her new sort-of boyfriend. But apparently, he had to work. It was a surprising response, seeing as how his work always took the backseat in his life. If at all. He was more of a *live for the moment* kind of guy. But he was responsible and intuitive as well. An old soul, even if he was only twenty-three. He was surprisingly in-tune to her deepest emotions. Well, usually. Today, he must've missed the longing in her voice as she'd invited him.

Bright yellow caution signs lined a particularly dramatic bend in the road, and she eased up on the gas. It was tempting to gaze out at the ocean, but she resisted. From that point in the road, it was an impressive lookout over the Pacific. There was even a wide dirt shoulder that nearly became a parking lot for travelers pulling off to enjoy the view.

Oncoming headlights brightened the road ahead of her, and Megan gripped the steering wheel, ready to move over should the driver require it. When the car came into view, she felt a wave of panic. It was clear they were going much too fast. They couldn't possibly make the curve ahead. She stepped on the brake and laid on the horn as it whizzed past her. Her hand fumbled with the levers until she was flashing her brights frantically. The driver, who she only saw half a second of, didn't look at her. He only glared down the road with a determined set of his jaw. His hair was dark and short, but it's all she noticed before he blurred past.

Slamming on the brakes, she turned in her seat with her heart pounding. He needed to slow down, or he'd never—

The car bucked as it raced off the road and onto the dirt turnout. Clouds of dust billowed around it. The headlights strobed up off the road, illuminating a few spindly saplings as the car bounced over the bumps in the dirt. Then they pointed straight at the metal railing.

"Oh my gosh," Megan gasped, unable to look away as the car smashed through the railing, and the taillights disappeared over the edge, sending it sailing down the cliff. There was a moment of terrifying silence. Then, the deafening sound of the crash had her heart nearly stopping.

She cranked the steering wheel, pressing on the gas. Following the tire tracks, she parked in the dirt lot and snatched her cell phone, dialing 911 as she got out. Fred was on her heels, watching her closely and taking in her panic. They hurried across the dirt turnout to where the guardrail was torn apart. Fred's big ears flopped aside his head as he searched their surroundings. Then he suddenly became more cautious and stepped carefully to the edge, sniffing the air.

Megan could hardly think straight, only imagining the man's face again and again. What had he been thinking? Did he just leave a fight? Learn of a death? Did he do it on purpose, or had he been ignorant of the curve ahead? Was he just not paying attention? Didn't he hear her honk?

So many questions as she leaned over the edge of the cliff, staring down at a twisted mass of metal that looked nothing like a car. It had landed on a pile of jagged boulders at the bottom of a two-hundred-foot cliff. Smoke trailed up from the car, and one brake light glowed amidst the dark scene. Light flickered among the broken glass and torn metal and a tendril of fire lifted from the heap. It grew quickly and tears gathered in Megan's eyes as the car was suddenly engulfed in flames.

Get the next book in the Megan Henny series, Dark Highways and Dogging Clues.

Also by Rimmy London

3947460BR00158